THE

Volume II

Comes The Dawn

*No Matter How Dark the Night Gets
The Dawn Will Come*

Joan Rossiter Burney

Library of Congress
Catalog Card No. 96-96835

ISBN 1-57579-022-x

1st Printing 1989
Christensen Printing Co.

2nd Printing 1996
Pine Hill Press, Inc.

Printed in United States of America

PINE HILL PRESS, INC.
Freeman, S. Dak. 57029

Comes the Dawn

Keepers II, Comes the Dawn contains columns selected by the readers of the following papers and magazines: *At Random and Joan Burney* in the *Cedar County News, the Maverick Media Newspapers, the Norfolk Daily News, the Hastings Tribune, The Kearney Daily Hub, The Sioux City Journal, and the Missouri Valley Observer; Comes the Dawn* in the *Nebraska Farmer* and the *Colorado Rancher-Farmer*; *Offer It Up* in *The Catholic Voice*, and *Over the Feeder's Fence* in the *Nebraska Cattleman*.

Also included are selected award-winning personality profiles which have appeared in the papers mentioned above as well as The Catholic Digest, and the Omaha World Herald Magazine of the Midlands.

"When the student is ready, the teacher will come."

Dedication: To My Teachers.

Illustrator: Mary Burney Sandberg
701 26th St., Minneapolis, Mn. 55418

Acknowledgments

Special thanks to my niece, artist extraordinaire Mary Burney Sandberg, who understands and interprets my thoughts with her art. Not an easy task. Mary, daughter of the late Dr. D.W. Burney, Jr. and his wife, Kay, is an award-winning professional artist with a special affection for cats.

To Vern Borer, without whom this book would not have been published. Life has come a full circle because Vern was the first editor to publish my column in the Cedar County News in 1968. It was his idea. I am grateful.

I also want to thank Joe and Brian Christensen, and the kindly people at Christensen Printing Company, who put up with my peculiarities and who do a masterful job of printing.

And I want to thank all the people who took the pictures used in my mini-photo album. That includes the amateur, but prolific, photographers among my family and friends, and friends who are marvelous professional photographers, the likes of Marianne Beel and Jim Denney, and the multitude of photographers, characters all, in the Nebraska Press Women. They have enriched my professional and personal life.

Photo by Jim Denney

Comes The Dawn

After awhile you learn the subtle difference
Between holding a hand and chaining a soul,
And you learn that love doesn't mean leaning,
And company doesn't mean security,
And you begin to understand that kisses aren't contracts
And presents aren't promises.
And you begin to accept your defeats
With your head held high and eyes open
With the grace of an adult, not the grief of a child.
You learn to build your roads on today
Because tomorrow's ground is too uncertain,
For plans and futures have a way of falling down in mid-flight.
After awhile you learn that even sunshine burns if you get too much.
So you plant your own garden, and decorate your own soul,
Instead of waiting for someone to bring you flowers.
And you learn you really can endure,
You really are strong.
You really do have worth.
And you learn and you learn and you learn.
With every goodbye, you learn.

Anonymous

Contents

Preface

The Road Less Traveled

I shall be telling this with a sigh
Somewhere ages and ages hence;
Two roads diverged in a wood, and I—
I took the road less traveled by,
And that has made all the difference.

Robert Frost 1916

Dear Readers:

I present to you yet another book to be read in bits and pieces. The columns and the essays in *KEEPERS II, COMES THE DAWN*, have again, for the most part, been chosen by my readers. God bless them all. As in *KEEPERS I*, they are a cross section of essays on this journey through life, sharing a few tools, some hard-won knowledge, the faith that lifts us up, and the humor that smooths our way. In this book, I am pleased to also be able to include stories of some of the people who have been an inspiration on my life's journey. Knowing their stories will also inspire you.

Somewhere along the road, I don't know just when it was, it dawned on me that I was never going to *get there* in life, that life was never going to be a destination, it was always going to be a journey—and not all of it interstate. Maybe it was after we got married and I learned that living *happily ever after* was not a foregone conclusion.

Maybe it was when my vision of myself as a perfect farmwife was shattered by the growing knowledge I had no knack for things like cleaning, making crisp pickles, or whipping little things up on a sewing machine, and, even more serious, I had no discernible desire to develop that knack. Maybe it was when we lost a son, and I found out how a person can hurt. Maybe it was when my beautiful, stately *on the road again* mother had a stroke and couldn't get on with dying until she'd spent five years in bed as an invalid, only able to say yes or no.

Or it could have been when the kids grew up and left home— and then came back again—and then left—and then came back—

trying sometimes painfully to find themselves, and we decided that the empty nest syndrome was not so much a problem as it was an accomplishment. (For all of us.)

It could have been when the farm economy went foul in the early eighties, and a lot of dreams came crashing down.

I realized it most profoundly when beloved friends and relatives we'd planned to have with us throughout our life's journey came prematurely (we thought) to the end of their road.

Along the way I witnessed pain. I felt pain. I saw people who were lost in prisons of their own making. It began to dawn on me, primarily a humorist, a person involved in making merry, that someone with a modicum of talent in communicating might be some help in this sad old world, if that someone had a mind to. It started with a still small voice somewhere inside, and built to an insistent nudging, doubtless from the Lord.

I had a mind to. The lessons I've learned in life are certain and sure. I've learned people can do what they set their minds to do, if they choose to. I've seen people with enormous problems rise above them, and not only survive but thrive. And I've seen people who would seem to have everything, who "poor me" themselves right into eternity.

The difference? Well—sometimes, to get on with this thriving business, we need a little knowledge, and someone to cheer us along the way. I decided to garner as much knowledge as I could, and— with my columns and speeches and counseling and whatever else it is I do—share it, and then lead the cheering. Albeit without pom- poms. (I'd always hankered to be a cheer leader.) So I veered off the road of domesticity I'd always presumed I would follow (but for which I was obviously ill-suited) and I started down a less-traveled road. It hasn't always been easy, but once I headed down that road I was bolstered by the sure sense that I was going the right direction.

I've had fellow-travelers along this way. In response to the death of our beloved friend, Marge Seim, I got involved in Hospice work, as did many of my friends. Responding to needs in our com- munity, many of us also trained to be Community Caretakers. And, to be more effective dealing with specific needs in our parish and our community, we responded to a call from the Archdiocese of

Omaha to be trained as Family Ministers under the auspices of Creighton University.

Problem is, it seemed the more I knew, the more I knew I didn't know. So on I journeyed, to a Masters in Psychological Counseling from Wayne State College. I was the oldest student in most of my classes. As a matter of fact, I was older than most of my instructors. Not to worry, I was also the oldest one in my class when I got my undergraduate degree in 1973. I am used to it. Besides, chronological age means nothing. I am young at heart, to say nothing of my other organs. Mark Twain said it best, "Age is matter over mind—if you don't mind, it doesn't matter."

I don't mind.

Then, responding to an expressed need in our parish for training in parenting skills, I got certified to teach parenting classes, a logical progression of my journey, don't you agree? So now I write and speak and counsel and teach, sharing my hard-won certain sure knowledge with anyone who will listen and with a few people who'd rather not. Mighty satisfactory work. Interesting thing though, on one of the rough spots along the way, I learned that you can't take care of the whole world unless you take care of yourself first. So now, I do that too.

Having set the scene, as it were, I share all this with you, and more, on the following pages.

None of this could I have done without the support of my husband, and the encouragement of my family, immediate and extended, who understand, because they've been known to follow a few inner nudges of their own.

I'm still heavily into humor. I wasn't able to shake that habit, and I have a great preference for merriment. My journey has been made merry and filled with intended and unintended humor by my husband, Kip, my children, Rob, Bill, John, Lou Ann, Juli, Tom and Chuck, (all of whom have found themselves), our almost perfect grandchild Kate, and the many characters who we count as our friends. My gratitude to these beloved people, who make my life rich beyond words, knows no bounds.

My fondest hope, dear reader, is that some of these words will spill into your life and help you on your journey.

Having done all this sharing, I have a request for you. As you read along, if something pops into your mind—an inspiring story, an amusing joke, a tiny tidbit of interest—it seems only fair that you share back. I would love to hear from you. My address will be lurking somewhere in this book. Because, dear reader, make no mistake about it, we choose our own road as we journey through life. We need to help one another. We are all in this together.

All for one and one for all.

Go Gang Go.

Joan R. Burney

CHAPTER ONE

Chapter One

Fellow Travelers: Family and Friends

This section of the book is dedicated to the people who accompany us on our life's journey, our family and friends. Nothing is more important to me in this whole world. They provide me with material, for one thing. For another, they enrich my life because they are in it. If someone were to ask me the most important accomplishment of my life, I would say "my children" without even a pause. Oh, I admit there may have been a few times in the past when I'd have given the whole passel of them to a passing stranger, but I can't even begin to imagine how dull life would be without them. As for my friends, they are so precious to me I puddle up when I think about them. They keep me sane, keep me entertained, and keep me humble. No easy task. What follows are little slices of life featuring the above mentioned characters. They'll pop up in other sections too, of course. Hope you enjoy them as much as I do.

"Here's My Joanie"

1976

Ethel Reifert died this week. You wouldn't have read this in the headlines of the major papers or heard it on the radio, but in my mind the Ethel Reiferts of the world are the stuff that Heaven is made of.

I can't remember a time when I didn't know Ethel. She was the mother of one of my best friends, Annelou. "Annie", as she called her, was her only daughter. They had a relationship full of honesty, love and laughter—a beautiful thing to watch.

But she was also the second mother to a crew of motley tom boys, scraggily half-formed girl-children whom she made feel like "somebodies."

2

We were silly, I think, but Ethel didn't say so. She clucked over us and gathered us close like a mother hen. She'd hike with us to the creek, build fires for wieners and marshmallows and dispense wit and wisdom the whole time. We were always welcome at her house. She seemed to sense a worth in us, mavericks that we were, which eluded almost everybody else.

Father Gerald Gonderinger gave the homily at Ethel's funeral Mass. In an apt analogy he likened our struggles here on earth to that of a butterfly in a cocoon. He told about a scientist who, thinking he would help the butterfly emerge, slit the cocoon. But the butterfly's wings were weak and they were not beautiful, and the butterfly died. We need the struggles of this world to be born again in the next.

If that is true—and I'm sure it is—Ethel would have the strongest and most beautiful wings in Heaven. Life was never easy for her; she seemed to have more problems than her share. But she raised her lovely family, and with common sense and a sure feeling for what is really important she *prevailed* in the strongest sense of the word.

Whenever Ethel saw me in these later years she'd put an arm around me and say: "Well, here's my little Joanie", and I would feel like snuggling in and just staying there. We'd usually talk about Annelou, plotting on how we would lure her back for our next class reunion.

Recently Ethel went east to visit Annelou, and she had a wonderful time. We talked about that too.

It was to be their last visit. She died suddenly, unexpectedly, making a terrible wrench in the hearts and souls of her family. She probably would have wanted it that way. She'd never want to become a burden to anyone. Even now she was to have problems, for a bad storm delayed the interment.

I write about Ethel today because I loved her and she was an important part of my life. As I sat at her funeral Mass with the snow swirling outside I found myself recalling our many hikes to our favorite creek. I could feel the warm sand curl up through my toes and the sticky marshmallows on my fingers and my mouth, and I could almost hear the laughter. And I wept. Not so much for Ethel as for the rest of us. She was such a nice person to have around.

She will be sorely missed upon this earth, but there can be no doubt that she's in Heaven and that she will be looking out for us again. That is comforting.

I hope all of you have an Ethel Reifert in your lives. They fill such an important need by just being there. I pray that someday, if I work very hard and flap my own wings against my earthly cocoon of problems, I will again be able to hear her say, "Well, here's my little Joanie."

Oh, For the Stream that Once Was . . . .

1977

Last week I went out with Kip one evening to help him check a field we are *FINALLY* flood-irrigating this year—after three years of drought. As he wandered down a row to see why the water wasn't coming through, I headed over a familiar hill to the wooded area where I used to take all of our children, when they were little, to fish and swim.

A swimming hole, which was way over my head, had been there, and I remember one wild occasion when one of the boys caught a snapping turtle. Lots of good memories, and I went prepared to be all nostalgic.

What happened was, I got mad. The creek wasn't even there. A thin trickle of water made its weary way through a weed-filled sand bed, but you certainly couldn't dignify it with the name "creek." It was pathetic. In my memories I could hear the rippling cool water and the splashing of the kids of yesteryear. Now you couldn't get your toe decently wet in this muddy little spit-bath of a stream.

It's because of the drought, of course. And because of all the irrigation. The irrigation is necessary, God knows, but it just gets so discouraging.

As of this writing we've had several days of above normal hot, hot weather. We're well on our way to our fourth year of drought. And this morning we had that cruel trick of Mother Nature, the dry thunder storm. Lots of thunder and lightning and about five drops of rain.

It's cruel because with the first faint rumbling of thunder in the distance you begin to have hope. By the time the clouds roll in with all their beautiful promising fireworks, you really get excited. Then it fools around and rains about five drops and goes its merry way, leaving one more disheartened and demoralized than ever.

The thing that made me mad about the disgusting little trickle of water which was masquerading as my beautiful stream was that it suddenly seemed to symbolize all that was yukky in the world of the farmer in this day and age.

You see, because of all these years of drought, farmers have been forced to go to considerable expense to put in irrigation systems. It was a sort of a *darned if you do and darned if you don't* situation.

But, to cover the basic expenses, the irrigating farmer has to have a return of at least $2 a bushel for his corn. So here's the irony. If we were to have a bumper crop, with corn coming out our ears, so to speak, the price would go down so fast you wouldn't believe it. And so, not only the irrigators, but all the farmers would be penalized because they did such a good job raising corn.

This in a world where a great proportion of the population is starving ─────────── so dumb!

In other words, it would seem the better job a farmer does, the worse off he is.

Still, if they do not go into irrigating, they go broke because they can't raise anything.

Now, wouldn't that frost you?

If it wouldn't, it should. Because whatever is happening on the farm, price-wise, ripples out into the rest of the economy just like the water when you toss a pebble in a stream. That fact is being brought home to me every week by a series of interviews I'm doing in Hartington for the local paper on our businessmen. One after another they mention that they are cutting back on their buying, or putting off thought of remodeling or expanding, because *things are tough on the farm.* As one of them said just recently, *"It starts with the land and it comes back to the land."* If the farmers can't buy, then the small town merchants can't buy; then their wholesale suppliers can't buy, and well, you can see the circle widening.

It's not that anybody is starving—yet. The land has risen so in value that farmers can borrow more and more on it to raise crops that bring proportionately less and less.

It's the weary, weary, weary truth of all the above statements that made me so blamed mad at that little trickle of water running through our creek bed. How much and how long are the farmer's of America going to be able to keep offering it up?

"Tennis Anyone?"

1978

I have a friend who keeps heckling me about playing tennis. It's the "in" thing, you know. I always tell everybody I used to play a lot of tennis as a kid. Truth of the matter is, I just used to go to the park a lot carrying my tennis racket.

Of course, we'd play. But the main thing was to go to the park and be available in case there would be any scraggly necked young boys around to pretend like we didn't notice.

So, our tennis playing was kind of like hit the ball and look around. But I do distinctly remember occasionally hitting the ball.

My first inclination that this might not have been the case was when I played a couple of years ago with my high school buddy, Libby Goetz Dale. She's a whiz, or so she tells me. I'll never know, because I rarely gave her the opportunity to show her stuff. After humiliating me for one set, she just walked off the court. "Are we done playing?" I asked pleasantly. "Did we start?" she countered. So much for old friends.

Then just a couple of weeks ago I set out on a luncheon venture with some of the gals, and I was informed it was to be an athletic type event, with swimming, tennis playing, etc. *Tennis playing?* I shuddered.

I carefully forgot my racket and went forward cheerfully. The rest would be fun.

The hostess for this olympic-like event has a beautiful home with a swimming pool and a tennis court. We shall call her Betty. People with tennis courts usually have more than one racket. Betty had several. So, while forgetting my racket was clever, it was not very effective.

Because after swimming and lunch and swimming, we HAD to play tennis. My friends Helen and Shirley, who have built in bounce, would have it no other way. However, they know about my athletic ability, so they gave me to Betty as her partner. Poor Betty.

You see, if I'm going to do something, I think what the heck, and throw myself into it with great enthusiasm. And hadn't I been watching Bjorn Borg and Chrissy Evert, or whoever those people are. So, I know how to bounce around at the end of the court in an alert position, and how to charge up to the net, and how to race to the side with a flashing backhand. So, as I was prancing around and bouncing and jumping, Betty said she thought, "Boy, have I got me a partner!" It's just that whatever I was doing almost always had no connection with what the ball was doing. And the more I flung myself into the game with great abandon, the less effective I was. And the more aware Betty was that she'd been had.

Even Betty's dog, Chris, was better at getting the balls than I was.

Well, we lost four games straight. I was exhausted. So was the dog. He'd been retrieving the balls. As the other gals bounced on to the next event, I said to the dog, "You know, I played a lot of tennis as a kid."

He didn't believe it either.

Hooray for the Homemakers!

1981

I've noticed in my travels around the country the emerging of a new kind of woman; the *militant homemaker*. These are women who are not only satisfied in their role of wife and mother; they are—thank you very much—fulfilled. They are experiencing life just the way they want to experience it. They are intelligent, their talents are many, their interests are diverse, and they are fully aware of their potential.

And just as the woman who feels trapped in the home resents society telling her she has to stay there, these women resent a society that seems to tell them what they're doing is not valuable. They heartily resent the insinuation that they are really miserable, but they are just too dumb to know it. They know how they feel. They feel good about themselves. And—by golly—they are starting to verbalize it.

There seem to be some figures to back that up. Insurance companies recently released a study that stated women staying at home—covering all the tasks such women cover—are worth a minimum of $355 a week, or $18,460 a year.

So while there are women who are in pain, who are suffering and who definitely need help—women who want to get out of the home, or are forced to get out of the home—we must also consider the fact that there are women who are tremendously rewarded by being wonderfully competent homemakers. And they are demanding to be heard.

Unfortunately I don't come under that heading. I do nothing competently in the home. I do not sew, nor do I reap. I'm a lousy housekeeper, and whenever I've papered a wall, grown men barf. However, I know women who do these things so excellently and so happily that I am envious. There is no greater talent than the wonderful one of nurturing your fellow human beings. None.

On the other hand, though I would go to the mat for women's rights, I'm not much of a feminist either. Like a lot of women, I have feelings of ambivalence.

When the six kids were all little, and I was sitting at home with them while Kip was cavorting about, I wanted to be a feminist. But when the blizzards hit, and Kip had to go out and feed the cattle while I stayed in the warm house, I didn't.

When he's sitting in the living room doing the crossword puzzle on a Sunday, while I'm cleaning up the dishes, then I want to be a feminist. But when we're driving down the road in a blizzard and we have a flat tire, then I don't.

When times are good and we're refurnishing the living room and he's insisting on things his way, then I want to be a feminist. But when times are bad and he has to go in to see the banker, then I don't.

Life is sometimes a balancing act, a series of compromises. A person has to weigh the things that are important, and make decisions accordingly. If you're willing to pay the price, almost anything is possible. In other words, whatever you really want to be, you darned sure have the right to be.

If you want to be a corporate executive—God bless. But if you want to be a homemaker, even a militant one, there is no greater profession.

But I don't need to tell you that! You're the ones who've been telling me.

Congratulations "Doctor John"

1982

The flat little paper owl that resides in the back of a kitchen cupboard has been called on to again preside over a graduation ceremony.

When you unfold his little round body, he's cute, although his mortarboard sits slightly askew now, and his little paper diploma is showing some wear.

No wonder. He has peered with his wise old owl eyes upon the festivities surrounding a multitude of graduations. Six eighth-grade graduations, six high school graduations, five college graduations (including mine), a couple of celebrations for Masters, and now—the ultimate—*our first doctor.*

Doctor John. He can't cure much, unless you have a problem with History, but he's worked long and hard for this Ph.D. and we are mighty proud.

His dissertation is impressive. A huge book, with a fancy black cover, about the students of Toulouse University in France. I said to John, "who cares?" but it turned out John did. He spent many years gathering the information, including a year at Toulouse University, most of the time in the archives and libraries. And the University of Kansas cared, for he was presented the outstanding dissertation award. And now even Toulouse University cares as they are interested in publishing it in book form. Quite a tribute to John's scholarly excellence.

Knowing all that, you will be as appalled as John was when he brought it home for our perusal and found an empty glass sitting on it. Clutching it to his bosom, he took it home with him. He was good humored about it because John knows better than anyone what a casual household this is. But he took it home nonetheless. So I haven't gotten to read it all, but I already know more about the students of Toulouse in the 19th century than most of their parents did.

The various graduates march through my mind as I unfold the little fat paper owl, and nostalgia assails me. Where has the time gone? When John graduated in '71 he was the first of the long hairs. Not really long, but gently flowing to his glasses. His two older brothers graduated with crew cuts. He looks so incredibly young in that graduation picture, but don't they all?

Now he looks like a history professor should. Nice haircut, neatly trimmed beard. His wife, Lou Ann, is his barber. Although John's gone all the way through school on scholarships, it's Lou Ann's nursing that's kept them in the frivolities—like food. So this Ph.D. is as much hers as his, and we are equally as proud of her.

John and Lou Ann traveled to France on a Rotary scholarship, which meant giving speeches to Rotary groups in both French and English. Harken you young people who are struggling with speech classes, or making up your mind about their importance, because John's speaking experience in high school and 4-H served him well.

And to think when he used to avoid *crowds* of two or more older people because "they expect me to talk, and I don't know what to say." He was our *thinker*, who—with his weird sense of humor—always kept things interesting.

The paper owl and I cherish these highlights. But when I dismember him, flatten his little body and put him back in his cupboard, I realize he doesn't know much about all the work and worry, the fun and games, that go on in between. There are times I envy that silly owl. But not for long. You can't really enjoy the high spots of life unless you've experienced the low.

So congratulations Dr. John!! (Can you do anything for this headache?)

When the Bus Goes By . . .

1983

There is something really good about all the different stages of our lives, and we should take time to realize it. No point in yearning for past years, or wishing for future years, when it's the time we're in that has to be the best time of our lives.

Always is. No doubt about it. For instance, I sat this morning with my second cup of coffee and watched the school bus sail by. I didn't mind.

Oh—I might allow myself a few pangs of nostalgia, as I sip away, for the days of yore, when that school bus dominated our lives. I might even relive momentarily, the years when our six kids dashed out the back door at the cry of "School Bus!"—grabbing shoes, books, pencils, etc., on the way out. I can almost hear their battle cry, "But I know I put it right there" when "it" was no place to be found.

Those were good years. Exciting years. The emotional cycle of our lives rose and fell with that of the kids in their various pursuits. Would they make the team? Get a part in the play? Do well in the contest? Pass? Oh, the sadness and the heaviness of heart when things didn't work out for them. Oh, the joy when it did!

In those years, as many of you know only too well, the job of *being parents* took most of your time, your energy and your thought processes.

Oh, you have your own pursuits, but your schedules are planned around sporting events, contests, plays, 4-H meetings and whatever else your little darlings are involved in. You may get away, but the umbilical cord of the phone always connected you to your family. And you got called! Forgotten books, sudden illnesses, broken bones, broken zippers.

Then, one by one, they march, young heads held high, thinking they know everything, down the aisle in their graduation gowns. It happens all too soon. And you weep copious tears and wonder where the time went. Then you learn that the *empty nest syndrome* is a figment of somebody's imagination because kids leave home, and kids come back—with dirty laundry, friends and kids of their own. It's amazing.

But time marches on, and most of us who have put our time in on the "being parents of young kids" progress, even somewhat merrily, to the "parents of grown kids" stage.

As our last one graduated from high school, Kip announced, "For 30 years we've wondered where you kids have been. From now on, you're going to have to wonder where we are." We've tried to keep that promise.

And it's good. When we meet our kids coming and going, we like them. They're nice adults to know. We laugh with them and cry with them, but we no longer assume responsibility for their lives. It's time.

So when the school bus goes by—I don't mind.

A Rare Find Indeed . . . .

1984

Some time ago I wrote an article here in TCV about how plants compare to people. Not in appearance, of course. (Although there are some people who would fit in a hanging basket better than others. And I do have a relative who resembles my purple passion plant when he gets mad.) It takes tender loving care to keep certain types of plants, and certain types of friendships alive.

I came upon this not-too-remarkable theory because of the problems I used to have raising plants. Even philodendrons died on me until I realized that even the hardiest plant takes a little consistent care.

So it is with friendships. The African violet, *for instance*, compares to a friendship which needs a lot of attention to survive.

On the other end of the spectrum, we have our *soul mates*, the *cactus friendships*, which endure with the least amount of care. They even seem to thrive on neglect.

I got a lot of comments on that column. It was reprinted and used as the basis for programs and things like that.

Proving to me that our friends are the most important elements in our lives on earth, and we know it. We just fail to acknowledge it very often.

And of those friends, the sturdy *cactus* variety seems the best of all.

Friends come in all sizes and shapes. Often they are relatives. Hopefully, we are married to one. But the *cactus* type is a rare find, indeed.

Sometimes the *cactus* friend is somebody you've grown up with or gone to school with. Sometimes it is somebody you've served with in the service of your country.

Going through harrowing experiences can weld *cactus-type friendships*—like serving in the war, or on a church committee, or getting married.

And sometimes, without ever understanding the why of it, you find out that somebody you just met is a *soul mate* . . . and they turn out to be *cactus* friends.

I'm not talking about so-called *love affairs.* There has been so much hoop-la in recent years about sex that it would seem to confuse the issue.

I'm talking about good, solid, laughing, enduring friendships. The kind that can occur between the young and the old, men and/ or women, regardless of just about anything. A gift from God, I would say. And you couldn't disprove me, and probably wouldn't want to.

I had a quotation once, which described that kind of a friendship perfectly. It occurred to me that it was from a person of note, and I probably used it and filed it, never to see it again.

But I ran across it in California, attributed it to the Arabs, and I thought I would share it with you, to put in your scrapbooks, or send to your *cactus* friends.

An Arabian Proverb:

> *"A friend is one to whom one may pour out all the contents of one's heart, chaff and grain together, knowing that the gentlest hands will take and sift it, keep what is worth keeping, and, with a breath of kindness, blow the rest away."*

A rare find, indeed. But one to be cherished.

A Family Is . . .

1984

The first definition of *family* in the dictionary is *parents and their children.* Which goes to show you that first definitions are not always best.

Ever since I dedicated a portion of my life to our "Family Ministry" program, I have been changing my idea of what *family* means.

For instance, families can, indeed, be *parents and their children.* They can also be people who are single, and a single parent and his/her children. A family can be two friends. It can be any combination of any amount of people who feel they belong together emotionally and spiritually.

It's possible that a person's *family* in the spiritual sense would not be their *family* by the traditional definition.

And it's possible that one could belong to a number of families, if one was very lucky. A professional family, a personal family, a church family, a hobby family . . . well, you see what I mean.

I was working with a bunch of people I've come to think of almost as family when one of them handed me a definition of family which is the best one I've seen yet. It dawned on me, as I read it, that I'd been trying to define *family* in 25 words or less. Not possible.

Here is what *A Family* is:

A family is a PLACE
  to cry
  and laugh
  and vent frustrations
  to ask for help
  and tease
  and yell
  to be touched and hugged
  and smiled at.

A family is PEOPLE
  who care when you are sad
  who love you no matter what
  who share your triumphs

who don't expect you to be perfect
just growing with honesty in your own direction.

A family is a CIRCLE
  where we learn to like ourselves
  where we learn to make good decisions
  where we learn to think before we do
  where we learn integrity and table
    manners and respect for other people
  where we are special
  where we share ideas
  where we listen and are listened to
  where we learn the rules of life
    to prepare ourselves for the world.

The World is a PLACE
  where anything can happen.
If we grow up in a loving family
  we are ready for the world.

A Parent's Reflection

1985

When I was a young mother, bustling about with the duties of taking care of six very active children, I would occasionally have visions of the time when they would be grown up and I no longer would have to worry about them. (Pause here for hysterical laughter.)

Most of the time I thought they were wondrous creatures, but not always. One day, when I was overwhelmed with the diapering and the spitting up and the rashes and the sleepless nights, a wise neighbor said to me, "Enjoy your kids now. Their troubles are little ones. You don't know what heartache is until you get grown-up kids."

And I thought, "How could they possibly be more trouble than they are now?"

Now that our kids are grown up, I know what she means. Little ones' troubles fill your days—and your nights. But wondrous though they still are, the troubles of grown up kids fill your hearts and your minds and upset your stomach. Although they are their troubles, and theoretically no longer yours, they hurt as much or more. And they aren't the kind you can kiss and make well. You learn, pretty quick, what *heartache* is.

With that in mind, I want to share with you a poem given to me by one of the young men who was helping with our filming at Cox Cable Company. We all shared in the growth of his darling baby, via pictures, during the weeks we were involved in the filming. I gazed on them fondly, with all the understanding and affection of an old pro at parenting.

I read the poem, and thought it was a perfect prayer for parents of young children. And then I read it again, and I realized that it was even more perfect for parents of grown children. I thought you might like it too:

It's called "Parent's Reflection" and its by Juli O'Brien.

> *Oh God, as I live this day,*
> > *Renew in me, a parent*
> > *The ability to laugh*
> > *At my children's antics.*
> *The strength to survive*
> > *Their cuts and bruises.*
> *The time to share*
> > *Their moments of pride.*
> *The need to praise*
> > *Their separate strengths.*
> *The faith to trust*
> > *Their growing judgment.*
> *The quality to love*
> > *Their changing moods.*
> *The virtue to forgive*
> > *Their disrespect.*
> *The openness to learn*
> > *Their ways and styles.*
> *The patience to hear*
> > *Their spoken words.*
> *The insight to see*
> > *Their doubts and fears.*
> *The tenderness to understand*

Their broken dreams.
And, Oh God, the Grace to let go
These Children are yours.

Juli—One of a Long Line of Hams

1986

When our daughter Juli was in the fourth grade she missed her very first starring role. She was to be the Blessed Virgin in the country school's Christmas program. Or perhaps it was Mrs. Santa Claus. Anyway, it was a major part. She got the chicken pox. As you might imagine, it was a time of terrible trauma. She was devastated. So was her mother.

Possibly because of that trauma she's become a professional ham. She's performed in and/or directed productions all over this area, all the way through grade school, high school, college at Wayne State, graduate school at Vermillion, and back to Wayne to teach. Now she's teaching theatre classes at Doane College, teaching creative drama for the Nebraska Arts Council, doing her own thing as a commedienne and directing the *Class Acts* improvisational troupe. She's been a part of a multitude of productions since the tragic night of the country school Christmas program. I haven't missed a one.

Last weekend in Lincoln was no exception. One weekend out of each month Juli's *Class Acts* Improvisational troupe puts on an original production at the Airport Holiday Inn at Lincoln. We were really busy, and Kip said, "Joanie, that girl is 30 years old. She probably could survive if you missed one of her productions." True. But could I?

There was no question of Kip's going along. He'd been there twice. That's more than anyone could ask. You see, he doesn't care for the theatre.

That might not be so bad if just one member of his family was involved in show biz. But not so. Our four oldest kids are all into theatre professionally or unprofessionally. (That means sometimes they get paid and sometimes they don't.) Kip does not understand how such a family could happen to a good, conservative Republican—whose idea of a perfect evening's entertainment is to sleep on the couch in front of sports on T.V.

I used to insist he come along. It was not a good idea. Maybe because of his grumpy demeanor—or because of the snoring in the second act—I learned that no Kip at all was better than a crabby Kip.

He's not too crazy about musicals, he can't stand plays, and improvisational theatre, wherein the participants respond extemporaneously to ideas, is entirely beyond him. The group collaborates on the writing of their own plays for the dinner theatre. Kip DID enjoy their melodrama. But he gets nervous when they start on the strictly improvisational stuff. They are wildly imaginative, and their humor gets somewhat irreverant on occasion. One of the "fun" things the troupe does is respond to ideas given to them by the audience. Kip had an idea. They should all go home and go to bed.

A professional director who attended the dinner theatre last week came up to me afterwards and said, "Have you any idea what kind of talent it takes to do this kind of live theatre?"

"Would you mind telling her father?" I said. "He's waiting for Juli to grow up and get a real job."

Advice to Newlyweds, Oldyweds, and Those of the Single Persuasion

1987

My best advice for newlyweds is to hang on to your sense of humor and hug a lot. That's also my best advice to oldy-weds, and to those of the single persuasion.

A sense of humor is an essential coping device for everyone. It is even more essential for a couple contemplating marriage, and it is overwhemingly essential for the parents of that couple.

Hugging is also very good, because you can say things with a hug which are hard to put into words. Emotions run high, because weddings change lives dramatically and feelings get all confused.

Even a couple blissfully in love may have niggly little doubts.

And parents! Well, they're beset by all kinds of fears. Mothers worry the most, which is why they throw themselves into wedding plans with such vim and vigor. Mothers also beam a lot. It's been said that the beam on mother's face as she contemplates her daughter's marriage is only matched by the sickly glow on father's face as he contemplates the bills.

And although bills can be a big problem, Dad's fussing could be the way he's contending with his emotions. Dad may want his daughter to get married, but there's never a man who's really good enough.

Watching children go down that aisle is a moment of truth for parents. Have we taught them anything at all? Parents desperately want their kids to be happy—because if they aren't, they might move back in.

I jest a little, but not much. A confusing array of emotions beset folks at wedding times. Sometimes a fit of crying can be set off by a disagreement over something as minor as the choice of a song, or the mints to be served. The crying hasn't got a lot to do with songs or mints.

I remember putting on my *going-away* dress in preparation for leaving on our honeymoon, and having Mom come upstairs to tell me that Dr. Dorsey had just arrived, and I should put my wedding dress back on so he could see me in it. I started to cry. So did Mom. We weren't crying about the late Dr. Dorsey. We were crying about us. She was scared for me. I was 18 years old, and as far as she knew I'd never had a serious thought in my life. I was scared for me too. We couldn't say those things then. Maybe we didn't even understand them. People understand their emotions better now. It's still tough to communicate.

Add to that emotional upheavel the Murphy's Law of weddings that seems to decree something *must* go wrong. Either the wedding dress or a bridesmaid's dress will not be ready, or the cake will tilt precariously, or somebody will forget to invite the minister, or some thing. And at least one relative will tumble face first into the punch bowl.

Being prepared for such events will help those of you, in the throes of marriage plans, to chuckle through them. I hope. Besides, if nothing untoward happened, what would you have to talk about in years to come?

I don't pretend to speak from a lot of personal experience, as only once have I been the mother of any wedding-type person, and that was a groom. I'm told that doesn't really count. However, I've watched friends struggle with the trauma of marrying off a daughter. I know it's not easy.

The memories of my own wedding aren't even too sharp, except for the trauma. I look at the home movies of that event and see two skinny people who look impossibly young, and who hardly knew each other at all.

But that was only the beginning. That's what weddings are— joyous beginnings. Then the work starts, the richer and poorer and sickness and health part.   The giddy *falling in love* feeling simmers down, and the real loving that lasts a lifetime starts to build. And if you're very, very lucky, some time down the road (maybe even forty years down the road) you'll look back on those wedding pictures and realize that skinny person next to you has become your very best friend.

Grandpa Burney Always Said, "It Doesn't Matter"

1987

Grandpa Burney used to say, with a shake of his head and a slight grin on his face, "It doesn't matter."

He'd be talking about the unimportant things in this world which get us in an uproar. He lived to be 95 years old because he understood that simple fact.

Grace, his wife, said he was always telling her that. She's having a hard time accepting the fact that he's gone. She worries about things she didn't do, and didn't say, like all of us. Because, somehow, in his case, we thought the Lord would make an exception.

But there are no exceptions—and the recognition of that, and the excitement and—yes—even the fun of thinking about the great adventure that death will be, has been brought home to me in the recent weeks by people of great faith, the hems of whose garments I truly feel unworthy to touch. So I haven't. I've hugged them though, pretty fiercely.

I sat through an afternoon that went by like a minute with Dianna Edwards, a music minister, whom Father Rick Arkfeld introduced as "a very talented person and very professional in her field of restoring dignity to people who are old and giving life to people who are sick and dying, and teaching all of us how to accept sickness and old age and death in her own beautiful way with music, and laughter, and tears."

The huge crowd at St. Francis church in Randolph simply loved Deanna, and took her message to their hearts. She showed us how dying is part of living, and crying is our way of saying I love you. She told us that people who are sick, or old, and especially people who are dying need acceptance and hugs and love. She also related how those same people are wonderfully capable of teaching us by *their* acceptance. Her poignant songs gripped our hearts.

The afternoon was made more memorable by the fact that one of the greatest living examples of everything she said was running around grinning, and hugging, and *being excited* about dying right in front of us. That's Father Rick, who has been teaching by his acceptance and excitement about his own death since he learned he had malignant tumors taking over his lungs. To those who love him, and can't seem to share in his excitement, he promises that even though he is physically gone, his love will still be with them. He'll still be "hanging around." When I asked him how he knew these things, he said, with absolute faith, "I just know."

What a gift these people are.

Their message has been with us, of course. In the bible we read about how we should be like the lilies of the field. We're told to have no anxiety about anything, but by "prayer and supplication with thanksgiving let your request be made known to God. And the peace of God, which passes all understanding, will keep your hearts and your minds in Christ Jesus." And we're comforted with "Don't be afraid, for I am by your side . . ."

But for mere mortals, these things seem hard to take in.

We want to fuss about unimportant things. We don't heed the Lord's wise words. We're like the little boy who was told not to be afraid at night because Jesus was with him, and he said, "but I need someone with skin on." Thank God for the likes of Father Rick and Deanna, who are Jesus' representatives with skin on. They get our attention.

And for the likes of Grandpa Burney, too. Although he is not hanging around any more *with skin on*, I suspect he's hanging around. Just like Father Rick plans to. Because Grace said, "The strangest thing happened. I was throwing out dozens of old Reader's Digests, and a caption *The Three Most Important Words* happened to catch my eye so I tore the article out. I don't know why I did that. What do you think they were?"

I replied, "I love you."

Wrong!

The words were the same ones Grandpa had said with gentle humor two or three times a week all his life. "It doesn't matter."

Claude Canaday's Name Leads All the Rest

1988

A hush fell over the village church in Bloomfield at Claude Canaday's memorial service as Genevieve Frerichs read the poem "Abou Ben Adhem" in an emotion-filled voice.

Claude would have loved this. It was his favorite poem. He was always negotiating with his friends to write a book promoting peace, with this gentle poem as it's base. You may remember it.

It was about Abou Ben Adhem (may his tribe increase), who awoke one night *from a deep dream of peace* to find an angel writing in a book of gold *The names of those who loved the Lord.*

"And is mine one?," said Abou,

"Nay, not so," replied the Angel,

Abou spoke more low, but cheerily still:

and said, "I pray thee, then,

write me as one that loves his Fellow-men."

Abou *was* Claude Canaday. During his 90 plus years of life, this humble farmer from Northeast Nebraska touched more lives than most famous diplomats. He was a man of extraordinary generosity, courage and wisdom. Because of his vision, Bloomfield adopted a town in Germany after World War II. In that town is a street named CANADAY.

Claude's peace-full accomplishments are too numerous to

begin to mention. His weapon was love and he never let up. In his 90's he still insisted on taking part in Bloomfield's Crop Walk.

Gently and persistently and with great good humor, he rallied others to his cause. I don't know when it was that I got my first letter from Claude Canaday, but by the time he recruited me in his fight for peace, he was no longer a young man. I was just one of many he emmeshed in the net of love he cast out in the world. He also caught my friends, Norfolk's Marie Huck and Mary Pat Finn. The three of us became *Claude's Girls.* The last few years we celebrated his birthday, and marched—mostly with joy—to the persistent beat of his drummer.

His letters to me were encouraging, and always filled with the things that Claude thought I could do to promote peace. I was having some trouble keeping peace in my own house, so Claude's vision of what I might accomplish far exceeded mine. Considering the world-wide task he set for himself, he really wasn't asking much of me. He simply wanted me to bring peace to Ireland. His persistence was such, that feeling a little silly, I finally wrote a letter to the Irish Prime Minister and to my great surprise, I received a letter in return, with special regards to Claude. I'd done what I could. Claude was thrilled with the reply, but wrote "Not bad for a start." He took no credit for himself. Not ever. He was almost infuriatingly humble. As the Reverend Robert Hopkins said at his funeral, "It was hard to even give Claude a gift. He never thought he was worthy, and he kept trying to give it back."

As I sat in his Methodist church in Bloomfield, listening to the warm homily of Reverend Gary Alan as he talked of Claude finally resting in peace, I knew suddenly that this might be far from true. I could almost feel the restless spirit of that man of great vision, freed now from the encumbrance of his aging body, ready to go to work at a celestial level. I wondered aloud to Marie and Mary Pat if we shouldn't just go home and start packing for Ireland. The conclusion of Abou Ben Adhem poem says it all.

> *The angel wrote and vanished,*
> *The next night it came again,*
> *With a great wakening light,*
> *And showed the names who the*
> *love of God had blessed,—*

And, lo! Ben Adhem's name
led all the rest.

Kate and the Library

1988

"This is going to be a very special day, Grandma Joanie" said three-year-old granddaughter Kate, "because I am going to introduce my two Grandmothers to my library." Pausing briefly for dramatic effect, she continued "Then, I am going to introduce my library to my two Grandmas."

A library is my favorite place, anyway. Libraries can be, if they are run the way they should be, the heart and soul of a community. We are very fortunate in Cedar County to have one of the top libraries in the state. Top librarians are running it.

The library in Dubuque has the same warm and welcoming atmosphere, as does ours. Like ours, it is so wonderfully *library-ish*. When we arrived it was abuzz with three-year-olds arriving for their story hour. Kate marched imperiously to a table, put a card with her name on it and a string attached around her neck and made a bee-line for a glass enclosed room. Her grandmothers were trailing in her wake.

Once in the room she picked up a pint sized rug, and plopped herself down amid twenty some other three-year-olds. The wisdom of each having his or her own rug became apparent when a tiny boy strayed, and the story lady—not missing a beat—gently placed him squarely back on his rug. Except for that one minor transgression—they all stayed put.

Today the stories were all to be about dogs, with a darling dog doing tricks, in person. The children, and the Grandmas, were entranced. Except this grandma had to get busy, because she had more important business at this library. She had to find a story about a donkey. A librarian found me on the floor in front of the confusing array of children's books, and lead me to "Donkey, Donkey," a morality fable about a donkey who learned not be to ashamed of his long, funny ears. Perfect!

The donkey book was a necessity because the night before, Kate requested a song I've sung to her for three years. Only suddenly she became a critic.   You doubtless know the song. It's the one Bing Crosby sang in "Going My Way" to encourage young people to go to school: "Swinging on a star." Or, he would croon, the unpleasant alternatives: "would you rather be a fish?" Or a pig. Or mule. I was singing "Would you like to be a star?" gently and soothingly, sure that Kate was dozing off, just as she's done for three years. Suddenly, she sat bolt upright in her bed and said "Wait a minute, Grandma Joanie, you can't swing on a star! They are way up in the sky."

We finally figured out a *good* magician, like the one in *Sesame Street*, could put a swing on a star. A ladder might get us up, and a *very, very long* slippery slide would get us down *right in the back yard.* Satisfied, she said "Go on singing Grandma Joanie."

I got through the parts about being a fish, and a pig, to "or would you rather be a mule," when up popped the head— "wait a minute, Grandma Joanie, I didn't ever see a mule."

So that is why I was on my hands and knees in the children's section of the Dubuque library.   Libraries—the font of all education—would certainly have books about mules.

I *just happened* to be passing through Dubuque on my way to a speech in Dakalb, rejecting the Dekalbites suggestion that I fly into Chicago *just an hour away* (any grandmother would understand). A car trip to Dekalb would go through Dubuque, wherein the almost perfect grandchild and her parents, John and Lou Ann, live. It is a *loooong* drive, so I invited the only other person I knew who might even consider making it, Kate's other Grandmother, Darlene Topp of Wayne.

And, I don't know how the library felt, but Kate was right, because for her two grandmothers, it was a very, very special day.

The Child in the Cemetery

1988

My three-year-old granddaughter, Kate, stood at the gate of

the cemetery and waved her little hands in the general direction of Heaven.

"Happy Memorial Day, Everybody!!," she shouted joyously.

Decorating the graves with your three-year-old almost-perfect-granddaughter puts a whole new slant on Memorial day. I was going through the *chores* that I feel I must on Memorial Day to honor the Burneys and the Rossiters who have died. This has always been a bittersweet experience, complete with a bucket or so of tears. The older I get the more bittersweet it becomes because we simply have more dead people to honor. That's life, you see.

And, as has happened for many of us, family members scatter hither and yon, so those who stay at home become the designated grave decorators.   That can make a person responsible for a lot of graves.

I sometimes ponder the whole process, preferring to give flowers to the living, and wondering if anybody cavorting happily around Heaven gives a hoot. Then I realize, that we do it mainly for us. It's cathartic. We touch base, as it were, with loved ones who have died. We acknowledge how we miss them, and then get on with the present.

Although I have no insight into just how Heaven works, I think our loved ones must be pleased.

I would be.

I think.

The flowers we use on the graves have become traditional. For my folks, it is always mums. Dad sent mother a dozen huge football mums on every anniversary, so that's what goes in the built-in container on their marker. For the Burneys, Grandpa liked red and as did brother-in-law Wid, so Wid's wife, Virginia, and I always orders masses of red geraniums, which—being practical folks—we then bring them home and enjoy them ourselves. And there are special things for Grandma Welch, and sister-in-law Pat, and our own tiny son, David, and on and on and on.

When I started amassing the flowers for my yearly assault on the cemeteries this year, Kate was visiting, and she was fascinated. She would go along, she decided. It sounded like fun to *decorate*.

She needed to know all about it. And what do you say about death to a tiny girl, who's heart breaks, when a kitten hurts its paw.

You tell her the truth, of course, but I knew I would be in for an interrogation. She's a child who probes. For instance, the other day she asked John, her father, to explain the circulation of blood.

I think she's going to be a reporter.

Meanwhile, back at the cemetery, Kate was fascinated. She interrogated me about my mother and father. She wondered why she couldn't meet them. I explained they'd gotten old and died, and were in Heaven. It was just their bodies in the cemetery, I explained, the important part of them, their spirits, had flown up to Heaven.

"We know they are really happy in Heaven," I told her, "but we like to let them know they are remembered on earth, so we set aside this special day. Kind of like a birthday party."

"But nobody is here," Kate said.

"Well, we can't see them, but they know what we're doing, and I think it makes them happy, don't you?"

What changed for me, because of Kate, was that instead of weeping around, I told her true stories about the wondrous characters who were her forefathers. What happened, you see, is that instead of mourning their deaths, we celebrated their lives.

Her "Happy Memorial Day Everybody!" was entirely spontaneous. The joyous outcry of a little girl who somehow seemed to understand, maybe better than her Grandma Joanie.

Then she marched out of the gate on her two sturdy little legs with great self-satisfaction.

"I think they are glad I came, Grandma Joanie," said Kate. I think so too.

Take Care of Your Earth Suit—Someone Else May Need Some Parts

1988

For years I have been looking for just the right example to illustrate the relative unimportance of what we look like, compared to what we are inside. One analogy I picked up somewhere is that we all arrive on earth with different packaging, but the packaging isn't the important thing, it's what's inside that counts. Beautiful packages can contain little or nothing, while brown paper bags can be full of wondrous surprises. Close. But no cigar.

Then came along the 15th annual meeting of the Kidney Foundation of Nebraska, and with it Milton Bemis and his poignant story. I am grateful.

I'm not sure how much I would be involved with the National Kidney Foundation of Nebraska if it weren't for my dear friend, Darlene Miller. There are a lot of worthy causes in this world. Darlene had a kidney transplant fifteen years ago, and—as she told the people at the meeting—she had 1700 people (population of Hartington) cheering her on. I was one of them.

She has involved most of the 1700 people in her enthusiastic attempts through the years to help the Kidney Foundation raise money. She thrust kidney candy upon us, along with donor cards and kidney literature. More recently, she has had a garage sale in which she and her relatives and friends have sold hundreds of dollars worth of homemade pickles, and pies, and candy, and aprons and decorated sweatshirts, and other things too numerous to mention.

The National Kidney Foundation of Nebraska is important, therefore, because of Darlene. We are grateful for what they accomplish.

The Foundation was so grateful for what Darlene accomplished, they presented her with a special award. She asked me not to mention that award because she's gotten a couple of others this year (LaVitsef and Good Neighbor). She thinks people will be getting sick of hearing about them. I would appreciate it if you didn't tell her you saw it here.

Be that as it may, the days when Darlene's non-functioning kidneys were replaced by one of her brother Leo's (Curley) perfectly matched and functioning ones, are vivid in a lot of memories. When it seemed that the body might reject the kidney, perfect match though it was, Curley sent Darlene a message: "That kidney has been trained on beer."

On the excellent morning panel, Darlene was the success story, as old as the foundation, and still going (in more ways than one) strong. Also on the panel was a young woman who described the frustration of waiting for a kidney, then having one turn up that was not a match. And a man who had had one failed transplant and chose not to have another as long as dialysis would let him function and be with his children. Then there was the experience of a man who'd donated a kidney. And then there was Milton Bemis. Milton had a five-year-old son who drowned, and his kidney and liver were donated so that a little girl could live.

It was difficult to explain this to the boy's two older sisters, Milton said, but they were determined not to in any way think that their boy lived on in this little girl. So, he said "We talked about how the astronauts couldn't live in space without their space suits. I told them that while we are on earth our body is simply our earth suit. When we die the essence of us, our spirit, goes up into Heaven, and we have no more use for our earth suits. So it is really a wonderful thing when somebody else makes some use of them." What a great way to explain death to kids. To anyone.

Doesn't it also make sense to do our best to keep our earth suits in tip top shape? Not abuse them, or take them for granted. Not only will they last longer, but when we shed the blooming things to begin our next great adventure, maybe there will be a part or two worth salvaging.   Something to think about.

In Appreciation of Ted

1988

I wish President Bush could meet my friend, octogenarian Ted Miller. Ted is a philosopher. Whenever you run into him—in the post office or just walking down the street—he greets you with poetry. He can recite almost anything, word for word, but I knew the minute he saw George, he would recite Rudyard Kipling's "If":

If you can keep your head when all about you
Are losing theirs and blaming it on you;
If you can trust yourself when all men doubt you,
But make allowance for their doubting too:
If you can wait and not be tired by waiting,
Or being lied about, don't deal in lies
Or being hated don't give away to hating,
And yet don't look too good, nor talk too wise;

Wise words for beleaguered politicians, or any of us. Ted recites all four verses, voice ringing with sincerity, bright eyes piercing yours to see if you're really listening. If your eyes light up when you hear those words, as mine always do, you'll be getting a copy of the poem, framed ready for hanging, to remind you of Ted's vast wisdom in case he isn't around to do it himself. The president's multitude of advisers could not speak wiser words.

The president needs Ted; needs him just hanging around, so he can pass by him in the Green Room occasionally and benefit from his wisdom. A lot of men get to be 80, but not all with such an understanding of the important things of life. Ted is as wise as he is because most of his life he's been a painter, and a masterful one. He also finishes old furniture. He's taken things that are downright ugly, and transformed them into things of beauty with great patience, inch by inch.

I think a painter, or a refinisher, learns all they need to know about life just doing what they do. They have to scrape off the old to make way for the new. They can't just cover it up. They tackle one portion at a time, doing it right, before they go on to the next. Just as one must tackle any task, or any of life's problems. It's the best way to go about life, patiently, not ramming through, taking time to smell the roses, hug a friend, recite poetry, finding out bit by bit the person it's in us to be, and then being true to that person.

If you can dream and not make dreams your master;
If you can think and not make thoughts your aim,
If you can meet with triumph and disaster
And treat those two imposters just the same:
If you can bear to hear the truth you've spoken
Twisted by knaves to make a trap for fools,
Or watch the things you gave your life to, broken,
And stoop and build 'em up with worn-out tools;
(Are you listening President Bush?)
If you can make one heap of all your winnings
And risk it on one turn of pitch-and-toss,
And lose, and start again at your beginning
And never breathe a word about your loss:
If you can force your heart and nerve and sinew
To serve your turn long after they are gone,
And so hold on when there is nothing in you
Except the will which says to them: hold on!

If you can walk with crowds and keep your virtue,
Or walk with kings nor lose the common touch,
If neither foes nor loving friends can hurt you,
If all men count with you, but none too much:

If you can fill the unforgiving minute
With sixty seconds worth of distance run.
Yours is the earth and everything that's in it.
And which is more you'll be a man, my son.

(And a darned good president!)

Kate's Imaginary Frog

1988

Once upon a time in a state called Nebraska, near a town called Hartington, there lived a seemingly mature lady who couldn't stop telling silly stories. Not jokes (Heaven knows!). But *Once upon a time* stories.

One night she started her story this way "Once upon a time there was a little girl named Kate who thought she was a frog."

The lady who has the story telling problem (whom we'll here-after refer to as Grandma Joanie, or G.J.) got addicted to it when she was very young, when she started telling stories to even younger kids. She always made the kids to whom she told the stories the heroes or heroines. She loved watching their eyes get big, and hearing them giggle. When the "and they lived happily ever after" part came (and they always live happily ever after) she loved to see how delighted they were.

To a point. Sometimes there are problems even for story tellers. For instance, as a very young girl, perhaps 11 or 12 , G. J. made up stories for her nephews, who weren't all that much younger than she was.   Little Micheal Rossiter, and his friend Toughy Renze, loved the story about the two little boys, Mike and Toughy, who saved the United states from the bad guys who were sailing toward it by swimming to the bottom of the ocean and pulling the plug so the water drained out.

Mike and Toughy loved the story so much they begged her to tell it again, and again, and again.

G.J. got tired of it and refused. So Mike and Toughy blackmailed her, saying that they would tell their grandfather Emmett (who was G.J.'s father) that a *boy* had walked her home. Grandpa Emmet was not big on *boys* being around any of his girls. So G.J., being no fool, told the story again, and again, and again.

Kate (the reason there is a Grandma Joanie) likes the same stories too. Especially the one about the three little mice who lived in the forrest and were visited by Kate, Winnie the Pooh and all the gang. G.J. never remembers all the gang.

However, not to worry. Kate, with her almost-four-year-old's insistence on accuracy, leaps in with details.

"Of course, that's it!" G.J. says, pretending to remember too. The latest story came about because Kate had spent part of the day pretending, for some reason no adult could fathom, that she was a frog. Kip, therefore, had to be Grandpa Frog.

In the story, Kate the pretend frog hopped down to the creek and ran into a real Grandpa Frog, who had a very deep croak, and said "ribit" a lot. Grandpa Frog was astonished to find a little girl with long blond hair claiming to be a frog. The little girl explained to him about how the *imagination* works. "We just pretend," said Kate. Grandpa Frog (the real one) wondered if he could pretend to be a real person. "Everybody can pretend," Kate said. And she and the frog came hopping home. That's why, on Christmas day, around the dinner table, there sat the whole Burney family, and one great big frog. Funny thing, he looked an awful lot like Grandpa Kip. (Ribit.)

And they all lived happily every after.

Angels in Nursing Homes

1989

Many years ago a good friend, Dr. Frank McCarthy, told me, "It takes a special person to work in a nursing home. It is an extraordinary gift."

The past few weeks I have had the opportunity to view these

special people in action. I've come to think of them as ministering angels.

Most recently my experience has been visiting my sister-in-law, Virginia, who is recuperating at the Coleridge Nursing Home.

This past week, I kept a silent vigil at the bedside of a Hospice patient in the Hartington Nursing Home.

Well, not so silent. My first task when I'm on this kind of a mission is to establish some kind of a link with the patient, so I can visit. Our patient this time was comatose. It's still important to visit.

Even in a small town we don't always know everybody, so I visited with the nurses, for whom the patients are part of one big family. I read her bulletin board. There I found my connection, a picture of the family of a friend of ours. I asked nurse Karen, one of the softly-gliding angels, what the link was between our patient and my friend. She said the friendship came out of a prayer group that just "hung out together."

I visited about all this with our patient, and found myself crying. Crying is okay. Crying is healing. But I wondered that I couldn't be more detached, given the circumstances.

Then it came to me that the people who work in nursing homes deal with this kind of emotional thing over and over. Though many people go home from nursing homes, using them as temporary places of healing, many others don't. And therein lies the great mission for the people who work in a nursing home. They assist these people in living out their last days with as much dignity and respect and love and humor as possible.

How do they handle this? I watched the nurses as they bustled in and out, and I pondered.

The bustling accelerated as morning came, and patient after patient had to be dressed and readied for the day. Then started a slow and stately procession to the dining room.

By wheelchair, walker, or on their own power, sometime hesitantly, sometimes with surprising briskness, the residents of the home flowed in an almost ritualistic procession towards their morning meal. Some were jovial, some silent, some just determined to get there.

The ministering angels hovered about, doing their job efficiently, with tender loving care.

I know many of the people who work in the homes. I know they don't get paid a lot. I know they work long hours, and then go home to families and chores. I know they are active in the community and in their churches.

I know many of the residents. Some of them are doing just okay. They maintain their enthusiasm for life and are a delight to work with. A nursing home is a great place to be when you can not take care of yourself. But for some, their spirits have all but deserted their ravaged bodies. They can no longer be the person they were, and so this is just a waiting period, until they get to abandon that shell of a body and become the person they are meant to be.

The *ministering angels* understand this, or so it seems to me. They treat these people with dignity and common sense, with compassion and empathy, understanding that this isn't who they were or who they will be, it's just one of the last stops on life's journey. And they are making it as comfortable as possible. As Dr. McCarthy said, "It takes a special person".

One Little "I Love You" Would Have Been Okay

1989

Father's Day is upon us, and I've been pondering it. As a counselor and a teacher of parenting skills, I've thought a lot about this business of fathering. I've come to realize, more than ever, how important it is. I've learned there are a lot of ways to be a good father, each one unique.

I've learned that most fathers really try.

Some fathers play games with their kids. Some teach them how to do things. Some sing to them. Some tell them stories, and some don't do any of those things. That's okay. The only thing absolutely necessary to be a good father is to give your children a foundation of love that lets them know you appreciate them as unique individuals, just as they are

That appreciation should go both ways, but it doesn't always— until children grow up and have children of their own. Then we begin to get some notion of what an unbelievable blessing and a bother children are. And we begin to understand the awesome responsibility of raising a child.

Fathers of today take a more active part in raising their children than the fathers of yesteryear. They are not afraid to tell their kids they love them. Nothing would be nicer.

At least, I think it would. I have no memory of that. I loved my father, and I'm pretty sure he loved me. But in my pondering I've come to realize I never heard him say those words. Not once. My father was Irish and a bona-fide character. And he was a crusader. Banging on his green-ribboned typewriter he took on the world, preparing for the depression he always thought was imminent, waging a constant war of vigilence against anything that threatened family farms. He lived life in over-drive and died in 1951 at the age of 63.

He handled stress with humor. In the midst of the drought he'd go in the bathroom, turn on the shower, and call his brother, Bert Rossiter, in Walthill, Nebraska, to let him listen to our "great rain". He and Uncle Charlie always had something going. I'll never forget Uncle Charlie Mullaney's pained outcry, "Emmett, Emmett, what have you done?" when Dad stumbled on the walk to Charlie's house, completely obliterating the fifth of Charlie's favorite whiskey which Dad cradled ostentatiously in his arms. Charlie never knew the precious liquid was really colored water.

My fondest memories of Dad were on Sunday afternoon when we took "THE RIDE". One of Dad's dearest possessions was a 1928 Cadillac convertible which he bought when the city of Omaha sold it after using it for many years as a parade car. My little sister Anne (Millea) and I used to argue about who would get to sit where President Roosevelt sat.

Dad would load up Mom and Grandma Welch and Anne and me (whether we wanted to be loaded up or not) and he'd head out over the hills of Cedar County. Hair blowing in the wind, we'd whoosh over the hills. I can still remember the tingling sensation in my tummy.

I'm sure Dad did the best he knew how. But in those days kids were seen and not heard. Fathers earned the living and mothers took care of the family. We didn't have much chance to get to know him.

I regret that. I think we all lost out.

I celebrate the fact this is changing. The young fathers I know communicate their love to their kids. They know how important that is. Of all the memories one has of one's father, the greatest one must be of a big hug, and an "I love you". I wish I'd had that. I wouldn't trade my Dad for any other one in the world, but one little "I love you" would have been okay.

If you are a father, and aren't already dishing out "I love you"s all over the place, I hope you take this to heart so when your kid gets to be 60 years old she won't be complaining in her columns.

Such a memory lasts a lifetime, and doubtless spills over into eternity.

CHAPTER TWO

GETTING ALONG

Chapter Two

Getting Along While You're Getting Along

Relationships

It comes as a shock to many, it certainly did to me, that people have a right to be different than we prefer them to be. Each of us has a unique personality, and we will not always understand the people who have different personalities than we do.

They will process information differently, laugh at different things, mourn differently, and enjoy different past-times. We do not have to understand another person to appreciate who they are, or what they do, or to work with them, or even to love them. If we just understand that, we will greatly diminish our stress load. The columns in this segment concentrate on relationships, and attempt to shed some light on this understanding process. I hope you understand.

Heading Around the Corner . . .

1982

The man wrote with great glee, "And it worked, too!" I'll bet it did. It even worked on me.

As often as I yammer away about remembering loved ones when they are still around to appreciate it, I don't always do it myself. Life gets busy. All those old excuses.

Sometimes we need to be reminded about things we already know, no matter how well we think we know them.

A friend of mine from Norfolk did that for me, and now I will do it for you. The quotation he sent me was powerful. It attacks you right in your heart and then goes to work. If it doesn't head a bunch of us right to the phone or the pen to set up a date with a beloved person we've neglected, I will be mightily surprised.

My Norfolk friend said he'd been looking for a quotation like this to shame his brother into visiting him and, "believe it or not, on one of the Sundays my spouse got me to church, darned if the minister didn't read the exact poem I needed from the pulpit."

Here it is:

Around the corner I have a friend in this great city that has no end;

Yet days go by, and weeks rush on, and before I know it, a year is gone. And I never see my friend's face, for life is a swift and terrible race. He knows I like him as well as in the days when I rang his bell, and he rang mine.

We were younger then, And now we are busy, tired men; tired with playing a foolish game. Tired with trying to make a name.

"Tomorrow," I say, "I will call on Him, just to show that I'm thinking of him."

But tomorrow comes, and tomorrow goes, and the distance between us grows and grows.

Around the corner, yet miles away.

"Here's a telegram, sir,"

"Jim died today,"

And that's what we get and DESERVE, in the end; around the corner, a vanished friend.

You might want to act on this yourself, or send it to your brother.

As for me—I'm heading around a few corners.

Fighters Can Turn Trouble Into Triumph

1985

A lot of painful things are happening in my hometown of Hartington.

The farm crisis is worsening and good operators are going down the tube. The Federal Land Bank is moving its office out of town, taking some fine people with it. The Neu Cheese Co. is considering locating elsewhere, which some would suggest is the begin-

ning of the toll of a death knell for our town. Jim Neu has been one
of the city's strongest supporters and builders. For him to make
that kind of a decision has to be like taking a slice out of his own
heart.

There doesn't seem to be any good news anywhere. So what's
a person to do? I have two suggestions.

Suicide is NOT one of them. A friend of ours who had to
declare bankruptcy told me that, for just a scary second, he had
contemplated suicide.

"Things seemed that hopeless, that terrible!" he said. "But
then I got to thinking about the things in life that really mattered. I
thought about the fact that I had pretty darned good health. I had a
wife and a family who loved me. I had friends and relatives who
stuck by me. I began to see that I had some riches that money can't
buy, that nobody can tax and nobody can foreclose on. I know
fighting our way back will be tough," he said, "but I have faith in
God and faith in myself and we're going to make it."

So my first suggestion would be to do what our friend did—
look around and count our blessings. As bad as things are, our
riches are many. Most people in the world would change places
with us in a minute for a chance to live in freedom and not fear for
their lives.

The second thing I think we have to do is get our creative
juices going. Our pioneer forefathers would look at all these difficulties as opportunities which they would get busy and surmount.
They would appraise the problem realistically, decide on their
options and get busy. There wasn't anyone around to help them.
No government programs, no nothing. They had only themselves
to rely on. Their hardships were many. They dried out and burned
out, got covered with grasshoppers, etc.

I'm getting my masters in psychological counseling. I'm getting it primarily so that I can write and speak with more credibility.
The one thing I have reaffirmed over and over again is that if a
person thinks only of disaster, disaster will surely be what happens.

But if a person thinks of all the difficulties as opportunities for
creating something new instead of beginning the toll of funeral
bells, then that person can learn and grow from each creative handling of the difficulty.

Towns are full of people with creative juices. Ideas waiting to be born. No one person can cause the death of a community if that community believes in itself. A person's not dead until they've stopped breathing. A community, especially a community like ours, has more life than it knows what to do with—with city fathers and mothers who work themselves to a frazzle in community projects, with two excellent school systems, a gorgeous park, a frustrating golf course, people as good as gold and kids as cute and healthy as exist anywhere in the world. With caring organizations and churches and people and vision.

As many of you know, my brother Vincent is a banker. And though bankers have had to assume the position as bad guys, they are in about as tough and psychologically destructive position as anybody.

Vincent is depressing and he's sincere about it. He knows the economy is headed for disaster and he's doing his best to protect his customers, most of whom would rather not be protected. Oh, they'll thank him if he's right. But they don't see that now. I'm considering setting up an office next to Vince when I get my masters in counseling. I should make a lot of money (only kidding, Vince!)

Anyway, both of us give speeches. And Vince pointed out to me not too long ago that taking everything into consideration it seemed strange that he, a well-do-do banker, would be going around giving depressing speeches, while I, the wife of a man who is a farmer, and a cattle feeder, both professions that are going down the tube, should be going around trying to make people laugh. I've thought about that a lot.

I know that it's just something I have to do, just like he has to preach economics. He knows his economics. But the thing is, I know my human beings and human beings are miracles. People are capable of infinite growth. Human beings can suffer the degradations of concentration camps and transcend the experience with faith and a sense of humor. That's a proven fact.

This is a long-winded column, but I've never written one with more sincerity.

As individuals or as a town we can fight or we can quit. We can moan and groan and complain and die a little every day, or we can take what we've got, and we've got one hell of a lot, and we can make the best of it. It's a matter of choice.

A Nice Cover Never Hurts

1986

This column is about books and covers and human beings and how everything is related, and nothing is for sure.

To start with, I had an experience in July which will ensure that I shall never look at a book again without a feeling of awe. Not because of what's in books, you understand, I've always been in awe of that. But because of their covers. For me that's a new kind of awe.

The old saying that you can never tell a book by its cover, meaning don't judge a human being by what you see externally, is certainly true in its usual context. On the other hand, a nice cover doesn't hurt, for human beings or books.

A visit to a book bindery made me aware of how much of a difference a cover makes. Recent studies attest to what human beings can do for themselves by working with their own covers.

All of this will make sense to you in a minute, I think. It came together for me in an "aha" type of experience because it happened that the very week I read about the studies I visited the book bindery.

Visiting a book bindery is a fascinating experience. Especially the historic Houchen Bindery, Ltd., located in the little town of Utica, Nebraska.

I felt comfortable the minute I entered Houchen Bindery because, to the unknowing eye of a bindery illiterate, the place was a mess. It looked a lot like my office with books piled everywhere. The startling thing was that most of these books were naked. They had no covers.

Now, many of you know what goes on in binderies, because you're in positions where you take a bunch of perfectly good but rotten looking books and have them recovered.

The Houchen Bindery is managed by the Osborne family, Don and Connie and troops. They're musical too. Besides binding new books, they take used books from schools or libraries and recover them. They also bind magazines into volumes. It may sound simple, but it's an operation that takes some thirty intricate and time consuming steps from the time they check the books in until, very carefully trimmed, sewn, glued, lined, back-stripped, covered with material which has been exactly measured and appropriately stamped, cased, creased, and pressed, they are packed and shipped home.

Some thirty-thousand books were being processed when I was there and the deadline for the Osbornes and crew was twenty days hence. It is organized chaos.

All that is impressive, but the most impressive thing for me was the visual evidence of what the cover did for the book. Cruddy-looking books came in, and they went out looking marvelous.

Unfortunately, there is no Houchen Bindery for replacing human covers. However, psychologists claim by consciously changing our exterior we can change how we feel inside. We're all convinced laughing is good for our mental and physical health. The studies take one step further. They say if you make yourself smile, especially when you don't have anything to smile about, the actual act of smiling itself will change the way you feel. In other words, if you change your cover, it will change you.

Try it. It can't hurt. If you're feeling grumpy trying to understand what in the heck I'm talking about, change the grumpy look on your face to a smiling one. See how much better you feel. Or, when you get up in the morning, instead of looking in the mirror and thinking, "Oh, my gawd!", try looking in the mirror and smiling. Even if you don't feel like it, and chances are you won't, you'll be amazed what it does for you.

We could go on and on with this cover business. Talk about how covers are involved in first impressions. Check responses to other people's covers. Think of how much better we like someone with a smiling cover than we do a grumpy one.

It's interesting. You may not be able to tell a book by its cover, but you can tell a cover by its cover. And if you like the cover, you'll probably want to get to know the book. Know what I mean?

Try Hugging, You Might Lose Weight

1987

Before I ever heard of Leo Buscaglia, I promoted hugging.

Now, I'm even more excited about it, and I'm sure Leo is too, because studies show that hugging can accomplish more things than we ever suspected. A warm and loving hug, my friends, can improve your outlook on life, fight depression, have a remedial affect on arthritis, diabetes and mental illness, and even help you lose weight.

"Wait a doggoned minute!!" you're probably thinking, "I understand all those other things, but loose weight?—How can that be?"

Well, I'm going to tell you.

I research a subject rather thoroughly when I get interested. Kip says, "ad nauseum." So it has been with losing weight, a heretofore illusive goal of my own, and possibly of yours.

For years Kip and I have been talking about our need to lose weight. We've discovered moving mouth muscles won't do it. This all came to a head (and a stomach) as we were waddling about the house after Christmas. We'd let Kip's pants out as far as they could go, and even the zippers on my *fat clothes* were beginning to groan. (To those of you who are lucky enough to stay the same size: many of us have two kinds of clothes, those we wear when we're at the weight we'd like to be, and those we usually wear).

Therefore, motivated by necessity, the mirror, and our pocketbooks, Kip and I have been on a diet and exercise regimen since the first of the year.

To the end of reducing our ends we re-activated our exercise bicycle (actually, reclaimed it from a kid) and even bought a gut buster. I got lower back pains, and Kip got sick in the very gut he was trying to bust. (Probably psychosomatic.) Progressing at a more sensible pace we have managed to rid ourselves of a modest amount of our vast collection of fat corpuscles.

But to get to the subject of this column, I learned through my research on ways to lose weight that a person MUST engage in the depressing duo of eating less calories and exercising more. But a person also needs something else, and that is affection. Translate that—to lose weight a person needs hugging.

Now, I'm not talking about sex—I'm talking about affection, meaning a loving, caring relationship. A survey conducted by Playboy Enterprises (could you doubt this?) found most males made a clear distinction between sex and love, and said that love was most important.

Experts agree. And they add that when we don't get that love, we reach for an Oreo. Everytime we go to the refrigerator to reach for food, what we may be really looking for is affection. If you don't believe me, you will perhaps believe Dr. Leo Wollman, an expert on weight-loss, who's in depth studies show that hugging actually helps people lose weight.

Not only that, according to Dr. William F. Fry, a psychiatrist from Standford Research Institute, "hugging is especially helpful to those who are depressed." So if it makes you depressed to pass up your favorite pie hugging could help.

Truly, hugging is essential. Harvard University studies show that young children who are cuddled frequently achieve better grades in school, and a baby who is kissed and hugged grows up to be a much happier adult.

If you aren't a hugger, it's almost as effective to create about you a hugging atmophere. A loving pat on the head, a warm shake of the hand, a caring smile, a few words of concern, an atmosphere of positive reinforcement can do wonders. It works in the home, at school, at your place of business, on a farm or a ranch, and up and down main street.

If you are a crabby person, not giving to kindly remarks, let alone hugging, I beg of you to try it. You'll be amazed. The people around you will be happier, more healthy, more productive, and even—perhaps—skinier. Besides, hugging is reciprocal. The same thing will happen to you. What have you got to lose—but weight. (I hope Kip reads this column.)

On Having a Wind-Up Mentality
in a Computer World

1987

Sometimes I feel as if I have a wind-up mentality in a computer world. That's okay. As long as I can keep winding myself up. We can't turn our clocks back—but, by golly, we can wind them up again.

I'm sure you've done some re-winding in your lives, too. There are a lot of reasons for a person's clock to run down. Life is full of hurdles and sometimes we just can't seem to jump that high. And occasionally life pops up with a wall which we can't jump at all.

Hurdles come in all sizes. Hurdles are problems which we can figure out ways to get over, or around, or under, as long as we have breath in our bodies. Hurdles can be pretty awful and pretty challenging. But they don't compare to walls.

A column about the farm crisis, for instance, brought a poignant letter from a farmer in the southeast corner of the state. His wife of many years had died and he said, "I think I might be able to hold on to my farm but I don't care any more. My wife and I were doing it together and, with her gone, it doesn't make any difference."

For many, the rules change in the middle of the game. Not for everyone, of course. Seemingly, there are those who, by a combination of wit, wisdom or luck, survive the rigors of life without having to negotiate even a bump. I wouldn't bet on it. Appearances are deceiving. No way do we know their secret sorrows.

I'm always echoing Grandpa Burney about the importance of living in today, because yesterday is over and tomorrow never really comes.

We have a friend from afar who is going through the painful process of losing his farm, adjusting to his loss, and starting life all over again—rewinding his clock, as it were. He'd stop to visit occasionally, and I'd listen and encourage. He told me recently that there were times he'd like to have "whomped me long side of my face." He said, "I knew I'd better concentrate on what I had and quit wallowing in suffering about my losses, but I wanted to wallow. Sure yesterday was over—and tomorrow would never come, but it seemed to me that today had been here too danged long."

That friend, by the way, has come out the other end of his personal crisis intact, psychologically and financially. Nothing easy about it. Lot of pain. Lot of healing. Now he says, "Sometimes I wake up and realize I have no interest to pay—and I just have to laugh. It feels so good."

In this day and age, many people are having to make tough decisions. Dreams of farms and businesses have been obliterated because of the economy. Dreams have been wiped out by illness and destroyed by death. We're constantly faced with the necessity of re-winding our clocks.

Women who'd planned to live and die as housewives, canning and gardening and cleaning, find that they have no choice but to go to work.

Men who's future seemed secure on the family farm, or in the family business, or any business, are having to contemplate a forced change of career.

We have to deal with denial, depression, anger and bitterness as we work through the grief process on the way to realistic acceptance . . . and getting on with life.

We can do it, because every fiber of our body is programmed toward survival. We WILL come out the other side. Things will never be the same but we might even be stronger in the broken places. We've taken all the buzzards can dish out, and, by God (because faith has a lot to do with it) we can survive.

This column is about re-winding your clock. Or, come to think of it, re-programming your computer. If you're down, this column may make you want to whomp me long side of my face, too. That's a good sign. Anger means you're getting better. Hang in there. To mangle a quote: "We can't keep the buzzards of misery from flying over our heads, but we don't need to let them nest in our hair."

Sibling Rivalry: Get the Book!

1988

I was waiting for an elevator when an angry family of two little girls, who appeared to be around eleven and nine, burst out of a hotel room, trailed by a younger brother.

"Go ahead and pout," said the big sister, giving the younger one a punch, "see if I care."

"Oh shut up!!," said the younger sister, punching back.

The little brother said, "you're both stupid."

The father, looking disgusted and embarassed, said in a menacing tone, "cut that out—or else!," and led his battling brood to a stairway, the sound of bickering fading as they went.

I had this overwhelming urge to run after that father and holler, "read *Siblings Without Rivalry*."

The sooner the better.

Of all the books I wished I'd had to read while we were raising our six children, this one tops the list. One of the greatest sources of stress in a famiily is the on-going strife brought about by sibling rivalry. As parents, we will do almost anything in the world to bring about peace in a household full of bickering children.

But sometimes we just don't know what to do. With the best intentions in the world, we simply aggravate the problem.   We forbid, and punish, and plead, and bribe. We yell and we take sides. And still the kids tease and tattle and battle.

The first thing that the authors in the above mentioned book do is attempt to make you understand how a little person feels when somebody new comes into the family. Children are not naturally receptive to a new brother or sister, any more than we would be if our spouse put his (or her) arms around us and said "honey, I love you so much I've decided to have another wife (or husband) just like you."

Instead of dismissing these negative feelings, parents should acknowledge them, and help their children put the feelings into words. Not till the bad feelings come out can the good feelings come in. Strange as it might seem, insisting on good feelings between children leads to bad feelings; while allowing for bad feelings between children leads to good feelings. For instance, if a young child says, "I hate my brother!," you don't say, "Of course you don't hate him, you love him, he's your brother." Instead you acknowledge how the child is feeling at that time, and say something like, "sometimes you get very angry at your brother, don't you," and then allow them to verbalize their feelings.

Encourage children to express their feelings in a creative way, by drawing a picture, or writing a letter. If children are allowed to get their feelings out in a healthy fashion, they will not act upon them in a devious or hurtful way.

Also resist the urge to compare. Every child is unique, with his or her own strengths and weaknesses. Instead of comparing children either favorably—or unfavorably—speak to them only of their behavior as it applies to them. For instance, try not to say, "Why aren't you neat like your sister," or even, "you're so much neater than your brother." Instead concentrate on the child's behavior that pleases or displeases you. *"I appreciate you're being so neat."*

It's important to realize, also, that positive reinforcement—sincere compliments—will go a lot farther to building a child's character than will criticism. Remember to concentrate on what the child does right, rather than harp on what they do wrong.

Children do not need to be treated equally, they need to be treated uniquely. Instead of, "I love you the same as your sister," you might say, "You are the only *you* in the whole world. Nobody can ever take your place."

The book also covers methods of handling conflict, and lots of other things that would be valuable for a parent who's being driven batty by sibling rivalry. If this is your problem consider yourself hollered at: Get the book. Get the book. Get the book.

I Love You Dear, But You Can Iron
Your Shirt Yourself!

1988

For years I thought the *empty nest syndrome* was a figment of somebody's imagination. Our six kids started to leave home on schedule, but they kept coming back, between colleges, between jobs, just "between." My concerns about how I'd be able to stand a house without children vanished before my concerns that I might never have that opportunity. When that time finally came, I didn't consider it so much of a problem as an accomplishment—more of a blessing.

And the children felt the same way.

Now, be assured, I love each one of our kids fiercely, and I am vastly interested in where they are and what they're doing. It's just that I'm just as happy it's not here. I get lonesome for them on a regular basis, but— after all—what are phones for?

However, this time of year new sets of parents view with alarm the graduation of a youngest child. A plaintive letter from a reader pointed that out to me, and asked "will you reprint the column you once wrote on the *Empty Nest Syndrome.*"

I will quote from that column, because what I said then is true now. Columnists often are called upon to muse about the same subjects, such as birthdays—Christmas—Memorial Day—Syndromes—. Hopefully, when requested to re-muse, they do it with a little more knowledge and from a different perspective.

So it is with me with the *Empty Nest Syndrome.*

It's all well and good for me to say, "It's a mistake to try to live through your kids."

And, "Develop your own interests long before the kids leave the nest."

But that's not much help for parents who have lived their lives through their kids, and who haven't developed those interests. They've had a wonderful time, but the time has come when their kids are desperately trying to grow up, and they need to leave their parents behind. Parents cannot continue to live their lives through their kids. It's not fair to them, or to the kids. So some parents panic, and feel pain. To get better, they will need to change their perspective. This isn't easy, but it is possible. I had a friend who was devastated when her youngest took off for college and all her kids were away from home.

She cried and cried.

"I can't live without my kids, I am so lonely I cannot stand it," she said. We talked about the importance of her getting some new interests, and finding out who she was apart from *mother.* There is no point in a person just sitting around wallowing in misery when there's a whole internal and external world waiting to be explored. She decided to explore. Boy, did she explore. She took some classes, did some traveling, eventually even got a fulfilling part time job.

The last time I asked her about her kids, she said, "What kids?"

There's another thing about thinking your kids have left home. Don't bet on it. Kids come back often. They come with friends and dirty clothes, and sometimes they come *between* to live awhile.

You'll find adult kids who come home often want the freedom of being an adult with the privileges of being a kid. Services, like laundry and cooking, are taken for granted. If Mom's are unhappy about this (some mom's don't mind) they will need to take a firm but friendly stand. "I love you dear, but I'm certain you can handle ironing this shirt yourself." It's not easy. Old habits die hard. And unreasonable and uncalled for guilt happens to one.

In reality, it takes kids awhile to really leave home. They do pop back often, and they like to keep their parents around for emergencies. But the pain felt by parents *losing* their children can be decreased in direct ratio to the excitement of developing new interests and talents of their own, and even becoming re-acquainted with each other. So, if the *empty nest syndrome* is a problem for you, enroll in a class, start an exercise program, develop a skill, join a club, volunteer for a worthy cause, and you'll soon be saying "what kids?" too.

The Miracle of the Encouraging Word

1988

Supposing you were driving down the road, minding your own business, and a patrol car came up behind you blinking its red lights. You knew you weren't speeding, and as far as you know nothing else was wrong, so you just can't figure out what's going on. You deal with a multitude of feelings as the uniformed man makes his way to your car.

But you feel a little better when you notice the patrolman has a warm smile on his face. He says, "I've been following you for a long time, and you are one of the best and most courteous drivers I have ever seen on the road. I was so impressed that I just had to stop you and commend you."

Or suppose you come home from a day so frustrating you can hardly believe it happened. You get in the door, and smell your favorite food cooking, and your spouse (in this day and age it could be either husband or wife) says to you, "I knew you were going to have a bad day, so I planned a special meal for you to show you how much I love you, and how important your feelings are to me."

How do you think you'd feel? You'd feel good, that's how you feel. Most importantly, you'd feel encouraged. An encouraged person is a person who can get on with life with enthusiasm.

Those of you who are long time readers know that I am an avid promotor of hugging and a hugging atmosphere.

And that I also stress the importance of humor, and being able to laugh at oneself. Now I come to my newest promotion, the root of all of the hugging and laughing. That is the importance of encouragement, for ourselves and for others.

In this land where supposedly "never is heard a discouraging word" we would be astounded if we really listened to some of the words that come out of our mouths. The constant barrage of negatives, the shouldn't, and the can'ts, that we heap on ourselves and on others.   These are the words that keep us from trying something new, or being somebody new, losing forever the wonders of what might have been.

Miracles happen in a home, or a class room, or a business, or a relationship, or a mind, where we concentrate on using encouraging words and positive reinforcement. Of course, sometimes constructive criticism is crucial, and discipline is necessary. But criticism and discipline are infinitely more effective when delivered in a *firm* and *friendly* manner, and sandwiched between encouraging words. Studies show business places that practice encouragement have marked increases in creativity and productivity.

The good feelings that are caused by saying kind words to one another trickle up and trickle down. An encouraged person becomes an encouraging person. Positive emotions generate positive emotions.

A driver who's been giving encouraging words by a patrolman drives down the road wearing this mantle of encouragment and radiates it out to his fellow man.

A tired spouse met by love, attention and encouraging words becomes encouraged, and a lot more fun to have around the house. Given encouragement, we can do nothing but improve. A writer who gets an encouraging letter from a reader, or the rare appreciative word from an editor, strives to be a better writer.

Parents find that the very atmosphere in the house changes and wonders occur when they replace criticism with encouragement. Rudolph Driekurs, noted child psychologist writes, "Children need encouragement like plants need water." *What is true of children is equally true of adults.* If you don't believe me, try this experiment. For one whole day say nothing but encouraging words to your loved ones or those you work with, or—for that matter—to yourself.

Build on strength, forgive weaknesses, and radiate warmth and loving concern. The atmosphere will change even as you speak.

Life will be a lot more fun.

Personality Peculiarities—Working Out Our Differences

1989

Interesting comments have come in from farm and ranch families who work together in various stages of harmony. This column will feature words of wisdom from a reader who's worked with family members for over 40 years:

> *"People need to understand each other's personalities. It's easier to work with someone with a personality like your own. But this doesn't always happen. One of our sons is like me, hyper. It's easier to trip our triggers. The other is like my spouse, laid back. We've learned how to work with each other, but it's too bad it's taken so long to learn . . . The important thing is to see things with a grain of humor. And to talk things out. We always have a round table discussion when decisions need to be made. There were times when the men got angry with each other . . . but there was never a thought of severing the family ties. They sit down in the shade on 5-gallon pails and talk over weighty problems."*

Solid advice. As the reader suggests, an important step in getting along is to accept the fact that each one of us has a different personality. We process information differently. We react differently to stress. We laugh at different things. Different things make us happy. Some of us are laid back. Some of us have triggers that are easily tripped. Trying to change someone else's personality is an exercise in futility. We are what we are. Learning to accept a person's personality, appreciating strengths, understanding weaknesses, is a great way to co-exist peacefully.

Anyway, wouldn't life be dull if we were all the same?

The variety of personalities in my own family is mind-boggling.

My sister, June, and I are the best of friends. But we have very different personalities. I tend to rush into things with great and foolish enthusiasm. She thinks everything through. I process externally, spewing out words as I'm thinking, changing my mind with every new bit of information. June processes internally. When she says something, it's all thought out.

We learned about ourselves when we took the Myers-Briggs Personality inventory along with other members of our church's Family Ministry team. What an eye-opener! We had 12 people in our group with 12 different personalities. The two who were exactly opposite on all points of this inventory were June and I, sisters, born of the same parents, raised in the same environment. What it made all of us understand is how important it is to have every combination of personalities in any group. One person's weakness is another person's strength. Different personalities complement each other. One can never predict. People who are alike don't always get along, and opposite personalities do attract.

Look how many neat people marry messy people, for instance.

The bottom line is people have a right to be different from what we prefer them to be. There are some people we will never understand. We just need to accept them as they are, appreciate their unique qualities, and live as harmoniously as possible. Just understanding that we won't always understand everybody, we understand them better than not understanding them at all. We keep trying to, but, we never will.

Do you understand?

The secret of getting along is communication. Having a *round table* discussion or sitting down in the shade and talking over *weighty problems.* Discussing differences, we work them out. Feelings stuffed inside fester.

Our reader came up with another piece of advice which I think is very timely, in case our memories of past difficulties are growing dim.

> *"If you can't afford it, don't sign for your children to borrow. If you want to help them, sign a note for a specific amount loaned to you and re-loan it to them. Then no banker loans your kid money on your assets."*

Thanks for sharing, dear reader, and God bless! Hopefully,

people will tune in. Unfortunately, many of us still seem to have to learn the hard way.

Secrets of a Happy Marriage: Compromise and Lowered Expectations

1989

I write this column looking out my office window at a bleak landscape. A kindly poet, whose name slips my mind, once described such a landscape as a *symphony in greys and browns.* Right now, to my not-so-poetic-eye, it looks simply dull. Not boring, just dull.

A little dullness is a good thing.   After the jubilance of the holidays, and before the wondrous awakening of spring, human beings need some down time. The problem is *down time* isn't what it used to be. When we first moved to the farm, some 40 years ago, the work was done in the fall and in the winter Kip's folks kept a table up for cards, and what's more—in the middle of the day—they played with whomever happened by.

Down time isn't what it used to be for another reason. For instance, completely destroying my delicious dull mood is the fact that behind me in this very office are stacks of things I am to sort through, toss out or file. This is Kip's idea. When he has down time, he attempts to organize me.

As many of you know, Kip is not only a cattle feeder but a cattle buyer. His greatest joy, as a young man, was to go to the sales and buy his own cattle. And he did a pretty good job. So, somewhere along the line his friends started asking him to buy cattle for them, and—well you know how these things go—this cattle buying business took over his life. And when there's a cattle sale, Kip is a happy man.

But when there isn't a cattle sale—look out. Two things happen. If the weather is the problem, Kip gets withdrawal pains. He rampages around the house like a caged lion, especially if he can't even get to town to heckle the businessmen. "I can see them canceling school," he will mutter, "but a cattle sale? Is that reasonable?"

His second reaction is even worse. He gets this look of mission-ary zeal in his eye and starts to attempt to organize me.

"Today we will clean out the hall closet," he will say, sending shivers of apprehension down my spine.

The worst thing he can say is what he said last week, which was, "I have some time today, so I think I will clean out the office."

Now—don't be fooled here—he doesn't mean HIS side of the office. His side never needs cleaning out. He's inherently neat. He's looking at my side. What he can see of it. I don't know what it is about people who are neat. They are always trying to change people who are comfortable being messy.

For instance, I—the messy person—never try to change Kip. I never say to him, "Mess up your desk, for Heaven's sake, it looks boring."

But he—on the other hand—is constantly trying to change me. I learned early in our married life that we had this problem, and so I have tried to set boundaries on my messiness. I think compromise is the cornerstone to a happy marriage. If you love a person, you try. I've really tried. Our office, for instance, has a divider in it. I thought it would help Kip if he didn't have to look at my side.

It does, except occasionally he peeks. It traumatizes him. "How can you work in that mess?" he will ask.

So on a down day, he can't help himself. He meddles. He does it, he says, "to make things easier" for me. He takes all of the things off my desks and tables and chairs (there is nothing on his, of course) and piles them up on the floor so I can't walk by them. Then he beams at the nice neat furniture. And he says, "Now you can sort all of these things out". For several days now I've stepped over those piles and stared out at my beloved bleak landscape. I have to explain something to Kip, you see. There's another great cornerstone of a successful married life. And that is lowered expec-tations. Not to worry, as I put all the piles back up on my desks and tables and chairs, I know that some day, maybe in forty more years, he will figure that out.

Marriage: It's Not Easy, But It's Worth It

1989

An older woman I know, who, even as I write, is happily traveling the world with her spouse of over fifty years, told me recently, "You know, there were some tough times in our marriage when we might have left each other, but neither one of us would take the kids". Then she added, "And we would have missed our best years".

I thought of her when I read the following letter:

> *Dear Joanie: I'd appreciate your thoughts on this. We have a large family, all married. But they aren't living happily ever after. One marriage is, in fact, heading for divorce. Our problem is, we don't feel they are even working at it. What is it with kids today? My husband is no jewel, but then neither am I. We've survived a lot of tough times together, and now we're just plain comfortable with each other.*
>
> *But we've worked at it. How can we get this across to our kids?*
>
> *Signed: Confused and concerned.*

Dear C. and C. I've written on this before, and I do it again with a sense of missionary zeal. If everyone contemplating marriage understood that the first exciting romantic love is transitory, they'd stand a better chance of getting to the place where *life is just plain comfortable.*

But, as you said, it takes work. Experts who know about such things say that there are four stages to any relationship, be it marriage or a friendship. The first stage is **attraction.** Somebody appeals to you. You meet them, and something clicks.

For a couple destined for romance I call this the *wow and whoopee* stage; a wonderful exhilerating infatuation that makes us act mildly insane. I can remember when just hearing Kip's voice would make my heart beat faster. Boy, was that a long time ago.

Dr. Scott Peck, author of *The Road Less Traveled* writes that "falling in love" is a myth. Characteristics of this myth, he says, are the belief that romantic love will last forever, and lead to perfect happiness. This myth of romantic love is a "dreadful lie," Peck says.

But it ensures the survival of the species because it *traps us into marriage.* What makes it not entirely "dreadful", says he, and I also believe, is that falling in love can lead us to make a commitment to somebody from which *real love* can grow.

Which brings us to the second stage, **attachment.**

For couples this means marriage, or sometimes, in this day and age, simply attachment. In a friendship it means you start hanging out together. Best buddies.

But there follows—in every relationship—the third stage, which is the most critical. It's a stage we call **adjustment.** This is where we realize perfection is not a human attribute. They may be messy, where we are neat. They may snore, or chew ice in public. They may have entirely different interests. They will, undoubtedly, let us down. In this stage it is necessary to lower our expectations. And probably, pray.

What happens with some couples, is that they start looking for that romantic love again, maybe with somebody else, not realizing that the best kind of love, the deeper more soul-satisfying love, is just around the corner if they'll just work at it.

If we understand this is a normal part of any relationship, and prepare for it, we won't be let down. We will just realize this is when we begin to relate to this other person on another, more realistic level.

We work through difficult times, as imperfect human beings must. We nurture ourselves as well as our spouse, or our close friends, and they do the same, so we can all grow and be what it is in us to be.

Then—as C. and C. obviously knows—we are able to move into the fourth level of marriage and/or friendship.

The *recommittment* stage. This is when we have learned to live with all of their faults and they with ours, and we love each other anyway. It is the very best stage. The most comfortable. *The stage you really don't want to miss.* It's not easy.

But it's worth it.

CHAPTER THREE
REST STOPS

Chapter Three

Rest Stops

It's the rest stops of life that give us the strength to journey on. The vacations, the hobbies, the sporting events, the naps, the pauses that refresh our souls, and invigorate us for the rest of the journey. They are essential to life, and allow us to be happier, more creative, and even live longer. I have friends who enjoy planning their vacations almost, but not quite as much, as taking them. And other friends who, I swear, would not survive if they didn't have a winter ski trip, or a summer fishing trip, to look forward to. Even a tiny rest stop, such as taking a nap, benefits us body and soul. Following are some of the columns about the rest stops on our journey, the four diamond ones—and the others. Glad to have you join us.

That's the Way It Should Be

1984

Above us, in the mountains, the snow was piling up to eight feet deep. Below us, in the foothills, winds were clocked at 70 miles an hour. But in tiny St. Paul's Church in Idaho Springs, Col., there was peace.

The cantor needed no microphone. She just stood up and turned around and called out the songs. She was seated in the front pew with her husband and two little children. We had the Glory and Praise Hymnal #1, the missalette, and a bishop's appeal-for-funds pamphlet in our pew. I felt right at home.

We sang the regular Lenten songs, such as "The Glory of These Forty Days," which I get so tired of before Lent is over that I can truly offer them up. My visit to Idaho Springs was on the first Sunday of Lent. Singing the familiar tunes was like the first time you meet beloved relatives whom you're really glad to see, though you know you're going to get tired of them before they finally go home.

Our realtor son Bill resides in Idaho Springs and thus was the cause of my visit. I've had several speeches in Colorado lately, and Bill always feels he has to haul me around. I'm sure he's about ready to equate me with "These Forty Days of Lent" at the end of Lent.

I always get a thrill at seeing the mountains. Attending Mass with Colorado Catholics and visitors in their colorful ski attire gave me a warm feeling. I felt a camaraderie with these glowing athletic types whose ranks I shall never join anywhere but in church, I certainly shall not see them on the slopes.

Though I love the thought of skiing—I even tried it once, getting almost inextricably tangled in the tow-rope—I've never had the urge to ski that some of my best friends have. It seems ridiculous to me to head out of this country in the wintertime and go some place where it's snowing.

Besides, I'm basically a coward. I agree with Betty Ford who says from her home in Vail, "I do not participate in any sport that has ambulances waiting at the bottom of the hill."

Many of you ski buffs are familiar with Idaho Springs. It's a quaint old mining town on Highway 70, three miles long and three blocks wide. Primarily, now, it mines tourists. The three blocks wide part is built up the mountain-sides, with St. Paul's Church being on the first tier. A beautiful mountain stream cascades through the town, and while I was there, a light snow fell, decorating all the evergreens up the mountain sides. It was like going to church in a picture postcard.

The peace of that place, surrounded on all sides by the wildest winter weather, seemed symbolic to me. In the midst of the storms of life, that's the way Mass should always be.

Doc says, "Why Don't We All Go"

1985

If you've never taken the trip I'm about to describe, I would encourage you do it. Often one procrastinates about the things which will bring him or her great pleasure. I wonder why.

For instance, for years Kip and I drove up and down Interstate 29 in Iowa, read the sign that said, "DeSoto National Wildlife Refuge," and said, "Someday we'll stop there." But we didn't.

We were interested because friends extolled the virtue of the place. They'd taken picnic lunches and binoculars and the time to admire the birds at the rustically beautiful spot with its handsome visitors center. They raved about the collection of artifacts from the excavated steamboat Bertrand, which sank in the Missouri River with most of its cargo in 1865.

Every time we got to that sign, we seemed to think it was more important to get to something at the other end. Therein lies an important lesson in life. It appalls me to think that we possibly pass by life itself in our rush to get to the other end.

Last Sunday we didn't. It was a gray and gloomy day, not one that would make one think of picnics or even watching birds. We were in Omaha visiting with Dr. Dwight Burney and wife Kay and getting ready to head home. We said something about always planning to stop at DeSoto Bend. Doc said, "Why don't we all go." It was remarkably easy. We just up and went—a great thing to do on a dreary day.

The refuge is located approximately 30 miles north of the Omaha metropolitan area via Interstate 29. Just follow the signs.

Our first glimpse of the place was wonderful. A field covered with snow geese. I mean covered! What a sight. The second was the center itself, and it's a delight. It is so suited to the surrounding area. It looks as if it grew there.

Viewing galleries overlooking DeSoto Lake provide superb opportunities to see waterfowl and bald eagles during the spring and fall migration periods. Rumor had it that a bald eagle was sighted the day we were there, but I stared until my eyes nearly fell out and didn't see it. Not to worry, we saw plenty of other birds and even if there had been none, the view is spectacular and soul-soothing.

Also fascinating were the tens of thousands of artifacts recovered from the Bertrand which are carefully preserved in a viewing area adjacent to the Cargo gallery. It is purportedly the finest collection of Civil War era artifacts in existence. I found it amazing.

A film in that area explains how the items were excavated and restored.

There is also an excellent 12 minute film in a comfortable open theater which depicts the beauty of the Missouri River basin and reveals the impact of western settlement on the Missouri River lands.

Young and old seemed equally enthralled with this fascinated place, and binoculars are available if you don't remember to bring some along.

Many more things of interest, but you'll find that out for yourself. This will be an investment of time that will refresh your soul.

Traveling the Dominican Republic with Mucho Grande Gringo

1986

Thinking back, I realize that we saw much of the Dominican Republic in a car, backing up.

It was hard for me to believe, as we crawled off the airplane in Sioux City and walked out into the frigid night, that only a few hours ago we'd been basking on a sandy beach at the Casa De Campo in the Dominican Republic. In fact, I thought I might freeze to death until we got our winter coats out of the trunk of our car and the heater started to work. Could their really be two such diverse climates at the same time on the same earth?

Following in the wake of the "Mucho Grande Gringo" from San Francisco, Charlie Cook, we saw as much of the Dominican Republic countryside as humanly possible in a week. Six-foot-four Charlie, of Scandinavian descent, was quite a contrast to the handsome but compact natives of the Dominican. The Spanish title, which roughly translates into "very great white man" was conferred upon him by the ever-present hoard of little boys who materialized out of thin air wherever we stopped, offering to wash the car, etc. (Bead salesmen also materialized, but that's another story.)

The Dominican Republic is one huge garden. Even the fence posts grow. The roads are bordered with palm trees and flower covered shrubbery, and distant mountains finish off the view. Kip played golf on a luxurious picture-postcard golf course called "The Teeth of the Dog," which is rated the fourth toughest in the world. He loved it.

The native homes were tiny, sometimes of rock, but often a ram-shackle affair of boards with thatched roofs and dirt floors. Dirt floors notwithstanding, children came out of these homes dressed in prim school uniforms as if they'd come out of a mansion and been cared for by a nanny.

Which, in fact, many Dominican children are. The rich are enormously rich, with homes that boggle the mind. Even the very poor seem rich here, because of the bountiful growth of fruits and vegetables, and the availability of all kinds of fish. The average temperature is 80 degrees all year around. So clothes are no problem at all for the littlest tykes. They just don't wear any.

The natives are a mixture of Indian, Spanish, Negro and whatever other nationality that happened by in a history that is full of gut-grinding violence and cruelty. Columbus landed here, and is buried in a cathedral in Santa Domingo. With him came the Con-quistadors, who all but wiped out the Indian population (from one million to three thousand) and then brought in Negro slaves. The cruel uprisings and wars continued until 1961 when Trujillo was assasinated. Since that time, the democratic process has been observed—more or less.

The people are beautiful. The women, because they carry loads of all sizes on their heads, walk with a regal posture. And they are so friendly, so willing to put things off (like plane departures) until manana, that it's difficult to believe their violent history. We toured the backroads, snorkled the Carribean above choral reefs, and toured a remote river atop a boat load of fish without ever being concerned about our safety. We watched a polo game (really inter-esting) and went to a wild baseball game, with some U.S. players involved. Baseball is #1—really big—in the Dominican, with fine stadiums in every town. Charlie says at least nine Dominicans are playing with our major leagues, usually short stop.

Charlie made all arrangements using his smattering of Spanish and a lot of hand waving. We wandered into the tiny circuitous streets of a village of huts to make contact with Charlie's deep-sea diving companion Pequito. Goats wandered free (Chevas—very good to eat) and pigs were on leashes. Pequito is the champion (Numero Uno!) shark fisherman (with a blow gun) of the area. So Charles worries not about being 70 to 100 feet below the sea perusing the personal habits of fish, one of his favorite pursuits. Kip chose to peruse the Teeth of the Dog.

We traveled the roads searching for parrots and orchids and giant tarrantulas (which are fuzzy and kind of cute). Problem was, we never saw anything until we'd passed it by. Jean would yell "Charles" and Charles would put on the brakes and proceed to back up. We spent almost as much time backing up as going forward. Our search for the perfect place (very dark) to see the Southern Cross got us into all kinds of trouble. After driving on forbidding looking country roads, and backing out, we ended up (not on purpose) on a golf cart path on the Teeth of the Dog. Nothing to do, of course, but back out.

Kip's favorite sight was—you'll never guess—a giant feedyard full of the islands famous horned Romano Red cattle. They are part Hereford and part Brahma and part something else. If it hadn't been for the trucking them across the sea we'd have had some.

The islands main crop is sugar cane. They are famous for their rum; also their fish. On Thanksgiving we had all the lobster we could eat ($8.00) in an open restaurant with a thatched roof overlooking the Carribean. (Eat your heart out!) Restaurants are not all that reasonable, but they have many and the food is good. (She says as she waddles about the house.)

One doesn't have to wander the countryside. It would be possible for a tourist to have a wonderful time and never leave the vast confines of the Casa De Campo where Charles and Jean have their golf villa. All kinds of vacation packages are available (such as golf and tennis and fishing.)

I'm sorry to say, however, that there's probably no tour offered, especially if you like to travel backwards, like the one with the Mucho Grande Gringo from San Francisco.

Golfing—"The Divorce Open"

1986

"You smell like a cake," Kip said. No wonder. I had dabbed vanilla on every exposed part of my body. It wasn't so that Kip would nibble my ear. It was so the gnats wouldn't.

The above scene took place at the golf course. For some reason, gnats swarm around golf courses, making the golfers even more miserable than they ordinarily are. Since somebody discovered that gnats didn't like vanilla, the golf course has begun to smell like a bakery. There is even a company selling a vanilla roll-on.

There are things about golfing even more remarkable than how golfers smell. For instance, guess what these folks have in common? Ninety-year-old Hobert Hunter, seventeen-year-old Sue Vlack, and never mind how old Kip and Joan Burney? Last week, amidst a group of 65 couples from all over the area, they participated in a two-ball foursome tournament on the Hartington golf course. And not only that, they all won awards. Golfing, it would seem, knows no age limits.

Hobert started golfing when he was 70, and shot a 45 on his 90th birthday. His partner was Sally Bart, a local golfer with a multitude of awards to her name. Sue, who's better known as a basketball standout than a golfer, played with Steve Miller, who's also well known for his basketball prowess. Kip and I, who are not known for much of anything on any ahtletic field, played together.

For those of you who do not know what a two-ball foursome is, (and probably don't care) it's a golf tournament in which a couple plays as a team. The tournament is run in different ways. The way we golf was both members of the team tee off on every hole. After that they take turns hitting the ball. Some people call them "divorce opens."

In spite of that, a lot of couples travel many miles in search of a tournament where they can play together. You meet great people. It's a lot of fun if you can keep your sense of humor and remember it's only a game. Kip and I have more fun when we're playing badly then we do when we're playing good. That means we have fun most of the time. When we're playing good Kip begins to think I need instructions. Which I do—I've golfed very little this year. But not from him. So, you see how that goes.

During the tournament mentioned above, we had another problem, and that was to avoid being struck by lightning. All the information that we get on the wisdom of golfers abandoning the course when a storm comes up went unheeded on that day. Golfers waited out the downpour under trees, or in golf carts with lids on, or—for eight of us—in a storage shed that smelled of decaying things. They'd come to play, and by golly that's what they were going to do. There's a streak of insanity in the avid golfer. One of the fellows in the shed said we should continue playing and use our one irons, because we wouldn't have to worry about lightning. Lee Trevino says even God can't hit a one iron.

"Unusual Weekend"

1987

From a Vietnamese kitchen, to a train speeding across a romantic landscape, to a shore lunch on a Canadian beach all in one weekend? Seems impossible. Well, it is, physically. Mentally, anything is possible.

The kitchen was actually in the home of Dick and Gwen Lindberg in West Point. It smelled Vietnamese, and it tasted Vietnamese. There was a distinct Vietnamese hustle of humanity. Gwen and Dick all but adopted a Vietnamese family some years ago, and Gwen has become an expert at Vietnamese cooking, and added Vietnamese cooking classes to an already overloaded schedule.

Nebraska Press Women organization, whose annual meeting was held in West Point, was treated to one of those lessons. Wielding a cleaver and bashing garlic in an old mortar and pestle that once belonged to her pharmacist father, Gwen barked orders like the commanding general she is in her heart, and molded the diverse and talented newspaper women (Marys in their hearts) into a troupe of chop-chopping, stir frying, meat stuffing, hard-working Marthas. This was Friday night.

The NPW workshops, held at Harold Schmader's antique-filled Neligh House restaurant, were excellent.

Saturday night we were already riding an intellectual high when we headed for our banquet, which was to be held on a train. Yes, you read right. A train.

While many of us were busily taking up the railroad ties to use in landscaping, the communities of Fremont and Hooper were raising money to put the Fremont and Elkhorn Valley Railroad in business. Fueled by the entrepreneurial spirit of Greg Webber and other far-sighted community leaders, the tracks between Hooper and Fremont were revitalized, and an excursion train started tootling back and forth. A few months later the Pathfinder Dinner Train was added.

I am crazy about trains. Remember the wonderful happily-ever-after movies of yesteryear where elegant people dined by candlelight to the romantic click of the railroad ties? My feelings blossomed into an almost unbearable ecstasy when we heard the whistle and saw the light of the train chugging in from Fremont.

It was everything we'd dreamed. Greg Webber, in his jaunty engineer's hat, was perfectly cast for this romantic saga. His brother, Kurt, dressed all in white, hovered over us, looking for all the world like a character out of the Great Gatsby.

"Is everything all right?" he kept asking. Well, I guess! My friend Mary Costello, famed columnist for the Sun papers, sipped her wine and announced dreamily, "I was born to this."

Cheryl Stubbendieck, Nebraska Farm Bureau vice president of information, cut into a king-sized portion of prime rib and said, "It's just so civilized."

On Sunday night, the shore lunch in the wilds of Canada, was a re-creation in the backyard of Clarence and Lenore Hoesing. Clarence is a hard-nosed, hard-driving contractor, but he has an awful lot of the kid in him. There was a time when our entire bridge club traveled to the Hoesing Canadian hideout, bucked the waves of the Lake of the Woods to fish for walleye and then landed on a tiny island and ate a shore lunch prepared on an open fire by a rugged Canadian guide.

We stuffed ourselves amid the rustle of pines, with the sun streaming down and a storm brewing in the distance. We watched pelicans do a stately dance on the waves, listened to the loons and savored such delicacies as crisply fried filets of fresh-caught (by us) walleye pike, fried in a giant black frying pan, potatoes and eggs all fried and mushed up together, peaches and baked beans warmed in cans on the coals of the fire. Delicious.

The chances of doing this again were remote. We often loudly regretted it, so Clarence brought Canada to his backyard. We had the beach (two pickup loads of sand incongruously piled on the luxurious bluegrass lawn) a lake (about the size, strangely enough, of a children's pool) complete with fish, an open fire, the large frying pan and all of the above-mentioned food. The spirit of Canada was upon us, and we enjoyed it. At one point I even thought I heard the distant cry of a loon.

These were *keeper* memories. You might want to try one out.

Appreciating Life's Special Moments

1987

As a young mother I was given advice that affected my whole life by two wise women, Lou Robinson and Wilma Bargstad. They taught me to appreciate life's special moments.

Lou, whose two little boys were just older than ours, pointed out how fleeting time is, and said, "remember to enjoy, because the problems with little boys are little. When they grow up, they aren't so easy to handle." Wilma, responding to my panic when Rob and Bill hit high school and I had my first look at them behind the wheel of a car, stressed the importance of keeping in perspective those years of sometimes painful growth for parents and teenagers. "Be sure and remember to enjoy," she said, "because these years pass so fast that you won't hardly believe it."

And they did.

But thanks to their words, I always appreciated the stage of life I was in, and thought it must be the *best* stage. I loved it when our kids were little. I could rock them to sleep, and feel their little soft heads on my shoulder. The growing up years, which were so exciting they almost did me in, were certainly, I thought, the best ones. Then, when they turned into interesting adults, and were so much fun to visit with, Kip and I began to have precious time to do our own things. I thought this HAD to be it. Until we became grand-parents, and our best times got even better.

The years passed so fast I could hardly believe it.

The happy people I've known in my lifetime have not necessar-ily been the ones with the most prestige, nor the most money, nor even the greatest health. They have been the ones who found great satisfaction in life's little pleasures, in the simple things that make up part of every day.

My friend, Marie Huck, is one of those people. She takes plea-sure in almost everything. Butterflies, bells, strawberries and tigers abound in her house, on her house and on her person. One of her pleasures which might be a mite irrational is her love of flashing red lights. I was in Omaha with her enjoying a spaghetti dinner in the Old Market, when a fire truck went by. She grabbed me by the hand and we chased that fire truck down the street. Now, I believe fire fighters have enough to do without me cluttering up the place. But chase it I did, never able to say no to Marie. Marie oh'd and ah'd while the firefighters put out a minor blaze. I shivered and thought about my congealing spaghetti.

Usually I can relate to Marie's excitement about flashing red lights. I wasn't wild about her delighted exclamations the evening we were driving through Madison and they showed up behind us. Fun for her, maybe, but it cost me money.

Another of my friends, Shirley, likes fire in fireplaces. She builds a fire with loving care, and then sits and stares at it, a happy person.

I like fires in fire places too—for roasting marshmellows, or reading in front of. Many people take great joy in music. I certainly do. I can listen or participate and be transported into joyous ecstasy. When the voices of our choir blend in perfect harmony, flowing from a gentle double pianissimo to a rousing triple forte, a thrill of pleasure courses up my spine. Water brings joy too, as in mountains and lakes and rivers and creeks. I like them all, a moun-tain stream frolicking, a shimering lake, a meandering creek. And best of all I like to be in water, sitting in an innertube.

It may be because of the summers my little sister Anne and I romped joyfully in the cold spring-fed creek at Long Pine until we were quite blue, and covered with a mass of water-induced wrinkles.

Days which become, with just a flip of my mind, the summer vacations we had with our own kids, and the days we hiked in our pastures and fished in our own little creek. Sometimes, when I'm pulling weeds, or reading a book, or eating an ice cream cone, or doing something which seems quite ordinary, I realize I'm having a good time. I pause to appreciate it. Life is full of good times. We just have to appreciate them.

Naps: Take 'Em!

1989

Herb Lingren, Extension Family Life Specialist at the University of Nebraska, had an interesting tidbit in his July newsletter. He suggested a nap might just "wake up your marriage."

My first question was, when one has been married forty some years, does one want to wake up one's marriage? Not a worthy thought, so I thought on.

I realized, if Herb is right, and napping does wake up a marriage, we must have the snappiest marriage in the midwest. Of course, we approach napping from different perspectives. Our marriage has always been a study in contrasts. Why should napping be different? Kip can catnap for five minutes and wake up completely refreshed for the day. I need a good hour, at least. Preferably, all afternoon.

I swear, Kip can look like he's been three day's dead, and after a five minute nap he's frisky as a puppy. He's always been able to do this. It's not just something that's come on with his becoming an official senior citizen. It's wonderful for him. He catnaps at social events and awakes the life of the party. (That may be a slight exaggeration.) He's notorious for his brief naps during cattle sales. In fact, it would probably be easier to get his intention while he was napping by just bellaring like a cheap steer.

What's more, it's a family trait. Most Burneys do this short snooze thing, especially the ones who live to be ninety-five years old. I can remember Dad Burney sitting straight up in his chair in the middle of a family reunion, nodding off. Not a bad idea.

Personally, I wouldn't dignify these little snoozes by calling them a nap. A real nap—to me—is lying down after lunch and sleeping an hour, or two. I wake up groggy, but after I shake that off I'm a new woman.

The problem with that, of course, is the only time I have to take my "NAP" is on Sunday. All week I perk along in high gear with no nap. But on Sunday, I can hardly wait to hit the couch. I pile the Sunday newspaper on my chest, put on my reading glasses, and go sound asleep. It's wonderful.

The nap thing, exciting as it is for our marriage, can get to be a problem. It's gotten so on the rare nights we're home we tend to take a nap in front of the TV to get enough energy to go to bed. So we've set a goal of staying awake at least until ten o'clock, so we can be horrified by the nightly news and the weather forecast, before we go to sleep. We've found we cannot do that if we take our usual nightly positions, Kip in the recliner, and me on the couch. So we've taken to walking around the farm, riding around the country visiting neighbors, or even (glory be!) going to a show.

So you see what I mean about napping. Herb's right. Naps have added zest to our lives. Only thing is, it isn't taking them that's done it. It's avoiding them.

Truely, naps are good for us. University of Pennsylvania sleep researchers have shown that napping is not only healthful and beneficial, but, more importantly "for many people, a nap can make the difference between vigor and lethargy, success and failure—even life and death."

My friend Kathy tends to doze off while driving, so she just pulls over to the side of the road, locks the car, and takes a little nap. Good idea, because after napping "people have quicker reaction time, make fewer mistakes, have better memories and feel more cheerful."

Besides that, "naps significantly improve a person's moods and presumably, therefore, benefit relationships." Such as marriages.

So take some naps out there. Life will be more fun.

Taking Time to Smell the Lilacs

1989

Every spring we drive up to the lake to smell the lilacs. It refreshes our soul. To do it we have to drop everything and go when the lilacs are ready to be smelled. Lilacs don't wait around.

My Dad was a work-o-holic. He thought he had to be. He barely survived the depression and knew the next one was imminent. He was a crusader, waging campaigns against the forces of evil, which he perceived as anything threatening to family farms, or independent banks.

He worked from the crack of dawn 'till the nightly news. He even had a phone installed in the bathroom, so he'd waste not one bit of time.

If you are a workoholic, this column is for you.

I don't remember my Dad ever holding me on his lap when I was a child, or hugging me as an adult, or telling me he loved me. When he died, in 1951, I realized I hardly knew him. I'm not blaming him. That's the way things were done then, by most fathers. He did the best job he knew how to do. Somehow, I knew he loved me. But I think we missed a lot. Nobody told him that work would always be there, but we wouldn't, and he wouldn't.

Just like the lilacs.

The economic upheaveal that we've just been through has taught us a lesson. Things don't necessarily get better just because we work harder. Work is good. It's necessary. But work, and only work, just doesn't work. We need to work smarter, and take time to refresh our souls.

All of which brings me to the following letter.

Dear Joanie;

Thanks for your column. It's fun, and has given us food for thought. My predicament is this. We have worked hard all of our lives on this operation. In thirty years we've only taken two vacations. Now our son works with us, and he's trying to talk us into taking every other weekend off. Besides that, he golfs, and he wants his Dad to golf. At fifty! Can you believe that? Now don't get the wrong idea, our son is a hard working boy. But golf? Hunting would be something else. At least he'd shoot something we could eat. But shooting golf seems the height of foolishness. And I'll bet you'd agree.

Thanks. J. and J.

Dear J. and J. Don't bet your farm on it. I agree golf is about as foolish as you can get, but we NEED foolishness in our lives. And fifty is a great age to start. That's when I started. You don't have to live up to how good you were when you were young. And, every other weekend off is a grand idea.

We live near a little town with a great nine hole golf course. Whenever you go out there, unless we're in the middle of planting or harvesting, the place is crawling with farmers *and* their wives. It's great!

Somehow, the frustration of getting out on that manicured pasture and attempting to knock a silly little ball in a hole puts other frustrations into perspective. Refreshed, you don't break machinary or blow up at people.

If golf doesn't do it for you, something will. Hunting might be it. Or fishing. Or boating. Or camping. SCHEDULE it into your lives. Otherwise, I know you workoholics, you'll feel guilty and won't do it. It will help if you remember that when you're refreshed, you work better. I promise.

I'm glad if you love your work, but you still need to get away. Kip is a cattle-sale-oholic. He gets withdrawal symptoms when he has to miss cattle sales. He LOVES his work. But too much, and even he gets testy.

Still have doubts? Here, slightly edited, is a poem by anonymous. Pin it up!

When I have time . . .

When I have time, there's a poem to be written, a song to
    be sung.
When I have time, there's a child to be led, a prayer to
    be said.
When I have time, I'll write down my story, I'll visit a
    friend.
Alas, time is gone
The child grew up to be a man, the prayer went unsaid,
The story untold, the friend is dead.

For what momentous affair did I neglect,
A poem, a song, a child, a friend
Was it a dirty dish, or an unmade bed?
Was it three more hours of work,
And then to bed?

The Power of Positive Thinking: Bowling 222

1989

Last night I bowled 222. I rest my case. If I can do it anybody can.

Three years ago I started using positive mental imagery to improve my bowling. It was a mini-experiment. I'd written a paper on this subject in pursuit of my Masters in Psychological Counseling. I began to wonder if the conclusions drawn from my own study could possibly relate to me.

I've shared this mini-experiment with many of the groups I've been speaking to, especially students. I told them that my ultimate goal was to bowl a 200 game, the fact that I'd been bowling for forty some years and never had a score even close to that notwithstanding. Now THAT's thinking positively.

What my research told me, you see, was that I was lousy at bowling because I thought I was lousy at bowling. But perhaps if I changed my thoughts—if I actually listened to the advice of my friends who were good bowlers—if I watched bowling on Saturdays, and then shut my eyes and imagined myself getting spares and strikes—could I—would I improve?

It seemed unlikely. However, what could it hurt to try? The use of positive mental imagery has gained wide-spread acceptance in three major areas, counseling, medicine and sports.

We use mental imagery all the time. For instance—how many windows do you have in your house? To tell me, you'll have to conjur up a mental picture of your house and count them. Yes you will.

The point of all this is if we go into any endeavor with our mind *programed* with negative thinking, that's probably how it will come out. But if we consciously choose to think positively—positive juices get to rolling subconsciously as well as consciously. And good things happen. It doesn't always work, but it works a lot better than thinking negatively.

T. Orlick, a well known Canadian sports psychologist, wrote in his "Pursuit of Excellence", that an athlete vividly picturing himself correctly executing the desired skill or response increases his chance of performing it in a competitive situation. The difference between doing his or her best and *choking*, say sports psychologists, is often in an athlete's *mindset*. One does not lose one's athletic ability. One loses one's mental sharpness.

Olympic teams use positive mental imagery. Jack Nicklaus uses it.

Why not me? So without telling anybody at first—certainly not my beloved Black Russians who'd put up with my 112 average for all these many years—I began watching bowling on Saturday and soliciting advice from my friends who are good bowlers. I put it all in my mind, and mentally envisioned myself getting spares, and even strikes.

My average started to raise, until at one time it was 149. Then I quit working at it—and it is work, you know. It came back down to 128. I started working on it again, and it began to rise, except that I kept getting splits. Big splits and little splits. Cousin Laura Lou Marsh, who along with her husband Dean, bowls with Kip and me on the Monday Night Couples League, kept encouraging me saying "splits are almost strikes. Someday they'll all go." But splits don't count up much, and I couldn't understand why I'd get such good hits, right in the pocket, and they wouldn't fall down. That's not the way it was happening in my mind.

I still don't know why, but last Monday night they all fell down, just like Laura Lou promised. I don't know what I was doing wrong, and I sure don't know what I did right, but glory, alleluia, I got the two hundred. And just in the nick of time. We only had two more weeks to bowl.

There are other things to take into consideration, of course. Basics must be learned. Practice is important. Concentration is crucial.

But—when you take care of those, the difference between winning and losing might just be happening in your mind.

So work on imagining things in your life coming out just like you want them too. Think positively. If you do that—amazing things can happen.

Just ask me!

The Vacation of '89—Compromise Pays Off

1989

After two and a half weeks journeying through the forests and mountain ranges of Utah, Wyoming, Montana, Idaho, Canada, and coming home through the Black Hills of South Dakota, I am completely out of oohs and ahhhs.

It was a trial run. If we survived, we'd probably do more. Survival was by no means certain. Kip and I rarely travel together. He heads out for his cattle sales, and I head out to do whatever it is I do. We have different driving habits. We listen to different kinds of music. He's neat and I'm messy. Could our marriage endure two and a half weeks in the same car?

With this in mind, we laid down the ground rules before we ever started. Kip promised to cease spitting sun flower seed hulls if I would quit leaning on his arm rest. When Kip quit smoking, five years ago, he took up eating sun flower seeds, the kind you mull around in your mouth, and then spew out the hulls. It was my fault. I read that sun flower seeds helped people get over craving nicotine. So he tried it. It must have worked. I could hardly complain.

I didn't, for five years. But it annoyed me. Eat and spit. Eat and spit. The thought of spending 6,000 miles with a sun flower seed fancier spewing hulls was more than I could stand. So I took it up with him. That's when he told me for years I'd annoyed him by leaning on his arm rest.

Both promising reform, we set out. Our first stop was Salt Lake City, where we attended the lovely wedding of Mary, the daughter of long-time friends, Gerald and Shirley Stevens, to Ken. We had the pleasure of sitting in on a performance of the Mormon Tabernacle Choir. For a music person like myself—a little taste of Heaven.

Then we went up through the Tetons, Yellowstone, across the

mountains and forests of Montana to Coeur d'Alene, Idaho, from whence we launched onto our exciting and traumatic bus tour into Canada, back to Coeur D'Alene for a National Federation of Press Women convention, and then home.

It's hard to convey the intensity of my feelings when I finally saw the Tetons in person. A painting of them, done by my mother, hangs above our fire place. On another wall we have a mural done by Nona Modde Albers, an artist friend. The Tetons were old friends; breathtakingly beautiful ones.

Yellowstone is still magnificent, but the ugly scars caused by the rampaging fires of 1988 are sad to see. Old Faithful Geyser was definitely a highlight. The most famous of some 10,000 thermal features sprinkled across Yellowstone, it has been seen by millions of people, of which I am now one. I watched it erupt seven times. One of the Rangers said it was slowing down, and may quit some day.

We saw so much beautiful scenery we nearly went into over dose, but the most beautiful sight of all, after 6,000 some miles on the road, was our own valley, especially after a blessed inch and a half of rain.

No place like it.

Home.

Difficult Persons

1989

"Anybody who takes a trip on a bus deserves what he gets," grumbled Bob Pond, retired A.T.&T. executive, and husband of Peg Pond, an award-winning press woman from North Carolina, who'd talked him into taking this trip.

Don't get him wrong. The tour part was great. We (two bus loads of press women and significant others from all over the United States) saw marvelous scenery, and did wonderful things.

But it wasn't easy. On the trip into Alberta and British Columbia the people on bus number one were beset with problems. That was us.

Trouble on a bus isn't all bad, you understand. It bonds the passengers. According to experienced bus travelers, it's also important for bonding to have at least one Difficult Person (hereafter known as D.P.). If you don't have one, they say, you need to designate one. We had volunteers.

Which is where the "beset with problems" started. We weren't on the road for half an hour before the D.P. made himself known, complaining about the air conditioner. There wasn't any. Sitting by an open window, we were not bothered. But D.P. was seriously distressed. Marching up and down in the center of the bus he decried and bemoaned, until they unloaded us all at a restaurant, and sent the bus back to change for another bus.

It was soon readily apparent that the second bus had terminal transmission problems. "If I had my choice in these mountains" said Kip to Bob, "I'd take a bus with no air conditioner." The back-of-the-bus-bunch (which included the Burneys and the Ponds) were seated over the grating and grinding gears, and we began to feel the distress of those gears somewhere in the pit of our abdomens. The "Little Engine That Could" came to mind.

Our next major problem, however, had nothing to do with the reluctant gears. It had to do with reluctant officials. We didn't seem to have a permit to get between the states in Canada. Somebody goofed "back at the office" we were told. After an hour or so, they fined the busses $500 and sent us not-so-merrily on our way. The bus drivers were really torked. (I think it was dumb not to have the permits, but I wondered why they couldn't have just sold them one. Strange way to promote tourism.)

We finally arrived at Cranbrook, our destination. We were served, with great flourish, a marvelous meal in the dining car of a restored Luxury Train, the "Trans-Canada Limited". Our enjoyment was enhanced rather than diminished by the fact it was 11 p.m and we were starved. Or so I thought anyway. I didn't bother to record what Bob and Kip thought.

The saga continues, with the D.P.s having trouble with their food, their rooms, and they heckled the bus driver (who was a fine man, but a little stressed). Up and down mountains, we went, touring Fort Steele, playing in a bell choir in Kimberly, with the gears groaning and rasping away until finally, driving up a slight incline out of one of the rest stops, we didn't. The gears quit. Thank God we weren't on our way up a mountain.

Taking a different route, downhill, we finally moved, to the cheers of the now firmly-bonded passengers. Things had become so ridiculous that the D.P.s, overwhelmed with problems, became cheerful. One of them said to me when it was all over "Isn't it great what good sports we all were." (Difficult persons can be very nice. They just shouldn't take bus trips.)

By now the bus was belching black smoke, and so we lurched to a station to pour in a ton or so of oil and attempt to tighten up gears. Another photo opportunity for the journalists that seemed to come with cameras welded to their chests. Finally, we called for another bus.

On the road again, we began to sing, the true sign of a bonded bus, and a great sign that I'm having fun. In this brought-on-by-near-tragedy relieved mood we arrived hours late at our last two stops, two tiny communities, not unlike those I know and love, whose exuberant hospitality seemed to have something I need to talk to you about. Sizzle.

But that, my friends, is a whole 'nother column.

Summertime—The Living Is Easy?

1988

Summertime—and the living is easy.

So says the song.

The question is "easy compared to what?"

I have a friend who spends every summer in something of a frenzy. She always says, "One thing I'm sure about is that this summer can't be as bad as last summer."

She's right. It's always worse. People work at their regular jobs in the summer, fulfill their regular community and church duties, and then add a multitude of other things, such as the care of gardens and lawns, weddings, anniversaries, reunions, the pursuit of summertime activities—and company.

In some households the company leaves, and even before the beds get changed more company comes. Each and every little group is a joy, but the cumulative effect makes a person testy.

The pursuit of summertime activities gets to be a special problem in the midwest because we know how long we have to put up with winter. So we cram into our limited time every warm weather activity we can think of. Golf, softball, baseball, tennis, boating, fishing, picnics and all of those good things.

Then, in the middle of all of it, we schedule vacations. Possibly so we can go visit people before they visit us.

I wonder about the mental health of people who get involved in programmed sports in the summer. Since we both do, I wonder about our mental health. Take daughter, Juli, for instance. (Please.) She's already got a terrifying schedule, so she's managing a soft ball team of comedians. If you can imagine a soft ball team of comedians. All of this in spite of the fact that the only good play her team has ever made was when a ball bounced off her head (giving her a mild concussion) and flew into a fielder's hands who threw it to a first baseman for a double play.

Our summers will never be so hectic as when we had to march to the tune of the schedule of our six children who were born in a twelve year time span, and—of course—went through life that way. When they were young, we had at least one kid in every summertime program. I would meet myself coming and going, and sometimes I would go out the door to go someplace and find no car, because everybody else had already gone some place.

This was the summer all of our relatives came home to visit, and most of our friends, and a few strangers.

Because this was the summer of the Whitenhellers.

Somewhere back in history Kip's father had a great-grandsomebody who was a Whitenheller. That one summer, for some unknown reason, the Whitenhellers were astir in search of their roots.

Wonderful people, but I had no idea there were so many of them.

Towards the end of summer, Kip and I were a bit testy. More than a bit. When the eight of us were sitting at dinner one night and a station wagon full of people drove in, we all groaned.

Turned out to be an old classmate, whom I was really glad to see.

All my summertime juices started to flow again.

Because all those things about summer I just complained about—well they are also the things I really like.

Summer's what it's supposed to be. I wouldn't have it any other way.

Besides—it's warm.

THE ROAD AHEAD

CHAPTER FOUR

Chapter Four

Tools for The Road Ahead

The mind, stretched. by an idea, will never return to it's original shape. This section of the book is into mind stretching. As I said in the introduction I firmly believe that no matter how dark the night gets, the dawn will come. I also know, in a psycholgical sense, at least, we sometimes have to help the dawn along. We can wallow in misery if we choose to, Lord knows we all have misery to wallow in. Or we can accept the reality of our situation, and get off our duffs and do something to make it better. If we can't change the situation or the person that's making us miserable, we CAN change our attitude, if we choose to. Key word here is "choose".

If you say "I can't" about anything, I would like to consider rephrasing that to "I won't" and see how it puts you in control. Then take it a step farther, if you choose to, and change "I won't" to "I'll try". Amazing what possibilities will show up.

Before you know it an "I can!" might pop up. It works. I promise. Miracles happen when you switch from a negative attitude to a positive one. Herein you have a few ideas.

Hope they help.

No Cross . . . No Crown!

1977

I think the hardest thing for young people to understand in this day and age, if you will forgive me for sounding like an old fogey, is that anything worthwhile is worth working for. That sometimes you have to go through something disagreeable to get to a goal you desire.

I've always put making chili sauce in that category. I really despise making home-made chili sauce. I don't like cutting up all those vegetables. I don't like the smell that permeates the house as you cook it for hours. I don't like canning the whole mess after it's made.

But I love the finished product. Since there's no way to have the finished product without going through the original hated process, I grit my teeth and do it.

I don't necessarily think its all that great an accomplishment, but it's a case in point. It's fighting life's little battles that make winning the big ones possible.

Like getting after your kids to brush their teeth, brush their teeth, brush their teeth—and all of a sudden discover that they are not only brushing them, but also flossing them, without being told. All the aggravation seems worthwhile.

Especially since there is nothing that I dislike personally as much as flossing my teeth. Do you do it? Floss, I mean?

I don't ever remember the dentist telling us to floss in the olden days. You know what I mean, don't you? Dragging that pesky little string through the crevices between your teeth to get at any hiding bit of whatever.

Since I didn't remember it as being important, the first time my dentist told me to do it, I just ignored him.

Well, I tried it several times and just couldn't abide looking at my gaping mouth in the mirror as I tried to guide the floss. All that gold and silver staring back at me was more than I could bear.

Besides, I told myself smugly, I have always been an inveterate brusher, if inveterate means it is engrained into me to brush all the time. I've always done this because I am sure (just as I can never find my glasses because I won't leave them on my face) that I would never be able to keep track of my false teeth, should I have to get them.

Therefore, to avoid the likely consequence of facing the world with bare gums, I have brushed and brushed all my life. Surely one who is so thoroughly brushed should not have to floss. Right? Wrong!

The next time I took my unflossed mouth to the dentist he told me if I didn't start doing what he told me, my jaw would fall off. Not right away, you understand—but slowly, and—doubtless—painfully (something like that.) Nobody " 'xplained" it to me that way before. So I commenced crabbily to floss.

And it paid off. Otherwise there would be no moral to this story. Last time I went to the dentist I got this wide, polished, white grin (from the dentist) and the good word that I was such a good girl I had no cavities (there's hardly room for another filling, anyway) and would not have to come back for a year.

How's that for doing something disagreeable to reap a desired reward!

It is not an easy lesson to learn, and we have to learn it over and over. Go off our diet, and we bulge in strange places. Smoke too much and our lungs clog up. Drink too much and our liver gives out. Don't floss our teeth and our jaw falls off. Don't make chili sauce, and regret it all winter. (Wait a minute . . . how'd that get in here?)

In any case, the point is that almost nothing worthwhile is achieved without some work, and even some heartache. For "he that hath no cross deserves no crown."

We can't really be the judge of the crosses others bear because some people's crosses are in plain sight, bringing sympathy and understanding from all. But others carry their crosses splinter by splinter, with no one the wiser but the Lord.

I'm Fine for the Shape I'm In!

1980

You know you're getting old when it takes you longer to rest up than it did to get tired.

Having just celebrated a 33rd anniversary, it comes to my mind that spring chickens we are not.

My kindly reader friend, anonymous, must have had the same thought. "I think you might enjoy this," he or she wrote. I like to think it was written with a chuckle. And also, since the post mark was from a somewhat distant city, that the kindly person was just sending the poem to me because of the desire to share, not because he or she had observed me creaking around somewhere. Anyway, I thought you might enjoy it, too. Chuckle.

I'm Fine

There's nothing whatever the matter with me.
I'm just as healthy as I can be,
I have arthritis in both my knees
And when I talk, I talk with a wheeze.
My pulse is weak and my blood is thin,
But I'm awfully well for the shape I'm in.

I think my liver is out of whack
And a terrible pain is in my back,
My hearing is poor, my sight is dim,
Most everything seems to be out of trim,
But I'm awfully well for the shape I'm in.

I have arch supports for both my feet,
Or I wouldn't be able to go on the street.
Sleeplessness I have night after night,
And in the morning—oh, what a sight!
My memory is failing, my head's in a spin,
But I'm awfully well for the shape I'm in.

The moral is, as this tale we unfold,
That for you and me who are growing old,
It's better to say "I'm fine" with a grin
Than to let anyone know the shape we're in.

I concur with anonymous' sentiments, if indeed these are they. I go even farther. I think we should do all we can to keep the shape we're in from ourselves.

We just have to develop Bernard Baruch's philosophy, which seems logical to me. "Old age is always 15 years older than I am."

When we get to the place where there's no one left in the world who is 15 years older, a position that some of us may be privileged to reach, or maybe have reached already, then we must realize the wisdom of the famed quote of Bacon, "Old wood best to burn, old wine to drink, old friends to trust, and old authors to read." (I especially like the "old authors" part.)

Presently, I'm battling my glasses. A recent necessity (just to read, of course) they are never where I need them when I need them. One doesn't read just books, as those of you who are in my shoes know. One reads recipes, directions, hymnals, parking tickets, programs, medicine labels, bills, prices, etc., etc. I have a friend who brought home a darling *little* lamp for only $15, and put on her glasses to discover it was $150.

Glasses are a blessing, of course. I see (through) them as such. The Lord in his wisdom lets your eyes weaken first so you can't see what's happening to the rest of your body. But—we're fine. Right?! (Thanks, anonymous.)

Ten Methods of Handling Stress

1984

Helen has a plane to catch, but the roads are closed. Shirley's just learned all her in-laws are arriving at noon and she's in the midst of cleaning house. Tom's been asked to give a speech before 500 people and he's never spoken before.

The people in these semi-fictional examples are under a lot of stress. Some of them may head for food, some for drink. Some may stuff all that worry inside and have a migraine, or develop ulcers.

We all handle stress differently. And most of the time, we don't handle it well. As you know, because I've told you before, when the body experiences stress, it goes into the *fight or flight* response. Scientists tell us that we react just like the cavemen, our blood pressure goes up and we produce adrenalin.

It worked for the cavemen, because they just had to fight a known foe, or outrun a wild animal.

It doesn't work for us, because most of the time, we can do neither. So we stuff the energy produced by stress back inside of us, and develop physical and psychological symptoms.

The reason I'm on stress again, is because I've come too realize how prevalent it is. A lot of people don't have time to go to stress workshops. They wouldn't if they could. But those people are sometimes the most stressed.

Now, remember, some stress is good for us. I'd never write a column without the stress of the deadline. I get so revved up before a speech that I'm wound tight as can be. But it works for me.

But when stress is negative—distress—is when we need to know methods to alleviate it. We have to learn a certain flexibility.

So, I've gone through a lot of my material and came up with ten methods which a multitude of experts agree are sure-fire stress relievers. I use all but one. A lot.

1] Have a good cry. Man, woman or child, you should know that crying is the greatest god-given stress reliever. Tears heal. Don't be afraid to let go and cry. Scientists even think that tears may relieve stress by carrying off far more than grief. They may be ridding the body of potentially harmful chemicals produced in times of stress.

2] Pray. Whether you're religious or whether you aren't, you will get great relief from praying to God, or your "higher power" as you know Him (or Her). Never underestimate the power of acknowledging that High Power and offering your troubles up to Him. Not just a recitation of a prayer, but a real sharing with God of your problems. Tell Him what your troubles are, and your weaknesses. If you're mad at God, tell Him so. Prayer comes in a lot of forms. I guarantee you, just turning things over to Him will help.

3] Talk it out. Don't bottle up your troubles, or you will explode. Acknowledge your anger, but keep your cool. Discuss problems in a detached way, with a willingness to solve them. Compromise and communication are two valuable problem-solving tools. Use them. If you can't talk them out with the person you are having trouble with, go to a trained counselor. Join Recovery, Al Anon, or A.A., or an appropriate self-help group. *Don't bottle up your troubles!*

4] Have some fun. "Recreation can be just as effective as drugs in treating certain stress-related illnesses, but without the dangers of side effects." Recreation takes your mind off the "self" problems. Movies, books, painting, needlepoint, spectator sports, sports (even bowling) are all great stress relievers.

5] Take a walk. I have good friends who handle a lot of stress by just heading out the front door and walking awhile. They don't know how smart they are. Moderate exercise is a great stress reliever. Heavy exercise just stimulates you more. But walking for twenty minutes significantly reduces stress.

6] Try a massage. I haven't done this, but it would be a great idea. A spouse could do this for you. Even a shower massage helps, the experts say.

7] Take a hot bath. Now—this I do. Not too hot—because

prolonged heat is a stressor in itself. Just body temperature. Then step in the tub, sink in, put a rolled-up towel behind your head and close your eyes. In a few minutes you'll feel like a new person.

8] Breathe slower. Next time you're stressed, check your breathing. Chances are it's rapid and shallow. Slowing down your breathing, "a seven-second inhale and an eight-second exhale" for a total of two minutes discharges stress immediately. This can be done any where and could become automatic in response to stress situations.

9] Learn to relax. We possess a natural and innate protective mechanism against overstress. It's called the "relaxation response." We start by sitting quietly and comfortably, with eyes closed, relaxing all of our muscles and breathing slowly. Then we repeat one word every time you exhale, like "one" or "love," and let our minds go blank. Try this for ten or twenty minutes. It works.

10] Turn to your friends. If you have a few friends whom you can trust; friends to whom you can say anything, they are invaluable to you. They can supply an objectivity and balance when you don't trust your own judgment. These are the people who know all about you and love you anyway.

This is a long column, but these suggestions will work.

If you can use even one, it will have been worth the reading.

Being the Person It's In Us To Be

1986

Sometimes when a person's writing, the words come forth like fresh water from a spring. Then again, to quote Ernest Hemmingway, "sometimes its like drilling rock and blasting it out with charges."

Like now, for instance.

I have an idea to share with you, and I can't figure out just how to do it. You see, we're up to our eyeballs working with high school students attempting to make them understand the importance of setting goals. We want them to establish long range goals about careers, and then work toward them with appropriate measurable objectives, such as getting better grades, checking into educational opportunities, and just generally planning ahead. We'd like them to be creative and imaginative, and then be practical and realistic. We'd like them to dream, and then think of practical ways to go about making that dream come true.

Yet how often do we who are adults set goals for ourselves? How often do we dream creatively and then figure out ways to make those dreams come true? We flounder around with no plan whatsoever, letting life do with us what it will. We put off doing this and doing that, and then stand wistfully on the side-lines while opportunities and life pass us by.

I can't even begin to count the people who've said to me, "someday I'm going to write," or "I plan to take a course . . . some day" or "next year we're going to take a trip . . . ." They have an inkling of something they need to be doing in life, but they put it off.

The big coach in the sky gives us our equipment, mental and physical, but sometimes we don't even get in the game. Think about these questions:

What do you want to do with the rest of your life?

What do you want to do for the next two years?

If you knew that in six months lightning would strike you dead, what would you do with those six months?

Maybe we adults should think about our own *career development.* According to statistics, lightning isn't going to strike. Many of us are going to live a long, long time. Are we just going to hang out and let things happen? Or are we going to set goals? Might be a good idea.

I have to admit the things I have done have not been part of a master plan. But I've remained open to change, taken a few risks, and things have worked out. I'm still open to change, because, although I'm 58 years old; I don't know what I'm going to be yet when I grow up. Keeps life interesting.

One can't, of course, plan the future with any degree of certainty. Lightning might strike. But for a person to become what it's possible for that person to be, it's going to take some planning. And, I should think, even if lightning did strike, we'd want to be in the *becoming* process.

It's not that we should do more. It's just that we should do what it's in us to do. We should work more effectively. Work towards something, rather than just getting so loaded down with stuff that we wear ourselves out getting nowhere.

I think we'd be pretty sure our life was going along just as the Lord intended it if—when somebody asked us the question, "If you knew in six months lightning would strike you dead, what would you do with those six months?"—we could answer, "I'd just keep on doing what I'm doing."

Something to think about.

Something for the Bulletin Board

1987

Many times people have written me, or met me hither and yon about the archdiocese, and they've told me that they have one of my columns on their bulletin board, or their refrigerator. Sometimes they've even taken one out of their billfolds, and shown it to me, yellowed and worn.

Well, that warms the heart, let me tell you. That's positive motivation at its finest.

All of which is preliminary to what I am about to write. Make room on your bulletin board. Move the stuff over on your refrigerator. Make a place in your billfold. I am about to share with you seven suggestions which I guarantee will make your life better.

Years ago I had the first six. I lost them, and lost the habit of doing them. Couldn't even remember, for sure, what they were.

You can imagine my delight when I ran across them in a recent Reader's Digest article. I memorized them. And then, just in case, I put them on my bulletin board. I have since passed them out to friends, foisted them on relatives and generally made a nuisance of myself.

The seventh one was suggested to me, after a griping session one cold day last winter, by a beloved relative who was sick of me being the griper, while she was the gripee. "Whenever you have a problem with a person," she said, "try this."

With that, I will give you my suggestions: Every day, say to yourself, Today I will. . . .

1. Do something for someone else.
2. Do something for myself.
3. Do something I don't want to do that needs doing.
4. Do a physical exercise.
5. Do a mental exercise.

6. Say an original prayer that always includes counting my blessings.

And, 7, If I am having trouble with some person, before I deal with that person, I will always say a prayer for him or for her. This may be hard to do, sincerely, depending upon how crabby you are with the person, or the person with you. But try it. The Lord's magic prevails.

As the Godfather says in the pizza commercials, "No thanks are necessary."

Worrying about Worrying

1987

The little portion of Northeast Nebraska that we call home has had a winter to end all winters. That is, we've had no winter at all. Even this past week when much of the country was wallowing about in snow banks, all we had was rain. We're worried. The winter was too nice. The thinking around here is, "we're going to have to pay for this."

We always worry about weather. Mother Nature has dealt us some blows. Of course, all of our worry never changed the path of a single cloud, diverted one snow flake, or stopped even an evening's breeze. Worrying won't change anything. And we could certainly think of jollier ways to use our time.

Some people, however, are born with more worry bones than others. My dear and beloved friend Shirley is a world class worrier. If they gave gold medals for worrying—she would have a wall full. I've been on her about it a lot, but it doesn't help. Now she is worried about worrying too much.

I realized something interesting about my friend, however. For her, talking her worries out is an effective outlet. When it counts she is a do-er, not a worrier. She gets her worries out in the open and—when things get tough (as she knew they would!)—she just pitches in and takes care of it.

Then there are those poor souls who are not only worriers themselves, but they aren't happy until they get everyone around them worried too. These often well-meaning types will come up to you on the street and say, "You should get more rest. You don't look well." Until then, you felt fine. They are the people who say, "I think you need to hear this for your own good."

Believe me, you don't. Their greatest delight is being the first with the bad news, especially if it concerns you.

I'm convinced these are not unkindly people, they just need to feel important. Perhaps they need affection. When they approach with some unsavory news or sad morsel of gossip, we should hug them. *Very* tightly.

The toughest worries to pare down to size are worries about our kids. When our kids are little, the worries are little too. Unfortunately, we don't appreciate that until they get big, and the big worries start.

A phone call from a grown kid with a truckload of concerns can wipe out a parents perfectly lovely day—or week—or year—or lifetime. I'm exaggerating, but not much. It helps keep the worrying down if parents realize they don't have much more responsibility for what their grown kids choose to do with their lives than they do for what Mother Nature chooses to do with the weather. You may find that hard to believe. But it makes a lot of sense, and it should be a relief. We can love them, and cheer them on. Once they are adults we can no longer assume the responsibility for their choices, anymore than they can assume the responsibility for ours. (Which is a relief to them, too!)

That's enough about worrying. I look out my office window at a picture of pastoral serenity and beauty. The sun is shining brightly, the skies are blue, and the grass is greening up. I can hear the Meadowlarks a'singing in the trees. We're going to have to pay for this!

Nebraskans Don't Have Less Stress—They Just Handle It Better

1987

A recent study suggests that of all the people in all the 50 states, Nebraskans have the least stress. As a person who's worked the past few years with young and old attempting to teach stress management techniques, I found that study amazing. Until I realized that they weren't saying we didn't have things to be stressed about, they were just saying we handled it better.

That I understand. I think we handle stress better for two reasons. One is our wierd weather, the other is our values.

Weather is something we often have to offer up. We probably do more praying about weather than almost anything, except our kids. Even kid-prayers are sometimes weather related, such as around the winter holidays when we have to pray them all home.

Except this year we didn't seem to have any winter. And then summer seemed to come before spring. Even the flowers were confused. That's what I mean. We've had to learn from early on that we must be flexible about the weather. We've prepared for anything. We dress in layers, so we can take things off and put them on as the weather dictates.

Our ability to adjust to the changes in the weather carries over to all the other changes in our lives.

We're good adjusters—very important in handling stress. The other reason, I decided, as I looked around me last Sunday at the good people in my own parish, is that we care about each other. We have some solid values. In this state, we are religious people. We have a firm basis in faith.

When I see the headlines talking about the sleaze, scandals and hypocrisy we've been assaulted by in the last few months, I weep for our country. Nobody gains from the treatment of televangelist Jim Bakker and his wife Tammy as buffoons, nor from the humiliating debacle of Gary Hart's downfall, nor from the devastating experience of watching the spectacle of yet another president involved wittingly or unwittingly in a cover-up. Everybody loses.

But in the midwest, these people are not our models. Not by a darned sight!! Our models are the deacons who serve selflessly every

Sunday. Our models are the people who rise out of their pews to take communion to the sick when Father says, "We, though many, are one body, who share the one bread. Go now to those members of our parish community who because of infirmity cannot be present with us this morning . . . the Lord be with you on your way." Our models are the C.C.D. teachers, the choir members, the family ministers, the priests, the nuns and all the people who serve on the multitude of committees in all kinds of ways without much thought of getting thanks, because we're not very good at giving it.

We've learned the important thing in teenage development is for teenagers to learn to stand on their own two feet and take responsibility for their part in whatever is going on around them. In addition, we've learned the overwhelming importance of their need for values, for a sense of God, and of right and wrong.

These things are no less important for those of us who are adults. They have become crucial for our country. If we are, indeed, people who can handle stress, it's because we have those values.

And we have wierd weather. We know how to offer things up.

The Healing Power of Tears

1987

When the congresswoman announced she was giving up on her dream of running for presidency, she was momentarily overwhelmed and shed a few tears. Some of the pundits in the media had a hey day, "Could a person who cried possibly be presidential material?"

What a bunch of rot! The better question would be, "Could a person who *didn't* cry possibly be presidential material?"

Some months ago I wrote a column about grief in which we discussed the healing power of tears, quoting Deanna Edwards, a noted music minister to the elderly and to people who are dealing with pain and grief. "We need to cry," I wrote. Even Jesus wept. Men and women, boys and girls, should welcome tears as a healing gift. Tears are our God-given human right. We need to cry alone, and we need to cry together as a family and friends. "Crying is a wonderful experience and a great way to say I love you," Deanna said.

I also stressed the fact that tears don't come on cue. Sometimes people feel terrible because they don't cry when they feel they should. Each of us experiences grief differently. Tears spill over when they need to—and sometimes when you least expect them. When they do—let them flow, and be grateful. This happened to me last week when I was driving down the road. A song came on the radio that rekindled fond memories of people long gone from this earth. I cried. Not for them, but for myself because I still missed them. I thought I'd shed those tears long ago. Afterwards, I felt—how can I express this—I guess the word "cleansed" describes it best. And I said, "Thanks Lord, I needed that."

That column, briefly recapped for you here, turned out to be one of the *keeper* columns, the ones reader's thought enough of to keep and send back to me. It comes back to me again and again, and has earned a place of honor in my book *The Keepers*, Volume One, page 10.

The letters which have come in have been as uplifting to me as any of my columns could ever have been to any of you. With one of those letters, from Joan Kaiser of Neligh, came a tiny poem. I will share part of Joan's letter, adding the poem at the end, because you may want to clip it. That's just what Joan did. She wrote, "The enclosed clip I send to you in response to your column in our paper regarding grief. Your statement about tears being such a necessary part of grieving and healing made me think of this clipping. I saw it in a paper or a magazine and it just begged me to save it. Though I could see no logical reason, I did cut it out and it hung on my fridge."

"This was in June of 1977. In November my husband was diagnosed as having leukemia and within a year he was dead. I read this clipping a lot in that year and did indeed cry a lot. Sure enough, the more the tears fell on the outside, the more often another tiny piece of grief and hurt was swept away. It has been nearly nine years now—time enough to wash away the lion's share of the hurt—to remember the good times—to find new ways to go and things to do—but the clipping remains, not only as a reminder to let the tears come in sad times, but as a seed for my *transfusion board*. That one clipping has grown to two sheets full of messages that are good for a transfusion of spirit or a kick in the pants, whichever seems right for any given situation." Thanks Joan, for sharing the poem. It will, e'er the night has flown, rest on a lot of other reader's *transfusions boards*.

TEARS

Tears on the outside
Fall to the ground
And are slowly swept away,

Tears on the inside
Fall on the soul
And stay, and stay, and stay.

Donald Wayne Rash

Changing Your Attitude—It Beats Tigers or Earthquakes

1987

Last week I got up one morning with an attitude problem. I was depressed. My feet hurt. The cat had ear mites. The weather was lousy. I was worried about some kids, overloaded with tasks. The world seemed to be going to hell in a handbasket. You know the feeling. I know you do, because at some time or other, everyone gets depressed.

According to eminent psychologists, "depression is the common cold of psychological disorders."

Something happened, however, that changed my attitude in a hurry. California had an earthquake. My problems paled in comparison to the fact that California might be falling in the ocean, taking son Rob with it.

A call from Rob assured me that he was shaken up, but still standing on solid (more or less) ground. I was elated. I was no longer depressed. I could handle any problem, as long as that earth quake hadn't swallowed up Rob. My attitude changed dramatically.

All of this made me understand better a point a psychologist had made at a recent meeting. He said one cure for depression would be to have a tiger jump through your window.

Seems a mite melodramatic. He explained that when we're depressed our body sort of shuts down. A tiger jumping through the window would rev it up again. Our body would automatically go into the fight or flee stance programmed into it from pre-historic times. Our blood pressure would shoot up. Our adrenalin would rise, and we'd be ready to fight the blooming tiger, or get the heck out of there.

"Nobody can stay depressed," said the learned man, "in the face of a tiger." I add to that, "or an earthquake." In pre-historic times, being able to fight or flee pretty well took care of your problems. Many of the stresses of today we cannot flee, nor can we fight.

But we can do *something*.

William James, in his *The Principles of Psychology*, wrote, "The greatest discovery in our generation is that human beings, by changing the inner attitudes of their minds, can change the outer aspects of their lives." Negative thinking is crippling. Expecting the worse from others and from ourselves, we usually end up with it. In many areas where our thinking goes awry, we can change those thoughts by making a conscious effort. The wonderful self help group, *Recovery*, stresses that 95 percent of the things that get us down are trivialities. If we handled them one at a time, we enhance our ability to cope. Piled up, they blow us away.

Dr. David Burns, in his book, *Feeling Good*, says that most depression arises from erroneous thinking. When it comes to curing depression, the best medicine, he says, is to change our thoughts. Nobody says it's easy. We need to be open and flexible. If we list the good things about our lives, and the bad things, we might be surprised at how many good things there are. We could decide to do something about the bad things—or, if we can't, change our attitude.

Attitudes change when we try something new—perhaps start an exercise program, or enroll in a class. Attitudes change when we talk things out with a friend or a confidant.

Changing activities changes attitudes. There are lots of ways. Of course, change can be uncomfortable. In fact, it almost always is. But harken to another *Recovery* quote, "Comfort is a want *not* a need." It's also important that we realize, just as the common cold sometimes turns into pneumonia, depression can become acute. That calls for professional help. Getting that help takes a lot of courage. But it makes all the sense in the world.

It beats tigers or earthquakes.

To Yell or Not To Yell—What To Do
About Anger

1988

"I'm so mad I can't even spit," bellowed a friend, and proceeded to keep bellowing until he got his mad out.

I was impressed, and envious.

When I was growing up, back in the forties, we were taught that one shouldn't be angry, or jealous, or have any of those "ugly" emotions. So we tried, not always successfully, to stuff all of our emotions inside. We got headaches and hives and nervous ticks. It's still hard for me to deal with anger. Although in recent years we have come to understand that emotions, all of them, are natural occurences, and during the course of just one day a human being will experience them all. We all handle anger differently. Some people just blow—like my friend. Other's swallow their rage and put a smile on their faces simply because they want to be liked. Or because they expect to be punished if they show their true feelings. Not a good idea. Psychologists warn, "Denying anger can lead to alcoholism, hypertension, or coronary disease—and turning the anger inward may bring on depression, migraine headaches, high blood pressure, even impotence."

People who do not find a suitable outlet for their anger get more angry, not less. They may go home and storm at their spouse or pets, and double their trouble.

The question is, what *IS* a suitable outlet for anger? How best can we express it at work or in a family or a social situation? Losing control can mean losing one's job or the respect of one's friends and colleagues, or someone's love.

The answer is there are ways, and anger handled properly can work for you not against you.

The first step is to *admit you are angry—even if doing so makes you uncomfortable.* Focus on the content of the situation, understanding that if your anger is unproductive it will lead to more problems.

We need to learn the words and skills with which to verbalize our wrath.

One way to deal with anger is to breathe deeply. Get hold of yourself. Another way is physical activity. A jog around the park, for instance. A brisk walk does wonders for me.

Once you're cooled off and become rational again, lock yourself into a "task orientation." Ask yourself what you want to accomplish from the situation. If you want to save a relationship, or solve an on-going problem, you may conclude that confrontation is no answer at all. Then you must use the energy from your anger in a more constructive way.

Or you may decide on confrontation. There's no reason in the world you can't sit down with the person you're angry with and say "I have this problem, is there some way we can work it out?" The best rule for expressing anger is to use "I" statements. Instead of Kip saying to me, for instance, "Your office is a mess," which is accusatory, and is also true, and would upset me. I'd start responding angrily about how busy I was. He needs to say, "I get very upset when I see your side of the office covered with papers." (Which he did, so now HE'S organizing my boxes of past columns.)

As with anything that's bad for you, prevention of anger is your best way of handling it. Not easy, but here are some ways that work. Take a look at your expectations of yourself and of your associates. If your standards are unrealistic and inflexible, you are setting your own self up for frustration and anger. Do what you can to mellow out. Look at what you're doing to other people. Your unrealistic expectations make it even harder for your associates to perform. It's not good business!

Notice how you appraise the incidents that bother you. If you can't change the situation, change your perception. You only control you. Put yourself in the shoes of the person who's getting on your nerves.

If your job is extremely stressful, set up ways to relieve it on a day to day basis. Start an exercise program. Talk things out constructively with fellow workers. (This is called "parallel suffering.")

Whether you're a boss or an employee, a man or a wife, a parent or a kid, a teacher or a student, don't just sit and suffer. Do the things necessary to relieve your anxiety. Let your needs be known. Keep open and honest about your feelings. Do whatever you can to keep the flow of communications open. If you occasionally break down and lose control, remember you're only human. Perfection is not a human attribute. Evaluate the experience, learn from it, and you will handle your anger better the next time.

Promoting Positive Expectations

1988

A portly fellow pulled into a filling station in a small town puffing on a cigar. He said to the attendant, "What kind of people live in this town, anyway? I'm thinking of moving here." The young man looked the fellow over carefully, "What kind of people live in the town you come from?" He asked. The portly gentleman replied, "The people in the town I come from are selfish, short sighted and stupid." The attendant shook his head knowingly, and replied "Then that's the same kind of people you'll find here."

Negative expectations produce negative results. Most of us bumble onto this truth as we go through life. We learn that it is much better to approach life with positive expectations. But sometimes we have to work at it. I, a peace lover and compromiser by nature, used to think that everybody had to love everybody. All we had to do was understand each other. Simple.

But I've learned that an idealic world is hardly possible. Personalities differ. Unavoidable conflicts arise. We just can't seem to understand some of our fellow man. We don't even understand ourselves sometimes. And yet I went on my pollyanna way, believing that at least I could *like* everybody, and—in turn—everybody would certainly like me. I learned this was hardly true one day when, in my bubbling busybody mode, I decided to cheer up a dour acquaintance whom, I thought, needed me to cheer him up. He looked at me with distaste and said "leave me alone, I hate you blankety blank happy people."

Some people, I learned, prefer to be dour.

Then, I met somebody I couldn't seem to like. The feeling was mutual. We grated upon each other's nerves like fingernails on chalkboard. This drove me crazy until I came to grips with the fact that for some reason I was *choosing* to work up a head of steam about this person. I was not even allowing myself to contemplate any redeeming qualities. I decided to choose differently. Now, while we will never be bosom buddies, we tolerate each other amiably. The writer of today's letter has a need to hear about the tactics I used on myself.

Dear Joanie; Please don't use my identification, because nobody knows I feel this way. I really like this operation I work for. I like my job. But there's this guy I work with who drives me crazy. He drives everybody crazy, except the boss. The boss likes him. It's getting so bad that I get sick to my stomach every time he comes around. I'd do anything not to feel like this. Have you got any advice? Sign me "Desperate."

Dear Desperate: You want to change, so you're already half way there. Nobody drives us crazy unless we let them. Stress isn't caused by a person, it's caused by our perception of that person. The only way to lessen the stress is to change our perception. It's not easy, but I swear it's possible. Some personalities just naturally grate on others. But, face it, people have a right to be who they are, even though that's different than we'd prefer them to be. Just accepting that fact and realizing perfection is not a human attribute is a good place to start. We will never understand some people. The problem is when we run into somebody we can't seem to like, we get so much emotion invested in not liking them that we won't even allow ourselves to look for redeeming qualities.

Amazing things happen when we start looking at this person from a different angle. Here are some things you can try. First, really try to look at life from the other person's perspective. This can be a real eye opener. It's the old "walk a mile in his shoes" idea. Try to learn what his problems are and something about his background. It may help you understand what makes him act like he does. You *will* find some redeeming qualities. Everybody has some. (There's some reason the boss likes him.) Then start some positive vibrations flowing between the two of you. Give him a sincere complement. Say some encouraging words. We need encouragement like plants need water. Change your negative expectations to positive ones, and sometimes magic will happen.

I know how hard this is, so let me know if these ideas help.

Life Is Too Important To Be Taken Seriously

1988

I woke up the other morning in a dour mood. I was crabby with myself for not getting more done. I looked in the mirror that very morning and saw a person who was older than I remembered being. It was depressing. My crabbiness lasted only until I sat down to drink my first mug of coffee. I read my mug.

"Life is too important," said the mug, "to be taken seriously." That's all it took. For a few minutes there I'd lost my sense of humor.

The quote was attributed, by the very mug it was on, to Oscar Wilde.

The ability to see the humor in life, particularly the ability to laugh at oneself, is—according to eminent folks who know such things—very good for our mental health. But sometimes we need to remind ourselves. The problem is as we get older we get more education and assume more responsibilities, and we begin to do a lot of what Sister Marie Micheletto calls "shoulding" on ourselves. We should do this. We should be that. Just when we need to develop more of a sense of humor, we begin instead to pile ourselves down with expectations of perfection. And perfection is not a human attribute.

We judge ourselves by other people's standards and other people's accomplishments, which is humorous in and of itself. The Lord never asked us to be anybody but who we are. Being the best of who we are is relatively easy, because that's who we are. It's when we're trying to be who we aren't that we get dour.

It helps if we can learn to chuckle at our imperfections, and smile philosophically at the things we can't do anything about anyway. Such as the older person who begins to look at us out of our mirror. But if you want more proof, how about the group of eminent psychologists who met in Wales a number of years ago and said, "more and more people are becoming sick today because they cannot laugh at themselves." They talked about our ability to "catastrophize" trivialities—to sweat the small stuff. If we only looked at everything with a "universal perspective" they said, we would realize how insignificant are many of the things which upset us. I prefer "spiritual perspective". But you understand. Adding more food for thought, Dr. Benjamin Lowe, the founder of that marvelous self-help group *Recovery*, says that 95% of the things that get us down are trivialities, (95%!). If we handled them one at a time, instead of letting them pile up, we'd do a lot for our mental health.

Dr. Joel Goodman, a psychologist who started a school to teach people to laugh, thinks the best way to handle them, or anything else, is with humor. He says, "Stress is not an event, but it is our perception of an event, and we can change that perception with humor."

Laughter is like a mini-vacation. It lowers the blood pressure, and even causes an immunological reaction that helps fight disease. It's good for handling pains in the head, pains in the back, and pains in the neck. The greatest proof of all, is in the bible, *Book of Proverbs*, 17:22. "A merry heart doeth good like medicine, but a broken spirit drieth up the bones."

We do have miseries to deal with, of course.

It will help us if we activate our sense of humor. How? Well, we can hang out with funny people, read funny books, go to funny movies, hang funny cartoons or sayings on our bulletin boards and refrigerators. Do something silly, even out of character, like hang an animal (stuffed) on your car window. Buy yourself a teddy bear. Look in the mirror and grin. When that older person grins back, she (or he) seems a lot younger. It's fun.

You might even drink your coffee from a funny mug. It's a good idea, because life *IS* too important to be taken seriously.

Life Is Not the Dreams We Dream, It's the Choices We Make

1988

"Our lives are not made up of the dreams that we dream. Our lives are made up of the choices that we make."

Thus a preacher spoke unto me as I drove home from Norfolk on a recent Sunday evening. I do not often listen to radio preachers as I am driving down the road, preferring instead to direct symphony orchestras on educational radio (one handed with great abandon and much imagined expertise), or listening to news broadcasts, or tapes (speakers, preachers or Spanish). A lot of the times I just ponder.

People who drive a lot are into pondering. That's what I was doing as I switched on the radio, thinking to check on the weather forecast because of the storm clouds on the distant horizon. Instead of the weatherman, I heard this voice with a ring of humble sincerity. And, strangely enough, or perhaps not so strangely, he was speaking directly to the very thoughts I had been pondering.

Why is it, I was pondering, that some people have the courage to make positive choices, while others sit on their duffs wallowing in doldrums, *poor me*-ing themselves into eternity.

I'd just spoken to two groups, back to back, as it were, who displayed this kind of courage. One group, celebrating a year of sobriety, had gathered at Valley Hope Treatment Center in O'Neill, Nebraska. Surrounded by loved ones, these folks of all ages and from all walks of life told soul-stirring stories of their near destruction from the disease of alcohol, and their subsequent revival because of their choice to go into treatment.

The other group, led by Norfolk's vivacious Mary Abboud, was a non- denominational support organization of single folks who choose to gather once a month for fellowship, education and inspiration. When the preacher spoke to me instead of the weather man, I was contemplating the bravery it took for each of these people to emerge from their own private hell, and choose—with the help of God—to survive enthusiastically.

I was thinking of the hope I'd seen in their eyes.

I was wondering what held the *poor me*-ers back. Mired in the muck of alcoholism, or caught up in self pity, doubtless they are afraid, laden down with unnecessary and self-imposed guilt. "Unnecessary?" you query. Yes, unnecessary! How can we not forgive ourselves, my friends, when the Lord himself forgives us? Listen to Christ's message via John 12:47, "I come not to judge the world, but to save the world."

That's us.

Not listening, many of us laden ourselves with guilt from the past. I do, anyway. It isn't easy to rid oneself of guilt. It helps to realize perfection is not a human attribute, and to understand that choices that bring about change, generate fear. As if reading my mind, the preacher boomed forth again, "We've all made some really dumb choices," he said, adding with a resigned chuckle, "I certainly have. It is important to forgive ourselves, as God forgives us."

My "Amen, brother!!" resounded in my empty car.

It is not enough, we find, to pray to the Lord, "take this problem away." What we need to do is pray, "God show us what we need to do, how we need to change, to help ourselves deal with this problem." Prayer helps us see our own short-comings. That's not pleasant. If we really want our prayers answered, we have to be prepared to do some uncomfortable things.

In fact, it sometimes calls for great courage to answer our own prayers; to make the choices and the changes necessary to set our lives in a positive direction. It calls for a "march into the red sea and know it will divide" kind of courage.

This week I had the privilege of seeing that kind of courage in action.

Prepare for Angry Grandparents on the March

1988

"I bet old people make a tough audience" said my friend who is very young. What a statement! As a person who is bordering on mildly old, I thought about resenting it.

I remembered how, in my youthful arrogance, I used to also stereotype *old people.*

As if people who were older congealed into some kind of a homogenious mass. If anything, the opposite is true. Characters become more defined and interesting. Many people never get *old* in any way except chronologically. That doesn't really count.

Dad Burney, for instance, lived with great enthusiasm until he was 95.   Norfolk's Margaret Agnes wrote a book at 90, and our own Aunt Lenyce Marsh played golf and edited and wrote for a newspaper into her seventies and eighties. At the Governor's Conference on Aging in North Platte, I met a woman of 90 who'd just gotten her Graduate Equivalent Diploma. Introduced as being 91, she rose up in indignation: "I am ONLY 90!" she said.

Which brings me to my favorite quote: "Nobody grows old by living a number of years. People grow old by deserting their ideals and giving up their enthusiasm. Age wrinkles the skin, but if you give up enthusiasm, that wrinkles the soul".

At the Conference for Aging, enthusiasm ran high. There might have been a few wrinkled bodies around, but not one wrinkled soul. Meetings were jammed with eager participants intent on soaking up information. But the fact is, *staying young at heart*, is nothing that anybody, or any agency, can *DO* for an older person. Older people do it for themselves. At any age, we can choose to wallow in misery if we want to, because there is enough of it around to wallow in. It's easy to get frustrated with the inevitable adjustments one must make just getting older. We who are more *mature*, so to speak, have already survived things we never thought possible.

A multitude of elderly people, including those taking part in that conference, make a different choice. They choose to continue to use their skills and pursue their interests. They may retire from a certain job, but they never retire from life. They understand that people rust out a lot faster than they wear out.

Many older people are gung ho volunteers. Worthy causes would surely collapse without them. Political activist groups are flexing their muscle in earnest, aware of the increasing power the growing numbers of elderly will command.

The challenge will be not to just concentrate on the problems of the older person. The challenge will be to use their (our) increasing political clout to bring hard-earned wisdom and solid moral values to bear on a country sadly in need of them. I expect to see them turn on such things as drug abuse, child pornography and political and religious corruption. Lord help the politician who doesn't listen to what they're saying. There is no greater force known to mankind than an aroused and angry grandparent who's grandchild is being abused or misused.

Trust me, I know.

This is bound to happen, because studies show older people are younger than they used to be when they were older if you know what I mean.   An article in Psychology Today states "the attitudes of a 70 year old today are equivalent to those of a 50-year-old a decade or two ago."

"Because of better health care, and increasing interest in physical fitness, more people are reaching the ages of 65, 75, and 85 in excellent health. Their functional age is much younger than their chronological age."

There used to be this mistaken assumption that old age brings on unavoidable mental decline, and people would atrophy just because they thought they should.

As George Burns put it. "I see people who—the minute they get to be 65—start rehearsing to be old. They practice grunting when they sit down and practice grunting when they get up, and by the time they get to be 70 they've got it made. They're a hit. They're old."

Not the newly young elderly. Not on your life. They're going to stand up and be counted, and they won't be grunting.

Are You Codependant? Check It Out!

1988

If you never say no, what are your yesses worth?

I have had reason to contemplate this in my lifetime more than once. Most recently, I contemplated it this spring, when I was spread so thin because of my own inability to say no that I lost my sense of humor.

Lost my sense of humor!!!! It was nobody's fault but my own.

There's an increased awareness now of a human condition called *codependancy*. The definition of this condition, according to a book called *Codependant No More* by Melody Beattie, is "A person who has let someone else's behavior affect him or her and is obsessed with controlling other people's behavior." Codependants are people who becomes so absorbed in other people's problems they don't have time to take care of themselves. Codependants judge their own self worth in the light of other people's behavior.

At first the term codependancy was linked primarily to people who lived with alcoholics—then it was recognized as prevalent in people who deal with any compulsive disorders, such as a gambler, a foodaholic, a workaholic, a sexaholic, a criminal, a rebellious teenager or a neurotic parent.

Dysfunctional families turn people into codependants, say the experts, and—get this—according to those same experts 97% of the families in the United States are dysfunctional. Some say 100%.

A column, by it's very nature, is limited. But it can whet your appetite to learn more. This is a subject you may want to learn more about if you are a person who is so busy taking care of everyone else that you forget to take care of yourself. Or if you are *wallowing in martyrdom and entangled in obsessions and worries about other people's problems.* Codependancy, in its most crippling form, requires treatment.

It's strange isn't it, because all the while we're being martyrs for somebody else we think we're doing them a favor. It's the worst thing in the world we can do for them. The greatest gift we can give to anybody is allowing that person the privilege of accepting the responsibility for his or her own actions. That is so hard. We want to help. We want to fix things. Letting go is the toughest thing we do. To allow people to work things out for themselves requires faith in them, faith in ourselves, and faith in God. We have to trust that sometimes the strangest and most painful things work out for the best.

Detachment doesn't mean that we don't care. It means we quit picking up after other people so they can begin to learn to pick up after themselves. It means that we establish a *healthy neutrality.* We live our lives without excessive feelings of guilt about others, or responsibility toward them. When we stop worrying about them, they pick up the slack and start worrying about themselves.

It's very simple.

We mind our own business. What a great idea. What an ultimately freeing thing it is to do. We can love our spouses, our kids, our friends. We can laugh with them and cry with them. We can cheer them on from the sidelines, but we cannot assume the responsibility for what they choose to do.

People who live with serious problems, such as alcoholism, or physical disabilities, or a teenager hell-bent on self-destruction, can (according to Beattie) grieve their losses and then find a way "to live their lives not in resignation, martyrdom, and dispair, but with enthusiasm, peace, and a true sense of gratitude for that which was good."

We can learn to hold **ourselves** in high esteem and survive with enthusiasm. We don't do this without effort, or perfectly, and certainly not instantly. But by striving to do it, we can **learn** to do it well.

So—are you shouldering burdens that aren't yours? Are you assuming responsibility or guilt for someone else's actions? Are you codependant? Something to think about.

Have You Checked Your Cholesterol?

1989

Cholesterol, the puzzle of the eighties, perhaps even the nineties.

You need it, but not too much. And—not too little. It's good. And it's bad. Everybody's talking about it. However—unlike the weather—which nobody *can* do anything about, people are doing something about cholesterol. Or so they say, "We used to talk about babies and kids at bridge club," said a friend of mine, "and now all we talk about is cholesterol".

We all know each other's cholesterol number.

When they go for tests, we can't wait to see if that number's gone up or down. Anything under 200 is good, as I understand it. When you get above that, you better beware. Some people are dieting, some are taking medicine, some are exercising more, some are eating oat bran, and some are doing all four. Kip's only done one, and that under protest. He's eaten oat bran. Lots of it. The conversation in our kitchen has gone something like this. Kip takes a bite of a cookie (or a muffin, or a piece of bread, or meat loaf, or whatever) and begins to look suspicious. "What's in this?" he asks. "Oat bran," I admit.

And he sighs.

"We're going to plant the whole farm to oats next year," he said, "The way you're using them there's bound to be a shortage".

Maybe I have gone a little overboard. When I read that oat bran might be effective in lowering cholesterol I started sneaking it into everything. I though cholesterol was boring until mine tested high, and then I got fascinated with it. I read all I could get my hands on, and the person I began to worry about was Kip. Here's a man who eats bacon and eggs every morning of his life, and beef at every meal he has anything to say about.

Cholesterol doesn't sound like anything you want to have, but we need some. According to the dictionary it's a fatty, monatomic crystalline alcohol, derived principally from bile, present in most gallstones, and very widely distributed in animal fats and tissues.

Our *Family Medicine Guide* (which allows us to diagnose all of our own ailments, and to worry ourselves through a few we never get) calls cholesterol a steroid chemical, small amounts of which are essential for making and maintaining nerve cells and for synthesizing natural hormones. Too much cholesterol could cause atherosclerosis.

Atherosclerosis is really something you don't want to have.

So it behooves one to look into this cholesterol business. There's good cholesterol and bad cholesterol. Exercise raises the good, and proper diet brings down the bad. Doing a little of both, and eating a lot of oat bran, I brought mine down from 260 to 239. It's still too high, but better.

I became a born-again oat bran enthusiast. Until Kip finally said, "Enough already, I'm going to the doctor for a check up and get me a number. I'm sick of you and your oat bran".

He admitted he'd felt out of it for some time because everybody had a number, and he didn't.

So he went. I waited for the bad news. You know what? With all of his eggs and his beef, his number is something like 167.

They say it's genetic. I say it's not fair. I'm going to munch on another one of these heavy, gosh-awful oat bran muffins and pout.

A Slip is Not a Fall

1989

Last week, in spite of all my resolutions to the contrary, I wolfed down deepfat fried mushrooms until I felt like I was one myself. Why did I do this dumb thing? What happened to the "sensible eating plan" I vowed to live by? I have such wonderful intentions.

Sometimes, however, I slip.

Do your good intentions fail in the face of "just this once" logic? One more drink can't hurt. A cigarette will calm me down. I'll have just this one mushroom, and then I'll quit. (And one more, and one more.)

I got some help understanding our problem just this past week from G. Alan Marlatt and his colleagues at the University of Washington. A slip can be valuable, they say, because it can be analyzed. And understanding why we slip will help us avoid it the next time. A little awareness goes a long way.

Marlatt writes in the "University of California, Berkeley, Wellness Letter" that people who are successful in ridding themselves of bad health habits, are those who anticipate difficulties and forestall them. He tells us, "As soon as you realize that, in defiance of all resolutions to the contrary, you've lit up, poured a whiskey, or wolfed down a dozen oreos (mushrooms), take a hard look at what you've done and why."

Ignore the feelings of guilt or inadequacy, they don't help. Instead, concentrate on the reasons why you're giving up tobacco, alcohol, or sweets in the first place: to avoid lung cancer, keep a clear head, lose weight.

Marlatt identified three primary high-risk situations that account for 75 percent of the relapses. See if these don't sound familiar.

1. **Negative emotional states.** Watch out if you're bored, tense, angry, or frustrated. That's when you're most likely to slip.

2. **Interpersonal conflict.** If you've had an argument at home or at work, you may return to your bad habits in compensation or in revenge.

3. **Social pressure.** It is not easy to avoid eating or drinking at a business lunch or a party. (My mushroom binge comes under this category.)

Would you like some strategies suggested to cope with such situations? Here they are:

1. **Develop a positive addiction.** Rather than rewarding yourself with a cigarette, a drink, or ice cream, become *addicted* to a healthful habit. Take up gardening, photography, walking, bird watching, anything that suits you, and start getting your daily *fix* from that.

2. **Stay away from temptation.** If you always smoke while playing bridge, give up bridge for awhile. Don't mosey aimlessly through grocery stores when you're hungry. Don't order deepfat fried mushrooms and think you'll just eat one. Don't stock up on goodies *you* can't resist.

3. **Learn to wait out the urge.** Ride it like a surfer rides a wave. You know that all waves subside. See through the things you do to undermine yourself. Don't bake cookies or keep a bottle around "in case friends drop by". They say five minutes and the urge is gone. (Try five years.) In any case, know what you can't resist. Then, avoid it.

Finally, according to the experts, be prepared to rehearse all these strategies several times. Only practice makes them work, and **they will work.** Allow leeways for mistakes, don't lambast yourself with guilt. A slip is just that. It's not a fall. Regard each slip as a fork in the road. One path leads to happiness, the other to continued change for the better.

Take the right path. Onward and upward.

We can do it gang.

Get with the Program—Prolong Your Own Life

1989

I was listening to Paul Harvey the other day, and he said something that really pleased me. He said a new study suggests you can significantly reduce your cholesterol count by eating two oat bran muffins a day.

I got excited. The cholesterol count didn't use to excite me—even after it got to be the main focus of conversation among my friends, and these were friends who had other important things to discuss, such as perfect grandchildren. I had, after all, never had any trouble with cholesterol. I have low blood pressure, too. And low everything else that is supposed to be low. I didn't mind telling people that, of course.

Besides ever since people started bad mouthing beef, the selling of which gives us (some years) our means of eating other things, I've never been tickled with all this talk about *healthy* diets. There would be no way in the world, short of making it illegal, that we wouldn't eat beef.

Recent years, however, I've gotten into health, because it has been discovered that nothing has as many nutrients as *lean* beef. The beef council has always said this but the latest word is from such unbiased sources as the Heart and Cancer folks. Their accent is on the "lean". I started muscling into the cholesterol-ic conversations over coffee, when my friendly doctor told me my cholesterol was elevated. I was outraged at the news, but I felt—well—"in".

The interesting thing was that many of my high-cholesterol friends have been able to control their problem with diet. As simple as that.

In fact, if we but choose to exercise that control, we have a lot of control not only of our cholesterol, but many other diseases including the dreaded cancer.

A recent article in the April *HEALTH* magazine says that 50% to 80% of all cancers are related to livestyle factors **in our control**.

They suggested a number of ways that we could exercise that control. Most difficult, I suspect, is to **quit smoking.** A 1985 study "blames cigarettes for one third of all cancer deaths." Also difficult is to **watch our weight.** But this is most important considering that there are more cancer deaths "among the too fat (40% over-weight) **and** the too thin." And we're told to **go easy on the booze.** Experts say if we do drink we should "limit our intake to four or five drinks a week."

Some things aren't that diffcult, but take conscious effort, such as the decision to **cut down the fat** in your diet (lean beef) and **eat more fiber and vegetables.** We are also advised to **beware of occupational hazards** and find out if we are exposed to **hidden carcinogens.** An example of this would be the present concern about asbestos at home, work or school, and the concern about the chemicals farmers deal with on a regular basis.

Something that no young person seems to want to listen to, nor do a lot of older people, is *stop worshipping the sun.* Most skin cancers are caused by prolonged exposure to the sun, besides it greatly accelerates the aging of the skin. For those of us who like to be outdoors, the advice is, "Use a sunscreen with an SPF of 15 or higher." *Keeping a lid on stress* is important, because stress makes us more vulnerable to disease. If our life style (eating, drinking, smoking, worrying) causes us stress, we need to look at making some changes. If we can't do it ourselves, there are self-help groups available. Most importantly, we need to see our doctor regularly. I won't name names, but some people worry so much about having a disease they do more harm to themselves then the disease would. When they finally see the doctor, they find out they didn't have it in the first place.

Of course, the doctor may tell us we need to do something about some problem we didn't even know we needed to do something about. So then we must change. Change can be difficult. Change can be painful. Change can be exciting. Change can prolong our lives. It could start with something as simple as eating two oat bran muffins a day.

Everyone Needs to Assist the President in His Fight Against Drugs

1989

I'm issuing a challenge.

President Bush is marshalling his forces and declaring war against drug abuse, and it's not a war we can watch from a distance, my friends. It's not for somebody else to fight. Politicians can prattle and prognosticators can predict doom, but this is a war we cannot afford to lose. Drugs aren't out there somewhere. We all know this. They are in our own hometowns. The battleground is our own backyard.

Whereas I think everyone has to be involved in this war, I think there's a powerful force just waiting to be mobilized—and that's grandparents. When the president says drugs are killing our children, he's talking about our grandchildren. I don't know what kind of mayhem I'd be capable of if I thought some drug-pushing leech was lurking around Kate. All grandparents must have that same powder keg of emotion ready to explode at the thought that their grandchildren might be seduced by these purveyors of potential death-dealing drugs. We just have to light our fire.

I propose to start Grandparents Outraged by the Abuse of Drugs with the appropriate acronym GOAD and set us on the warpath.

The thing that blows me away about this problem is that in almost every small town, certainly in ours, everybody seems to know who's selling drugs. It's talked about, around card tables and at the coffee shop. They must not be able to prove it because nothing ever happens. But in a small town, somehow, some way, everybody knows. They see for themselves places where cars drive up with suspicious frequency. They hear rumors from the kids.

A lot of things stop people from doing something about drug pushers in their hometown, especially if it is a small town. Sometimes, the person who is suspected of selling drugs is someone you really like, so you don't believe it even if people swear it's true. If this person is exposed, it will bring tremendous hurt on people you love and respect.

Not being able to stand the thought of that, good people sit by and do nothing—and pray it will go away. *But it doesn't go away.* I am overwhelmed and appalled when I think of the consequences of that inaction.

I have heard the argument that illegal drugs are no worse than alcohol, and so, therefore, people who drink alcohol have no right to say anything to those who simply smoke a little marijuana for recreational purposes. Some think smoking pot is cool and do it as a kind of sophomoric rebellion.

Alcohol is a destructive drug when it's abused. It is a serious problem. But unless marijuana is legalized, people who smoke marijuana, even for recreational purposes, are breaking the law. They are also giving a rotten example, and supporting the very drug pushers who are supplying death-dealing drugs to our kids. That's not cool. I don't think they really want to do that. Besides the latest studies show that marijuana can have devastating effects on reproductive systems and minds. A mind fried on drugs is terrible. A child born afflicted because of parents' drug use is a helpless victim.

So you ask me, what can we do? I'm suggesting two things. One is this: If you have any solid information whatsoever that you believe indicates somebody is selling drugs, for the love of God and your fellow man, present it to somebody. Do it anonymously if you have to, but do it. Or tell me, and I'll do it. Drug pushers will not quit pushing drugs if no one every threatens them with exposure.

The second is to activate GOAD—which I have now done with a membership of one person, me. One person can make a difference. If you want to join forces with me, drop me a line, Route 2, Hartington, Neb. 68739. I don't know where this is going, but I, for one, am fed up. I'm also scared silly for our kids and our grandkids. I know that with our political clout, and the fire of our moral outrage, we can make things happen. Maybe we'll march, maybe we'll petition legislators, maybe we'll just make a heck of a lot of noise, or maybe we'll run over them with our wheelchairs and whack them with our canes. But we can, by God, make a difference. *LET'S DO IT!*

Family

1. Joanie the speaker
2. Juli the comedian
3. Kate the Dancer
4. Everybody: Bill, Chuck, Rob, Tom, Lou Ann, Kip, Joanie, Kate, John, Juli
5. Four Burney boys with Mom and Dad
6. Rob at Taos
7. The Burney girls
8. Kate patiently waiting for the fish to bite

Fellow Travelers

1. Kip, Doc and Kay Burney
2. Dad and Grace
3. Virginia's Birthday Party
4. The Graduates: Marlene Uhing, Jean Doyle, Joan, Dr. Cathy Conway
5. June and John Stockwell
6. Connie
7. Lib Goetz Dale, Bill and me
8. Harold, Gerald, Dad, Don, Doc and Kip
9. Dwight I, and Dwight II
10. Mary and Bud Gengler
11. Vince and Rhea Rossiter
12. Crew Cut Kip and Eldon Hartman
13. Florence and Joan celebrating
14. Anne and Bill Millea

Rest Stops

1. The golfers: Kay Burney, Barb Schultze, Darlene Miller
2. Black Russians: Helen Dwyer, Marg Miller, Rhea Rossiter, Evalyn Peterson
3. On Mardi Gras cruise with Nebraska Livestock Feeders
4. The Fudds: with Gwen Lindberg
5. Smelling the lilacs, Lenore Hoesing, Jean Carlson, Darlene Miller, Shirley Stevens & Evie Litz
6. Going to the Sun Road, Canada, with Bob and Peg Pond and Kip
7. Ireland, with Bob Riley & Kathy Wintz
8. Jubilee Program, with Marge Seim
9. Dominican Republic, with Charles and Jean Cook
10. Nebraska press women whooping it up.
11. Lewis and Clark Bunch: Bob and Phyllis Karolevitz, Phil and Pat Knerl.

Inspirational People

1. Governor D.W. and Edna Burney
2. Auctioneer Ferdie Peitz
3. Whittler Hugo Wuebben
4. Claude Canaday and Marie Huck
5. Kathy Frank
6. Class of '46, 40th Anniversary
7. Jim Denney, Father Rick Arkfeld
8. "Duchess" Margaret Agnes

CHAPTER FIVE

SPIRITUAL JOURNEY

Chapter Five

Our Spiritual Journey

I believe, dear readers, that we all need a spiritual connection, and it's there for us, if we just choose to connect up. I speak to the Lord in Catholic, where I was raised and feel most comfortable. But I know, whatever religion you are in, we speak to the same Lord. We have the same needs, the same doubts, and He loves us the same. And, believing this, I have ecumenized, if there is such a word, all over the place.

I directed a Lutheran choir for five years. I have spoken for, and been in retreats with Lutherans, Episcopalians, Methodists, Baptists, Congregationalists, to name a few. I believe one day we're all going to meet up in Heaven, and wonder what the fuss was about. So, although most of the columns in this section were written for the Catholic Voice, I know they speak to all Christians, indeed to anyone who acknowledges their spiritual connection.

I confide in you that my spiritual journey has not been all beer and skittles. (Did you know "skittles" was a game of ninepins?) I have experienced a few dark nights of the soul. But, especially in recent years, I have come to understand that coincidence cannot account for my many answered prayers. I am convinced that the spirit of God lives within us, and that we can tap into that spirit if we choose. There's that word again. "Choose." These last few years I have chosen. Whatever turmoil I'm in externally, I am at peace with my soul.

It's a nice place to be.

Looking Beyond the Masks

1976

Once in awhile I need to remind myself of this. There is within

120

each one of us a core of strength. Some people are not aware of this, but sometime in their lives they will need to be.

Because, not knowing, we can flay around for quite awhile, wallowing in whatever misery is confronting us. Realizing its presence, however, we can tap into it before we drown, and start the process of surviving.

It's a sense of self-worth, of inner dignity. We accept ourselves for what we are, work with our own gifts, and become the very best *us* we can be.

Too often we base our lives on what other people think we should be. Or we measure our accomplishments by what other people have accomplished. This is a mistake. The Lord did not mean for us to be brain surgeons if our gifts are in merchandising or cooking or whatever.

There is dignity in everything if we believe in the essential dignity of ourselves. Booker T. Washington said, "There is as much dignity in tilling a field as in writing a poem."

It is essential that we are true to what St. Teresa (the Little Flower) calls our "inner flame."

It's a cinch that the grumps of life, the people who go about flaying out at others, blaming everybody and everything for their problems, haven't made contact with that "inner flame." What they actually need to do to find the source of their troubles is to look in the mirror.

Many people wear masks of grumpiness, arrogance, cockiness, anger or silence. Too often we don these masks ourselves. We need to look beyond the masks and recognize the pain inside—pain that the mask-wearer often cannot even acknowledge to himself.

I know that you have felt this "inner core," this guiding "flame." It's that gut feeling for right and wrong which we sometimes follow and sometimes ignore.

The "flame" is fueled by the acceptance of God's will, of course, and knowing his guidance will be there. It is also fueled by our willingness to accept the challenges of life which are meant for us . . . to kick over the bushel and let our light shine.

His guidance is hardly ever as obvious as a road sign. Sometimes we stumble into something backwards, and then we figure out we are where we're supposed to be. Sometimes we have to hit bottom to tap into that inner core and realize we can and will survive. It helps to remind ourselves of this once in a while.

Healthy Pink Souls Need *Rain*, Too

1977

Last week I wrote this very crabby column, pounded a stamp on the corner of the envelope, tromped out in the searing heat across the drought-parched front yard and mailed it in the mail box.

I was crabby because of our creek being nearly dry, and because of the "going on" four years of drought which caused our creek to go dry—because of all the irrigating and just plain dry weather.

Which brought on a lot of other complaints, which I unloaded on my poor readers.

Well, it wasn't but a few hours later when the clouds started building up in the west, and rumbling away to their silly selves. I didn't get excited, because they'd been doing this for several days, and we'd had five and one half drops of rain and one bug in our rain gauge.

But the little rascals meant business. We had one and one-quarter inches of rain. It was unbelievable.

Everything perked up—fields and flowers and farmers alike. The pasture outside our house, which had been a yellowish-brown, immediately took on a tinge of green. And again, as always, I likened it to what grace must do to the soul. I can see this gray, yukky looking soul drooping away in a very dismal fashion—then grace comes and it pinks up and starts looking glowing and healthy.

The nice thing about grace is that you can go out after that and pink up your soul any time you take a notion. Rain comes when it pleases.

All of which brings to mind another analogy which I think is apropos. It was suggested to me by a wise priestly religious instructor and I've never forgotten it. Every time I pull a weed in our garden it comes to mind. Since I've been pulling a lot of weeds this summer, it's come to mind a lot.

He said that keeping our life free of sin is a lot like keeping a garden free of weeds. It's a constant battle, and just when you've got one section cleaned out, something pops up somewhere else.

If you turn your back and think you can let up a little, the whole garden is soon overrun with weeds. The worry being that you'd give up the weeding and let the garden go, just because it seemed like too blamed much work.

His point was, if you just keep pecking away at the weeds when they are little, they won't ever get big and take over your garden.

Just as there are a lot of times when we let the weeds get ahead of us in our garden, there are the times when we let the spiritual weeds get a hold on the soul. I suppose, combining these two analogies, we could liken grace to weed-killer, but somehow that gets to be a bit much.

We deal a lot with symbolism in the Catholic Church, but somehow I can't visualize a banner with a sickly gray soul covered with weeds being compared to a lively pink one full of flowers, with "Amazing Grace" cascading down the middle in felt letters.

On the other hand, if a wise religious instructor implanted (!) this weed analogy in my mind 30-some years ago and it has given me food for thought ever since, that can't be all bad. To say nothing of the added zest it gives to weeding my garden.

Praying Is Good for What Ails You!

1979

An elderly friend of mine used to say (when anyone was confronted with a problem): "Try praying. It's good for what ails you."

A recent UPI release backs her up although I'm sure none of us doubted the wisdom of her statement in the first place.

To quote: "Prayer, taken twice daily, is good for high blood pressure, anxiety and other ailments and has no bad side affects," a Harvard University physician told the annual meeting of the New England Hospital Assembly.

The report went on to say: "Dr. Herbert Benson, associate

professor of medicine, said he discovered the physical benefits of
prayer while teaching patients how to use the 'relaxation response,'
a 10-to-20 minute exercise that combines meditation and deep
breathing.

"The person seeking deep relaxation as a stress-relieving mechanism sits quietly, closes his eyes, inhales deeply and repeats the
prayer to himself as he exhales slowly."

We've talked about that "relaxation response" in this column
before. Many books have been published that include the activity—
or rather, lack of activity—as part of the program.

You re-program your sub-conscience while you're in it (the
relaxation response, that is) and it helps solve whatever problems
you might have. Over-eating. Smoking. Drinking. Whatever.

But even if you don't do the reprogramming, the very fact that
it lowers the blood pressure and relieves stress is terrific.

Boy, do we need to concentrate on lowering stress in this day
and age!

But the point of all this is that all the new theories that people
are developing are really just basic common sense. Some people,
like my elderly friend, knew them all the time.

Basically, every one of the massive amount of self-help psychology books now in print have to do with accepting yourself for
what you are, with developing self-respect, with appreciating your
own self-worth, and therefore being able to accept others.

And that was in the Bible. "Love others as you love yourself,"
the Lord told us, perhaps forgetting to stress that the hardest part,
the one we were going to have difficulty with, was the part about
loving ourselves.

Because of all the people we are crabby with, we are crabbiest
with ourselves. We are not perfect. Others are fallible human creatures just as we are.

We are too concerned about what *other people* think. I've
learned, perhaps the hard way, that the people who are important
are always supportive, no matter what your problem might be. The
people who get their kicks from kicking other's while they are down
are not worth the time of day. They are to be pitied and prayed for.

I've also learned that there's nothing that the Lord won't help
us through, if we really turn to him. He's always there. We just

sometimes forget to ask. Like my friend said: "Try praying, it's good for what ails you."

Recycle Your Pastor . . . ?

1980

I ran into a Catholic Voice reader in Omaha this week who said: "What are you doing here? I thought you were flying over Ireland."

I know it must be confusing, but my chronicle of events on our trip must necessarily be interspersed with important things like basketball games and chain letters so it will probably be fall before I take you through the customs with me and get home. (Suggestion, never put plastic bags of soap powder in your luggage. Causes thoughtful inspection.)

For instance, this week I was going to take you to France, and you would have enjoyed it, I think. But something came into my possession, via a dear friend, which I think we just all might need. Hence the above reference to chain letters.

I've got to tell you that I think we lay people sometimes make impossible demands of our (mostly) beloved priests. I've never had that brought out so succinctly as it is in this chain letter.

You won't want to send it on, I'm sure. At least, I think you won't. But it should cause you to laugh a lot and think a lot and maybe get a few pointers in perspective. It did me.

Dear Parishioner:

The results of a computerized survey indicate the perfect pastor preaches exactly 15 minutes. He condemns sin but never upsets anyone. He works from 8 a.m. to midnight and is also the janitor. He makes $50 a week, wears good clothes, buys good books, drives a good car and gives about $50 weekly to the poor. He is 28 years of age and has been preaching 30 years. He has a burning desire to work with teenagers and spends all of his time with senior citizens.

The perfect pastor smiles all the time with a straight face because he has a sense of humor that keeps him seri-

*ously dedicated to his work. He makes 15 calls daily on
parish families, shut-ins and hospitalized parishioners. He
spends all his time evangelizing the unchurched and is
always in his office when needed.*

*If your pastor does not measure up, simply send this
letter to six other parishes that are tired of their pastor too.
Then bundle up your pastor and send him to the church at
the top of this list. In one week you will receive 1,643 pas-
tors, and one of them will surely be perfect.*

*Have faith in this letter and don't break this chain
under any circumstances. The results could be disastrous.
One church broke the chain and got its old pastor back in
less than three months.*

> *Sincerely yours,*
> *A perfect parishioner.*

Of course, this is just a joke! We never make those kinds of
demands on OUR pastor.

Or do we???????

A Warm Place in Our Lives . . .

1981

The letter read; "We are told that the Ancient Church had a
custom that was both beautiful and meaningful. When a member
died his or her name was not removed from the membership list but
following the name, a notation was added: transferred to the
church above. So sure were they of the unity of the Church above
that death was merely a transfer. This is how I feel about Marge."

The letter was from a Lutheran pastor's wife in Lincoln. She
was writing to express her feelings about our friend, Marge Seim,
who died Sept. 22.

On Sept. 22nd my friend Shirley and I were in Omaha. I was
giving a little talk at Mary Our Queen Parish. On the way down we
stopped in Sioux City at the hospital and spent an hour with Marge.
She was in intensive care. On the way back we stopped again. It
was the middle of the night, but we knew that wouldn't make much
difference in intensive care wards. She was no longer there.

We walked out of the darkened halls of the hospital and to our car in stunned silence. We knew this would be a possibility, of course, but the reality was unbelievable. Our calmness belied our inner turmoil. I wanted to scream. I did not want to accept this. I wanted to ring the doctor's neck and tear the hospital down. I wanted to blame somebody.

To what avail? None. We started to talk about all of the good times we'd had with Marge on the way home. She was a unique person. One who fomented the craziest kinds of events. Shirley remembered the night Marge's gas pedal got stuck and she roared through the streets of Hartington with a car seemingly totally out of control. "I kept hollering, Whoa!," Marge said, in regaling us with the story after the event. We drove down the road laughing with tears rolling down our faces. We must have been a sight.

We lost another close friend this year—a man of tremendous compassion, charm and wit, Dick Wintz. He died a beautiful death surrounded by family and friends, and supported by his faith. His funeral was a triumphant one—alleluias proclaiming victory. Marge's was too. For both of our friends, their faith was as natural as breathing—deep and abiding. No doubt in our minds they've simply been "transferred to the church above."

As all of you who've lost loved ones know, we don't mourn for them; we mourn for ourselves. Always and forever we will miss the warm place in our lives where they used to be.

Always Enough for Everybody

1981

The most enriching ingredient in our life is love, and the only way we can get it is by giving it away. A much beloved friend said, "Love is a basket of five loaves and two fishes. It's never enough until you give it away."

It is the greatest gift we can bestow on anyone. On our friends, our spouse, our relatives, mankind.

Yet it is impossible for us to give away unless we first learn to love ourselves.

For a long time I didn't understand that. I'd berate myself for this and chastise myself for that. I'd wallow in the guilt of not being perfect. I'd compare myself to others and always come up wanting.

Until one day I learned that perfection was not a human attribute, and I came to understand that in order to live in this confusing and mind-boggling world with any degree of sanity one must accept the fact one is worthwhile just by virtue of the fact that one is.

To accept ourselves for the imperfect being that we are, and learn to have the kind of self-acceptance that lets us—in turn—accept others, is the great lesson of life.

Because of all the people we are hard on, we are hardest on ourselves. And being filled with doubts about our own self-worth, we lash out at others.

We're not talking here about a kind of self-love that is egotistic or narcissistic. We're talking about the ability to approve of oneself quite apart from the need for anybody else's approval.

I've sometimes thought of the world as a gigantic jigsaw puzzle in which every piece is important to the whole. If you've ever put one of those 1,200-piece puzzles together and ended up without just one piece, you know how upset you get.

Without that piece, the jigsaw picture is a failure. It doesn't make any difference if it's a piece of a rock, or a tree, or a ship, or a person . . . the fact that it is missing means the puzzle is incomplete.

As long as we're privileged to be on this earth, we are a crucial part of God's jigsaw puzzle. Whether poet or farmer, executive or dishwasher, we are an important part of the whole. We are relative. We do not need any other affirmation.

God does not want us to be anybody else, or to achieve like anybody else. He wants us to be the best we can be.

I believe that to the depth of my soul. And once we accept the fact of our own self-worth, once we love ourselves, the rest is easy. We accept everybody else too. Then, as we smile benignly at the world about us, our love will bloom and grow and, like the loaves and the fishes, there will always be enough for everybody.

Look for the Jeep or the Helicopter

1983

Did you hear about the fellow who lived beside the river? Seems there had been a lot of rain and the river just kept rising and rising. Some officials in a jeep stopped by, and said to the man, "You're going to have to get out of here; the river's reaching flood stage."

He said, "Don't worry about me, the Lord will take care of me."

The water rose and rose until it reached the fellow's second story window, and he was looking out that window when a boat came by. The fellows in the boat said, "This is really serious, you better come with us."

He said, "Don't worry about me, the Lord will take care of me."

The water just kept rising, and the fellow was now out on the roof of his house clinging to the chimney. A helicopter swooped down, and the guys in the helicopter yelled at him, "We'll drop a line to you, and you come with us. You're going to drown!"

The fellow said, "No, I have faith in the Lord. Don't worry about me. He will take care of me."

The water kept rising, and the fellow drowned.

He went up to Heaven just mad as hops. He couldn't wait to get to the Lord. When he found Him, he went up to him and said, "Lord, you just made me look like a fool. I had faith in you. I thought you'd save me from the flood. Look what happened to me . . . I drowned!"

The Lord looked at him and said, "Well, my son, what do you expect? Of course you drowned . . . First, I sent a jeep, then I sent a boat, and finally I sent a helicopter!"

Sometimes, don't you see, the Lord's help is right there, and we're asking for miracles.

I have great faith in the power of prayer. I've seen its wondrous works. But I also think that the Lord expects us to pitch in on our own behalf. Sometimes his help isn't so obvious as the jeep or the boat or the helicopter.

Sometimes it's a self-help group that's available, or a class that's offered, or a counselor who's waiting to help us. But we have to have the courage to take advantage of that help.

Our Lord gives us the paints and the brushes, and the whole world as our canvas. But it's up to us what the picture will be. If your symbolic water is rising and you feel like your drowning—as we all do sometimes—look around for the jeep or the boat or the helicopter. You can be sure, it's there some place.

The Role of a Serenity Apprentice

1984

It could not have been just a coincidence. I was asked to give a speech on "change" and in going through all my resources gathering information dealing with change, I ran across—again and again—the *Serenity Prayer*.

I attended some meetings to learn how to cope with a family member who is chemically addicted. The meetings were opened and closed with the *Serenity Prayer*.

I gave a little talk in Kearney, and in front of my plate was a miniature plaque—the kind with a magnet that you can put on the refrigerator. There was some favor in front of every plate. But mine was this little plaque with a butterfly on it, and—you guessed it—the *Serenity Prayer*.

No doubt about it. Somebody Up There was trying to tell me something.

You know the *Serenity Prayer*, of course. It goes like this: "God, give us the grace to accept with serenity the things that cannot be changed, courage to change the things which should be changed, and the wisdom to know the difference."

Serenity comes with the ability to live that prayer. But it does not come easily. We acquire serenity through apprenticeship.

I like to equate the things that can be changed to stumbling blocks which we can let trip us up if we choose. Or we can turn them into stepping stones. If we are honest and listen to the rumblings of our inner soul, we know what these things are. Over-eating, over-drinking and over smoking all can be stumbling blocks.

Anything that causes us stress, such as being taken advantage of by family or friends, or a bad work situation, are stumbling blocks and, as such, need to be confronted constructively and taken care of.

We can do something about anything that has to do with ourselves. Our problems often lie in the fact that we spend a lot of our lives trying to do something about other people's problems.

We can love them. We can pray for them. But we cannot change people who are not willing to change themselves. Just realizing that is part of the serenity apprenticeship.

The things we cannot change are walls. We'd just as well sit in their shade and have a picnic. Walls are other people's problems. Walls are incurable diseases.

Walls are things over which we have no control, and we sometimes beat our heads against those walls. If you observe carefully, you can see the flat spot on my forehead that indicates I've done a little of that.

Accepting your personal "walls" is a big step for a serenity apprentice. "The wisdom to know the difference" is the most difficult part of the *Serenity Prayer.*

Help comes from God in a lot of ways; people you love, support systems and learned counselors. Sometimes He just slaps the *Serenity Prayer* in front of you so often you begin to get the message.

Nobody said it would be easy. Nonetheless, it is the only way to go. I am a serenity apprentice. I hope you are too.

Say Thanks by Singing

1984

I am declaring October *Hug Your Cantor* month. Cantors are generally, if you'll excuse the expression, unsung heroes. Week after week they give their all to encourage the congregation to sing. But who encourages cantors?

I am not doing this from a selfish motive. The fact that I will be cantoring in October, and that hugging is my favorite sport, notwithstanding.

The revival of the cantor has been one of the most positive things in the liturgical renewal. The cantor's job is to give constant encouragement to the worshipping community. Cantors are not necessarily vocal soloists, although they need to be people who can carry a tune with authority.

Cantors have to learn to rejoice in small gains, and to overlook great failures. It's great fun to be a cantor when everybody knows the hymn, and they sing with great enthusiasm. It's not so fun when the congregation is apathetic, if not downright surly. They tend to get that way when you bring in a new hymn.

Cantors do not get many compliments, but they always get two kinds of criticism. Half the congregation criticizes them because they are always singing the same old thing. The other half criticizes them because they *aren't* always singing the same old thing.

Himself, my friendly husband, is one who wants nothing new introduced into the liturgy. Less is better, as far as he's concerned, and he takes it as a personal insult when the cantor, however enthusiastically, presents him with a new hymn. He clamps his mouth firmly shut and replaces the missalette or hymnbook firmly in it's rack. That's it for him.

As a cantor, I am well aware that half the congregation is following suit. And yet, three Sundays later, when a dozen or so cantors have wrested this new song out of the congregation, it will suddenly sound familiar to Kip, and he smilingly joins in the singing.

It's not easy.

Cantors also have obligations. They have to be prepared. They have to remember they are song leaders, not soloists. They have to give the congregation lots of sincere praise. They have to avoid the tendency to fret over mistakes. It helps if they look nice, and speak well. They must never get discouraged.

If a service goes well and the singing is joyful and you are involved, chances are the cantors had something to do with it.

You can say "thank you" by singing. But a hug couldn't hurt.

The Teacher Will Come

1984

"When the student is ready, the teacher will come."

That might sound like a prophet speaking from a mountain top, but it actually came from Mary Nolan at St. Margaret Mary's Parish.

I was there to participate in the Silva Mind Control classes taught by Father Justin Belitz. An immense intellectual curiosity about the workings of the mind brought me to this place, and it was a gratifying experience.

A bonus was partaking in slices of life of the parishioners of St. Margaret Mary's. We saw the beginnings of three beautiful weddings, and went to a Mass that celebrated the 55th anniversary of a darling couple whose name, I think, was Borland. Just touching the edges of all that joy was a privilege.

The next weekend, we heard Father Dunne give a stirring sermon, in which he discussed the problems of being a pastor. He said, in great good humor, that he'd told one of his parishioners that he was going to pray for rain, and the parishioner said, "Oh, don't do that, Father, I want to go fishing tomorrow." With an eloquent shrug of his shoulders, Father asked, "What's a priest to do?"

My curiosity about the mind began in earnest some 15 years ago when I was studying for my degree. A book by George B. Leonard, called *Education and Ecstasy*, said that we use only 10% of the capabilities of our mind, and that for all intents and purposes, the capacity of our mind for creativity was infinite.

Infinite! That's pretty heady stuff.

Since that time I've taken every psychology course I could reasonably get into, studied all the books telling about how mental imagery could improve you physically and mentally, worked with the "relaxation response" and meditation, and gradually became aware that behind every "method" that people subscribe to was the dynamic meditation system of Silva.

My friends, the Rueves, used it to battle cancer. The Olympic athletes used mental imagery to achieve perfection in a variety of sports. Major league teams use it to improve performance. Could a simple farm-wife in northeast Nebraska tap into this information? Well, it's available to anybody with a mind. Even me.

The course is totally based on love and enhancing our relationship with God and our fellow man. It's also based on solid research, and teaches you methods to train your brain to train your body. I'm working on a number of physical and spiritual goals. I'll let you know how I come out.

There's Work To Be Done

1985

"You have a mission to fulfill, a mission of love which must begin in your homes, in the place where you are, with the people you are closest to; and only then spread out."—Mother Teresa

This past few months I've been asked to speak to various groups on the Archdiocesan Family Ministry Program. I tell them up front that I am no expert. I am simply someone working in the trenches. The gigantic effort to promote family ministry which is being made by the archdiocese is being noted in other places, however, and there's a great deal of interest in seeing how it works *in the trenches.*

The more I'm involved, the more I'm aware of how many wonderful people are loose in this world, just ministering away. Whether we acknowledge it or not, more and more we're becoming convinced and acting out what we know in our hearts—that each and every one of us is a minister, so designated at our birth.

It makes no difference if we've had special training or whatever. We all have what one writer says is the "call to mission" that is to "listen to the voice of Christ in the cry of the poor, the lonely, the fearful, the distrustful, the misled, the despairing, the abused, the neglected, and exploited—to encourage those who have lost hope, whatever their economic condition, and to know that this voice is also the one we hear in the deepest part of ourselves."

Some people try to hide this goodness, embarrassed that it's there. When you catch them at it, they mumble away like, "Oh heck, it's nothing." In truth, it's everything.

Clarice Flagel, the family life minister at St. Pius X Parish in Cedar Rapids, Iowa (who is an expert) says that many of the problems stem from the fact that people have no support. Isolated from one another, they "go it alone," and in that aloneness they lose the potential for creative and productive lives.

There are times when we've all felt that aloneness. Our response to that cry from our very being is "a call to people of courage and hope. It is a challenge to reconstruct where culture and society have broken down."

By concentrating or ministering to other (and "family" in family ministry includes every member in our parish and our community), we can make our parishes places of welcome and of love.

We must start first with ourselves and accept ourselves lovingly, with all of our many faults and peculiarities, just as Jesus accepts us. Perhaps that's the hardest part. After recognizing our own worth, we turn that same warm light of Christ's love on those closest to us, and open up our hearts and hold out our hand to others. Remember, we all need love most when we are least lovable.

Mother Teresa has shown us the miracles that can be wrought with love. It's in our power to work a few of our own.

Many of you are doing just that. Keep up the good work! Those of you who aren't, look around and get busy. We ministers have work to be done.

No-Frills Catholic Suspicious of Being Renewed!

1987

We're going into RENEW now, and it's making a lot of people nervous. Including me. It shouldn't, because it is simply a spiritual exercise in which all of us work and pray together to bring our church community closer to God, and closer to each other. In the long run it will make us feel good all under.

Even Kip.

But we are creatures of habit. Even in church. Especially in church. At a recent teacher's meeting, a nice looking fellow from Scotus High brought this to my attention. He said, "If I sit on the

left side of church I'd just as well go home, I can't even pray. I
always sit on the right side." I thought about that, and you know,
it's true. Most people sit in about the same place every Sunday.
They stake out a little area where they feel most comfortable, and
there they light, Sunday after Sunday. There was a time when families actually purchased pews, and even had their names on them.
That is no longer true. At least, not in our church.

This has nothing to do with politics. Kip is a conservative. In
fact, he's so conservative he's just to the right of Ghengis Khan. We
sit on the left side of the church, somewhere in the middle. If I look
across the aisle I always see members of the Stevens clan, who sit on
the right side of church, toward the middle. I can be assured sometimes during mass I'll hear my brother Vince cough or harrumph,
because he and Rhea sit behind us. I can check and see if Kathy
Wintz is there, because if she isn't in the outside row of pews near
the front, she isn't in church.

You see what I mean.

Not only that, people habitually go to Mass at the same time of
day.

When I go to mass on Saturday night I feel as if I should go
back on Sunday morning. I don't, of course. Not that I couldn't use
it, but I only go on Saturday night when I can't get there on Sunday. And yet, a lot of people are more than comfortable with the
Saturday night Mass. They love it.

There were years when Kip and I never went to church at the
same time because I directed the choir at 10:30 Mass, and Kip—
when he has a choice—only goes to 8:30 Mass.

Kip is a *no frills* Catholic. He doesn't need a choir. The less
commotion he has during mass, the better he likes it. He will sing.
In fact, he has a good voice. But he does not ever want to sing a new
hymn. He especially doesn't want to practice a new hymn before
mass.

I know when one of our *new* hymns has become acceptably old
because that's when Kip will join in. He is, in fact, the kind of
Catholic who is the bane of any creative Liturgy committee. He's
never gotten over the Sunday morning we who were on the Liturgy
committee saw fit to have John the Baptist come down the aisle in
full regalia and exhort the sinners to repent.

"Repent you sinners!!," the young man who was playing John cried, poking his staff in Kip's face.

"Who's idea was that?," he asked me crabbily.

"We hoped it was the Holy Spirit's," I responded sweetly.

"I doubt that!," he said.

The point of all this is, I don't think the Lord cares what kind of habits we have in church, as long as we go. But He appreciates it when we put up with each other with love, understanding it takes all kinds to make a parish. I know He will be especially pleased that we're making an effort to do a better job, by getting closer to him, and closer to each other. Even if it makes us a little nervous.

Offer It Up?

1988

This morning, even as I write, my jaw is swollen to the size of an orange, and I am offering up the pain for a variety of good causes. The reason it is swollen is that a wisdom tooth (which I thought was long gone) decided it wanted out, and was moving into another tooth's territory. It seemed reasonable to me that at 59 years of age my teeth should have long ago become permanently settled. But a dentist, a periodontist, and finally an oral surgeon, convinced me the wisdom tooth would have to go.

I was dubious about it, because I don't suffer pain gracefully. My last wisdom tooth experience was not a pretty one. The oral surgeon scoffed at my concerns, telling me this wouldn't amount to *a hill of beans* and proceeded to yank it out.

It didn't come willingly, and hence the pathetic looking (and feeling) jaw.

The comfort I get from this whole necessary experience is that I could offer it up. I had a number of worthy causes waiting in line. When I started writing this column for The Catholic Voice in 1974 the title "Offer It Up" just came to me, providentially I believe. I was surprised and amazed when my non-catholic friends professed not to understand. "Offer it Up?" said my friend, Marge Seim, "What does that mean?" I explained how when I was a youngster

and anything happened that was physically or psychologically painful, my parents or the good nuns would say, "Just offer it up."
Meaning that I should endure the pain with forebearance realizing
that my very endurance would earn points in Heaven for me or the
cause for which I was enduring it. Therefore the pain served a good
purpose, which made it easier to bear.

Marge was not convinced. "In my faith," she said, "we believe
that Jesus earned our way to Heaven for us when he died on the
cross, and it doesn't make much difference what we do, it's still
earned. We don't need to earn points in Heaven."

"Well, I'm sorry about that," I told her, "because *offering it up*
seems to help one suffer through painful experiences with some
sense of purpose." A couple of weeks after we had this conversation
she and I headed across country on a mutual speaking jaunt. I was
driving, and somehow got so engrossed in the conversation that I
drove many miles down the road less taken, which wasn't going
where we wanted to go. We had limited time, and when we discovered what had happened, Marge couldn't believe I'd been so dumb.

She sat there fuming away at me, and then—suddenly—she
brightened up, "Burney, I know now what you mean."

I looked at her in some confusion. Usually, I was able to follow
the peculiar twists and turns of that fertile mind. But here she lost
me.   "What I mean about what?" I asked.

She sat back in the car seat and grinned a huge grin, and with a
great sense of satisfaction she announced, "I'm offering you up."

Are You a Chicken, a Goose, or an Eagle?

1988

The minister's sonorous voice rang out, unfolding the story of
this eagle who thought it was a chicken. It was brought up with
chickens, so instead of fulfilling it's potential by lofty soaring, it
scratched at the ground and pecked at corn. A passing stranger was
appalled at the sight of a mighty eagle pecking and scratching. He
went to the farmer and said, "Don't you know that that bird is an
eagle, not a chicken."

The farmer looked at him as if he was very stupid and said "It acts like a chicken. It thinks it's a chicken. So it's a chicken."

The story was being told at a meeting of a group of Northeast Nebraska Singles at the Methodist church in Osmond.

I will explain later what I—a survivor of 40 years of marriage—was doing at a singles meeting. For now, we'll get on with the story.

The passing stranger's every effort to convince the eagle he was not a chicken failed. He climbed to the top of a barn, and then to the roof of the steeple, throwing the eagle into the air. The eagle would start to soar. But then he'd look down at his chicken friends, and he'd swoop back down to resume scratching and pecking.

As a last resort the man took the eagle to the top of a mountain, and tossed him into the air again. This time the eagle soared, and soared, and realizing, finally, that it was an eagle, it soared out of sight.

The point of this is that a lot of times we of the human race just keep pecking and scratching when we have the capability of soaring. We don't try soaring, even though we might like to, because we don't realize we can. And we'll never find out if we don't try.

I was pleased with this story, and said so when I got up to give my little talk to the impressive group of single folks, which is why I was there. I have never felt reluctant to speak to singles, because in my own life I have learned that one has to learn to understand oneself as a single, before one can function effectively with others. To operate at our peak level we must figure out our own identity. We may team up with others for awhile, but these unions are seldom forever. If our understanding of who we are is dependent upon another person, well we're just picking and scratching at life, never learning our own ability to soar.

Is this making any sense?

Still, we can't always soar. Even eagles need to roost occasionally. Soaring can wear a person out. My friend Marsha Baumart pointed this out to me on the way home from the meeting. She explained it with another bird analogy. "I think," she said, "that human beings should really strive to be more like geese than eagles." Geese?

"Geese still soar," she said, "but they take care of each other." The lead goose in a flight, for instance, creates friendly air waves which make it easier for the other geese to follow. Each following goose does it in turn for the geese behind him.

What a great idea.

Occasionally we may soar like eagles, but more often we need to soar like the geese, making waves for others to follow. This is interesting to think about, especially when I've lapsed into my pecking and scratching moods. Sometimes we get tired of challenging ourselves. Our "chicken side" says "why stick our necks out, again?" It doesn't last for long, because it's innate for human beings, at any age, to strive to be the best the Lord intended them to be. We all have a drive to fulfill our personal potential. But sometimes we get scared. And sometimes we get lazy.

That's when we need to take ourselves to the mountain top, whether we're eagles, or geese, or adventurous chickens, and get to soaring again.

Sometimes we just get tired. That's when we can happily get in line behind some other goose. Not to worry. We'll get back to soaring when it's time for us to soar. Helen Keller explained it, "One can never consent to creep, when one has the impulse to soar."

Keeping Awake Going Down the Road

1988

"Are there any questions?," asked Father Rick Arkfeld. Nobody had any. I might have, but he couldn't have answered me if he wanted to because I was in my car, listening to him on tape. I was listening to talk #7 of thirty, the tapes of classes he held in Randolph for his multitude of converts. Some of my tapes, the Berlitz Spanish ones, for instance, demand that I talk back to them. I do, when I can understand what they've demanded.

But Father Rick's questions were more or less rhetorical, so I comfortably let them slide by. I was having a fine time.

Due to a multitude of commitments up and down life's highways and by-ways, I spend a lot of time in my car. Though that time is not wasted in that it is getting me from here to there, it can get boring. One tends to doze off. In fact, a couple of times I did just that. Those of you who've had that happen know what a scare it puts into one. Fortunately, veering off the side of the highway startled me into instant wakefulness, not veering into another car.

In any case—not a good idea. So, I attempt to keep myself mentally stimulated while driving. If I can, I con somebody into riding along with me to keep me awake.

But my friends have gotten so that they can come up with excuses not to come with me as fast as I can come up with cons.

In casting about for something else to keep me stimulated, I came up with the idea that I should learn a second language. Kip thinks, because of the slang I've picked up working with high school kids, that I've already learned a second langauge.

But my goal was slightly more elevated than that, I wanted to learn Spanish. I got the Berlitz tapes and learned, to my chagrin, that the only language they used to teach Spanish was Spanish. They asked questions in Spanish, and you were to answer. Turned out to be a problem. I've gotten good at the first lesson, but never made it through the second.

I found it all very frustrating. I'd say "say that again" but the tape would go merrily on, assuming I was with it. I wasn't. Abandoning this form of self-abuse for something less formidable, I began to purchase motivational tapes. Well, actually, "borrow" would be the better description of what I did. I borrowed Father Joe Miksch's ten tapes of John Powell, which were delightful. In fact, they still are delightful. I borrowed them ten years ago, and haven't given them back yet. (Yes, Father Joe, this is where those tapes are.)

Then, while interviewing Father Rick one fine day, I noted the piles of tapes he had all over his office. He allowed as how these were tapes of the thirty classes he'd put on for his converts (and a multitude of others who just came to listen). He said he's copied hundreds of them for people who were interested. I was interested.

Cradle Catholic that I am, I am learning a multitude of things about my faith and experiencing a spiritual rejuvenation as I go up and down the road. Every once in a while I come up with an Alleluia. I recommend this highly. We all need to be re-converted on a regular basis. It certainly keeps one awake. Thanks Father Rick.

Hugging Atmosphere: What's It Take to Make a School Christian?

1988

It is the job of Catholic Schools to present a "unique Christian school climate," said Father Vincent Mainelli in his "state of the union" homily to his Cathedral faculty, "if that isn't present there is little left which can make the school Catholic."

All schools could benefit from this message. Father was quoting from a missive titled, "The Religious Dimension of Education in a Catholic School", subtitled, "Guidelines for Reflection and Renewal" sent from "ROME 1988" by the Congregation for Catholic Education.

You may wonder what I was doing at a meeting of erudite Cathedralites, and then again you may not, but I will tell you anyway. I was giving a little talk because my friend, Father Ron Noecker, suggested gently that I owed him one. (Through the years Ron has consented to be in a number of my in-depth cultural productions, including singing World War I songs in Kip's World War II Air Force Uniform.) (Not a dry eye in the house!)

However, Father Ron was not the reason I went about this task with a sense of missionary zeal. In a world where some of our political and religious leaders are displaying all the ethics and morals of sewer rats, we desperately need the kind of role models who will believe in and teach lasting values to our young people. I believe that education based on the Lord, schools teaching Christianity, is an important way to go about that.

I have learned that nothing much works for long in this life without some basis in faith. People go through life looking for happiness and peace in all kinds of peculiar places. They end up—if they're lucky—coming home to the Lord and saying, with some surprise, "Oh, here it is." When it was "here" all the time.

Kids need to know this.

In a school system where a loving and forgiving God is a part of the curriculum, I've seen this *hugging atmosphere* demonstrated from the Administrator to the Janitor.

Father Mainelli's missive continued thusly: "The prime responsibility for creating this unique Christian school climate rests with the teachers, as individuals and as a community. The religious dimension of the school climate is expressed through celebrations of Christian values in Word and Sacrament, in individual behaviour and in friendly and harmonious interpersonal relationships and ready availability. Through this daily witness, the students will come to appreciate the uniqueness of the enviroment to which their youth has been entrusted."

If the atmosphere in a school (or a home, or an office, or a town, or a country) is punitive and expectations negative and everybody operates out of a *fear* mode, creativity dries up, and people become robots. Or rebellious. A *hugging atmosphere* promotes creativity and growth. We're not talking about an atmosphere without discipline. The Lord is kind and loving, but He's no whimp. His expectations are clear. Young people respect boundaries even (especially) when they fight against them. Students need to know what's expected of them, and what the consequences will be if they don't live up to those expectations. Teachers need to say what they mean, and mean what they say.

The responsibility for the *unique Christian climate* in schools rests on the teachers, but that does not let the rest of us off the hook. No way! Teachers also need to work in a *hugging atmosphere*. Administrators, boards, parents, priestly people, Education Departments, Bishops, Archbishops, and the "Congregation for Catholic Education" in Rome, must remember their own responsbility for providing a *unique Christian climate*. This is a trickle down theory that really works.

It is my firm belief that we who work in and around schools must never lose sight of the necessity of providing this unique enviroment. If we do "there is little left which can make the school Catholic."

And we'd just as well close up shop.

Of Course Jesus Laughed!

1988

According to eminent psychologists and psychiatrists, the ability to laugh at oneself and with others is a sign of mental wellness.

A laugh is like a mini-vacation, they tell us, it reduces stress and relieves tension.

It's a message you've heard before. In the Bible, for instance, Proverbs 17:22, "A joyful heart is the health of the body, but a depressed spirit dries up the bones."

What it doesn't say in the Bible is that Jesus laughed. And yet, you know he did. He came to bring the Good News, and that had to be fun. He must have chuckled with satisfaction when he changed the water into wine at the wedding feast at the request of His mother. And certainly He laughed with joy when they brought the little children to Him.

I have oft pondered on this, and my pondering was greatly helped by Elton Trueblood's book "The Humor of Christ". Trueblood says we view the Bible with *excessive sobriety*, and suggests when we free ourselves from this we will realize that Christ did not always engage in pious talk. In fact, he points out that Christ's messages are made more understandable when we understand their humor.

Only in this erudite and carefully researched small book, complete with footnotes, he put it this way, "there are numerous passages in recorded teaching which are practically incomprehensible when regarded as sober prose, but which are luminous once we become liberated from the gratuitous assumption that Christ never joked."

Luminous. I like this Trueblood fellow. It is unthinkable that Christ didn't laugh. He cried freely, and he showed his anger, flinging people out of temples. Of course he laughed.

Trueblood points out that Christ consistently used the humor of irony, satire, and paradox in his statements and his parables. Paradox—a statement absurdly self-contradictory—is always potentially humorous. The blind leading the blind, for instance, "is absurdity as far as it can go". His appendix lists thirty *humorous passages* in the Bible, including the one about the speck and the log in your eye, straining a gnat, swallowing a camel, a lamp under a bed, begrudging generosity, etc., etc.

Christ got people's attention with preposterous statements which they could not forget, no matter how hard they tried. So they wrote them down. He is still getting people's attention. Had these parables been couched in some less attention-getting form of rhetoric they would have fallen by the wayside, according to Trueblood.

He writes that Christ's irony is "marked with the subtle sharpness of insight, free from the desire to wound," which distinguishes it from sarcasm.

Christ often allowed the logic of a situation to demonstrate itself by the use of an ironic question. His pragmatic teaching that any system is to be known primarily by its consequences is brought out by, "Are grapes gathered from thorns, or figs from thistles?"

Trueblood says, "A misguided piety has made us fear the acceptance of His obvious wit and humor would somehow be mildly blasphemous or sacrilegious." There are those who feel religion is serious business, incompatible with laughter. Not true. Religion is the most joyful business we go about. However, this conclusion cannot be forced upon those who refuse to contemplate the possibility.

Christ enjoins us, does he not, not to waste precious words or time or effort on those who are *chronically impervious* when he says not to cast pearls before the swine. But those interested in pearls might try this: In your quiet meditative moments—*just listen.* You can almost hear Christ's warm hearted chuckle. Christ was a man of great charisma and great joy. *Trust me. He laughed.*

How To Make Sure Nothing in Your Community or Your Parish Ever, Ever, Ever Works

1988

In our community, and in our church family, we have a multitude of wonderful people who donate their time unselfishly, and who are spontaneously enthusiastic about everything. But occasionally, we get a complainer, a do-nothinger, who nobody quite understands.

We don't have many people like that in our community, or our parish.

I'm certain you have none in yours. But just in case some happen to be lurking about, perhaps these ten commandments will help you recognize them. Perhaps we should realize that once in awhile, this negative person might even be us. Heaven forbid!

"Ways to Make Sure Your Community Doesn't Succeed"

1) Attend no meetings of any kind. Sign up for nothing. Criticize the way *they* are doing things. (It is important to remain uninformed.)

2) Be sure to constantly bring up any past problems the community or parish has had. Try to keep old wounds from healing.

3) Complain about all the committees, and be absolutely sure not to get *stuck* on one. Then, be the first to gripe if the committees don't do the things you think they should.

4) Keep convincing yourselves that your attendance at city meetings, church services, community betterment meetings, etc., etc. is not important—convince yourself you'll never be missed.

5) Knock all the councilmen and the Mayor. Be sure and put down the parish council, and the faculty of your schools any chance you get. (When you need a special favor, be sure and ask for it.)

6) Better yet, stay away from church altogether. You might just attend on Easter or Christmas to reassure yourself that all who attend are hypocrites. (But if your pastor isn't right on tap when you need him, yell loud and hard.)

7) If you have any talents, hide them under a bushel. If you have a good voice, don't sing in the choir. If you're good at organization, don't offer to help. That would never do.

8) Always be the first with the bad news. Remember all clergy are suspect, all kids are delinquent, all politicians are corrupt, all businessmen are crooks, and uncomplimentary remarks are expected.

9) Don't get active in the community either. Purchase everything out of town and from firms that never come forth with donations.

10) Above all, always be skeptical, cynical and negative about

anything that is designed for community improvement or the parish's spiritual betterment.

I share this in good humor . . . . . by simple deduction, dear Watson, I'm sure gentle readers of this book would never be guilty of any of the above.

We Can Choose How We Respond

1988

President-elect George Bush lost a daughter, Robin, born in 1949. She died at the age of three, from leukemia. He said "to this day, like every parent who has lost a child, we wonder why; yet we know that, whatever the reason, she is in God's living arms."

Losing a child is the toughest thing that can happen to a person. I've been there. But what better place to be than "in God's living arms."

I came to closure with my grief at the loss of our infant son many years after we lost him. It happened when Father Rick Arkfeld told me about a homily he gave at the funeral of a young girl. I don't remember his exact words, but I know he felt those words were directed by the Holy Spirit. He told the grieving family that their lost child would not want them to ask her to come back, such was her happiness in Heaven. He said, "and if we are very quiet, we can ever hear her joyous laughter." Then in an awe-filled voice, he said, "You know, we could."

Chills went down my spine. I'd wasted a lot of time grieving not only for our child, but other loved ones who had up and died, who I'd hoped would hang around and get old with me. It was legitimate and necessary to grieve for my own losses. But I'd also grieved for them, for their "loss."

Suddenly I knew, as sure as could be, that if I was very quiet, I would be able to hear their joyous laughter.

Isn't that what we're all about?

Sometimes we forget to believe what we believe.

One of our *RENEW* prayers said: "Father, we move and stray in so many directions. We tread tiresome and lonely paths and do not know when we are lost. You will find us somewhere between faith and unbelief; somewhere between hope and despair; somewhere between care and indifference.

In my journeys around the country doing whatever it is I do, I have come across people of great faith who have survived enthusiastically in spite of overwhelming obstacles. I have run across people, who seem to have everything, who are "poor-me-ing" themselves right into eternity. They wallow in despair, blaming somebody—anybody!—for their ills. Sometimes, even, God.

I hang out somewhere in between these two groups. Striving to be the one, but slipping into the other when I'm not really careful.

The difference, I have come to understand, is one of expectations. Expectations are things that happen in our heads. The people who thrive on this earth choose to have positive expectations. The "poor-me-ers" choose to have negative ones.

The key word here is "choose."

We cannot always choose what happens to us, or to our loved ones, but we can choose how we respond. The thrivers on this earth hold tightly to their faith, not only in God, but in themselves, and their fellow man.

They accept the reality of what's happened, and then get on with their lives. They pray as if it was all up to God, but then work as if it was all up to them. They don't wallow in it, they transcend it with faith.

Life is difficult, filled with stumbling blocks, and sometimes walls. But stumbling blocks can be turned into stepping stones, and, with the help of our partner, God, we can learn to live with walls. Plant vines on them, have a picnic in their shade. We've all had our stumbling blocks, and we have our walls.

God does not *DO* these things to us. Things happen to us because of imperfections of mankind and the happenstances of nature and the decisions we make which wreak havoc on our own bodies.

But he's always there beside us. Loving us. Showing us the way.

If we choose to tap into that love.

Some day, in joyous reunion with all of those who've gone before us, we will also rest in his loving arms. And if you're very quiet, you'll hear our laughter.

Keeping Your Torches Lit

1989

It wasn't necessarily the Olympic runners who got to the finish line first that won the race in Ancient Greece. It was the ones who got there first with their torch still lit.

To my mind, the recent day-long meeting at Creighton University called "Work and the Family: Christian Discipleship" was all about keeping our torches lit.

You've read about the meeting, but I'd like to tell you what it meant to me. My part in it was tiny, almost undetected. I was to present a workshop on "Work and the family in the Rural Setting".

Either people were not interested in the subject, or in me, because only four people came to my workshop, *including* the person who was to introduce me and myself. Not to worry, we had a great visit. However, coming under the "Lord works in mysterious ways" heading, I found I *needed* to be at the workshop to hear what the others had to say. But I wouldn't have made the three hundred mile round trip if I had not been requested to present the workshop on two of my favorite subjects, the family and a rural setting. (Not necessarily "work".)

I needed to hear the key note speaker, Arthur Jones, a Washington Bureau Editor of the National Catholic Reporter because he clarified some issues for me in the keeping our torch lit department. And the panel, which included Portia Anderson, Beppie Aube, Steve Kent, Terry Crosley, William A. Fitzgerald and Pat Gannon, did a superb job of putting personal faces on the issues involved. As did my fellow presenter Roman Uhing. (Who attended the same school I did long ago.)

The subject of this whole day, as I understood it, was to give us a better understanding of the Bishops' "Economic Justice for All". The Bishops would like us to consider—in keeping our torches lit— that we might be hindered by the "cult of having".

We seem to be loving things, and using people. They'd like us all, including presumably themselves, to get back to loving people and using things. *Things* are not much help when we lose our health. All the accumulation of wealth in the world will not make up for the loss of a child or someone we love. *Things* don't make us happy. Not that we shouldn't hanker after a few, and enjoy them when we get them, but when the accumulation of wealth and *things* becomes our main goal in life we need to step back and take a look in the mirror. *Our flame is in danger of going out.*

No matter how much we accumulate, we'll still be searching for something until we understand that happiness comes from tapping into that spiritual flame and giving, as Jones said, "not just of your affluence but your substance". Jones suggested we may sow the seeds for peace and justice in our family, or on our farm, in our business, in our parish, in our community, in our nation, knowing we probably won't be in on the harvest. *He suggested that we didn't need to take on the world, but that we could change that world by starting within our own hearts in our own community.* Patience is essential, along with the willingness to adjust. Quoting Sinclair Lewis, Jones said, "Sometimes the person who turns back sooner and starts again makes the most progress." Fulfilling our potential may mean we build up great wealth, and accumulate many things. That's wonderful, if we've gotten there with our flame still lit.

Christians are in a "no win" situation, said Jones, because "our responsibilities are in direct relationship to our awareness". "Work and the Family: Christian Discipleship" heightened my awareness. When I reach the finish line, I want my torch lit.

Merry Christians!

1989

For many years, perhaps even decades, I have attempted to eject the mental image I have had of our Lord as a stern disciplinarian, which was implanted in my formative years, and replace it with a picture of the Lord as I have come to understand Him now, a loving and joyful savior. The more I knew of the Lord, and the more I read the Bible, the more it seemed to me that Christians should be the most joyful people in the whole world.

So why aren't we. Why the dour face and woeful expectations? (I said, looking in the mirror.) Though I desired it, and prayed for it, my metamorphosis from a frightened Christian into a joyful one seemed to me to be slow in coming. I knew in my heart that the Lord was not so much interested in showering us with rules and regs as he was in showering us with love. Lord, I kept saying, help me get that belief into my head.

Some weeks ago I began to metamorphisize in joyful leaps. Our friend, Father Thomas O'Brien, sent me a picture of Jesus laughing. And there it was. The mental picture which had been eluding me. I loved it. I ejected every other mental picture of the Lord, and inserted this one.

The biblical quotation on the back of the picture said it all. Jesus said, "I have loved you—I have told you this so that you will be filled with my joy. Yes, your cup of joy will overflow." John 15: 9,11.

Ellen McVay, a Christian Counselor from Yankton, South Dakota, helped me emerge further from my dour cocoon. She'd heard me speak on the importance of humor, and asked, "Have you ever heard of the Fellowship of Merry Christians? It would be a perfect organization for you."

I hadn't. I know a few *Merry Christians*, but we have no organized Fellowship. Perhaps we need one. The information Ellen provided me included, "An Invitation to Make a Joyful Noise." And I was hooked.

Easter Monday was traditionally a "Day of Joy and Laughter" for the early Christians, the invitation explained. They "went to church to frolic, tell clean jokes, play merry pranks, feast on lamb, sing and dance and have a lot of fun." With Eastertide, wrote Jurgen Moltmann, began "the laughing of the redeemed, the dancing of the liberated."

Doesn't this make all kinds of sense?

The invitation went on to say that this theme echoed through the centuries in Christian experience. Francis of Assisi advised: "Leave sadness to the devil. The devil has reason to be sad." Martin Luther wrote: "God is not a God of sadness, but the devil is. Christ is a God of Joy. It is pleasing to the dear God whenever thou rejoicest or laughest from the bottom of thy heart." It is said that the devil can't stand the sound of Holy laughter. In their monthly publication, "The Joyful Noiseletter", the FMC says it's not claiming that laughter is a cure all. Nor that it will save anyone from the consequences of his or her sins. The Lord is consistent and no way whimplike when it comes to his positive expectations for even Merry Christians. Its only claim is that when a sense of humor is combined with Christian faith and a Christian life-style, it's a combination that will triumph over all trials and tribulations.

I concur. Even as I write I see before me the faces of a multitude of people (merry and dour) whom I would like to personally enroll in this fellowship. But it costs $16.00 and I am more merry than I am generous. Knowing most of these people read this paper, and might even, if they're not careful, read this column, I will accomplish my goal in my own cheap way, by giving you this address so you can enroll yourselves. The Fellowship of Merry Christians, P.O. Box 668, Kalamazoo, MI. 49005-0668.

It doesn't really matter to me if you actually enroll, as long as you allow the merriment of Christ to seep into your soul. Eastertide is coming, my fellow Christians. See to it that *thou rejoicest and laughest from the bottom of thy hearts.*

CHAPTER SIX

COMES
THE DAWN

Chapter Six

A Few Travel Tips

Comes The Dawn

Several years ago, after I completed work on my masters in counseling, I was urged by my friend, Sally Schuff, editor of the Colorado Rancher-Farmer, and Bob Bishop, then editor of the Nebraska Farmer, to write an advice column, of sorts, for their magazines. They thought with the tempestuous state of agriculture it would be a good idea to have a columnist in place who could respond to readers who might have problems they wanted mulled over. I was hesitant, at first, attacked by a giant case of the unworthies. But I'm a great muller of problems, if I do say so myself, and that still small internal voice started nudging me again. What more effective way could I do what I claimed I aimed to do with all my hard-won education, and looooong years of experience; be a little help to my fellow travelers on this journey through life. So "Comes the Dawn" column was born. What follows is a sampling of those columns, which will give you a chance to do a little mulling right along with me.

Making Friends Out of Enemies

1986

In his book, "How to Stop Worrying and Start Living," Dale Carnegie says, "When we hate our enemies, we give them power over us; power over our sleep, our appetites and our happiness. They would dance for joy if they knew how much they were worrying us. Our hate is not hurting them at all, but it is turning our own days and nights into a turmoil."

One of the things we have to deal with, especially in times of crisis, is hate. We're imperfect human beings and we do get angry, and anger engenders hate. We get angry at ourselves (depression is anger turned inwards), angry at our friends, angry at our family, and angry at our bankers. We allow ourselves to wallow in that anger.

Sometimes it's justified, of course. But whether it's justified or not, it eats at our innards and takes the joy out of life. We can't afford it. We need to decide, up front, that we're not going to let it get the best of us. Sometimes we need to be creative, but since studies tell us we only use 6 percent of our creative ability, that shouldn't be a problem.

What usually happens when we're angry is we plan and plot our revenge. I don't know about you, but I build up scenes in my mind in which I am brilliantly triumphant over my adversary, making witty come-backs—all a day later. "I should have said's" go on and on in my head. "Boy, would that get them!" I think.

And boy does it get us! It gets obsessive, and it's dumb.

But what can we do? How do we talk sense into our own heads?

Well, in the first place, just by doing that. We will have emotions. That's a given. But we can keep ourselves from getting worked up. We can replace negative thoughts with positive thoughts.

Counting to ten is a good idea. It gives us time to take control. Then we can start taking deep breaths. That gives our body a message that it should calm down. And we can force ourselves to smile. According to a recent study, just by making ourselves smile we feel better. Try it. Yes—right now. Smile! See what I mean? Humor is a wonderful tool.

It's all up to us, because our mind is our own personal library, and we stock the shelves. (I used to tell that to my sons when I found girlie magazines under their mattresses.) Whatever the subject matter, this is an obvious truth. Trash in, trash out.

Although it can be almost impossible, we can develop great and healing insight if we look at the situation from the offending person's point of view. Not easy, but effective.

We also have the ability to mentally transport ourselves to a place of calmness. My personal favorite is a cabin on the shores of a lake in Canada, with a roaring fire in the fire place and water lapping cheerfully against the rocks out the window. I've only been there a couple of times in body, but, oh my, have I made mental use of that place. For you it might be a fishing hole, or a mountain, or a meadow. We all have somewhere.

We can stock our shelves with inspirational people and inspirational reading. Abraham Lincoln's wise words stick in my mind. Lincoln was chastised by some of his political cohorts for being so nice to his enemies after he'd gotten into office and had the power to destroy them. Lincoln said, "if I make a friend out of an enemy, haven't I destroyed that enemy?" He also said, "A person is about as happy as he makes up his mind to be."

There are times when we simply have to have faith. Many of the people I've interviewed for my book on the Farm Crisis tell me that God got them through.

The way I look at it, it's His job.

Which brings me to our letter for this week. This letter needs no commentary, it stands on it's own. I'm delighted to share it with you.

Dear Joanie:

"I am truly overjoyed by your column. I wish you well in this undertaking. I want to share with you a prayer I've had for many years. It meant a great deal to me when we were going through our farm crisis and has continued to have meaning in other adversities. Over the years, I've discovered it is completely there.

Signed: A former farm wife.

"Do not look forward in fear to the changes of life; rather look to them with full hope that, as they arise, God, whose you are, will deliver you out of them. He has kept you hitherto and He will lead you safely through all things; and when you cannot stand it, He will bear you in His arms.

"Do not fear what may happen tomorrow; the same everlasting Father who cares for you today will take care of you then and every day. He will either shield you from suffering, or will give you unfailing strength to bear it. Be at peace and put aside anxious thoughts and imaginations."

A prayer of Francis de Sales (1567-1622)

Read the Handwriting on the Wall

1987

My Dad was a banker who lived through the depression. From that time until he died, he was positive the next depression was just around the corner. Our family never spent a nickle we didn't have to answer for three times over. No temporary *good times* ever caught him off his guard. According to my Dad, the only goal for a farmer was to get out of debt. It was as plain as the handwriting on the wall. He was so sure that he painted on the wall of his bank: **"Read the Handwriting on the Wall."** And—just in case the message wasn't as obvious to the people who read it as it was to him—he added this explanation: **"This is the year to get in the clear."**

So for the first 18 years of my life I was never confused. I knew *debt* was a bad word. You only spent money on necessities—and you felt guilty about that.

Then at a very young and impressionable age I married Kip, the friendly cattlefeeder. And confusion set in.

His dad used to say: **"You can't make money with your own money."** For the Burney family, borrowing money was a way of life. Business as usual. Kip's dad believed that people were too cautious with their own money to be good cattlemen. His only advice to Kip as a cattlefeeder was **"Buy 'em low, sell 'em high."** (Preferably with the banker's money.) I've been a cattlefeeder's wife for some forty years now. Some years my Dad's been right. Some years Kip's Dad has. So, I'm still confused. I'm not alone. Witness the following letter.

Dear Joan: I like your column, and appreciate what you're trying to do. A lot of us don't have any idea how to talk about what's bugging us. We think we have to be tough. So it helps when we see that somebody else has the same things bothering them. Sometimes, it's as if you were talking right to me.

The thing I wonder about right now is this. We can see some light at the end of the tunnel. But we're really playing our cards close to our chest. We've looked at all sides of this thing, and we think it's smart to be cautious. However, some of the guys around us are jumping right in like good

times were here forever. They are paying big prices for live-
stock and buying stuff they don't need. They don't seem to
have learned. But what if they're right? I guess maybe I feel
bad because I might be missing the boat. You know what
I'm saying? I know you're no financial advisor, but I'm
wondering—why is it we never learn? Signed: Troubled
Cattleman.

Dear T.C.: Boy, do I know what you're saying. But, look at it
this way—**you** learned. Congratulations. Hang in there. One thing
that has come out of our problems in agriculture is that farmers and
ranchers are a heck of a lot more astute about the business part of
agri-business. They are also more knowledgeable about their psychological needs. Your letter is a case in point. For instance, you're
making your business decisions after looking *at all sides of this*
thing. We need to do that. Farm magazines have knowledgeable
people analyzing all sides of this frustrating business. I read everything I can. As you said, I'm certainly not a financial advisor (ask
Kip!) but only a dodo-head would think good times are here
forever.

So we need to do what we have to do to assure that the light at
the end of the tunnel doesn't go out. We need to do what you've
done, make **informed** decisions. Nobody else can do that for us. Not
even our Dad's. For instance, this really might be the year to get in
the clear. But then—last year was definitely a "buy em low, sell 'em
high" year.

With all the education in the world, it's still never a sure thing.
But in this day and age, with no education—it could be a disaster.
Sounds as if you're on the right track. Thanks for sharing.

Insomnia

1988

One never knows what will pop up in the mail, and therefore,
one never knows what will pop up in this column. A letter from a
kindly but apparently sleep-deprived reader brought up a subject
we've discussed before. *"Your columns are great! But how about*

one on insomnia?" Funny that subject should come up again. Lately, friends have been complaining about insominia. And the other night I woke up at three o'clock and could NOT go back to sleep.

The more I told myself that I had to, the wider awake I got.

Enter first cause of insomnia. According to sleep researcher Peter Hauri, "Fear of insomnia becomes its own self-fulfilling prophecy." For example, one of my friends said, "I go to bed at night scared to death I won't be able to sleep." Guess what. She doesn't sleep. She isn't alone. Thirty million Americans suffer from what is called "disorders of initiating and maintaining sleep," or DIMS.

Virtually everyone suffers from the least serious kind, the kind that bothered me, which is an occasional sleepless night. This might be caused by worrying about some temporary stressful situation. It can also be caused by something you eat or drink.

More serious is "short-term insomnia", which can last days or even weeks and is fueled by such factors as on-going psychological stress of bereavement, divorce or relocation.

The most serious type is chronic insomnia, which may last for months or even years. No case is the same, and in more serious cases the key to helping insomniacs is careful diagnosis.

Sleeping pills are NOT the answer on a long-term basis.

Hauri has the following suggestions for dealing with DIMS:

- Never oversleep because of a poor night's sleep. Get up at the same time every morning.
- Try to set a regular bedtime, but delay it if necessary so you go to bed only when you are tired. If you awake in the night, relax in bed for awhile and let sleep return. Try reading or listening to music. If this doesn't work and you grow tense and frustrated, get out of bed and do some quiet activity until you're sleepy once again.
- Cut down on alcohol, smoking, chocolate, tea and caffinated soft drinks at night. Avoid them in the afternoon, or elminate them completely.
- Schedule a time in the early evening to write down worries or concerns and what you will do about them the next day.
- Experiment with your bedrooms noise level and temperature.

- Avoid heavy meals too close to bed time or snacks during the night . . . .
- **Unless** you want to try a snack of hot milk and crackers. That seems to help some people.
- Stay fit with regular exercise, but *not* too close to bedtime. Keep as physically active as possible the day after a bad night's sleep and *avoid napping* unless you're sure that will help you sleep at night.

Try each of the above suggestions for at least a week before discarding it. If nothing helps, it is advisable to get professional help in dealing with life's stresses. Learn bio-feedback or get training in relaxation techniques. Join a self-help group, such as "RECOVERY" to learn how to cope. Find out if something physical is bothering you, or if prescription drugs (including sleeping pills) could be keeping you awake. If your sleeping problem is a long standing one you may want to consult a sleep-disorder clinic. For a list of those you can write The Association of Sleep Disorders Centers, National Office, 604 2nd St. S.W., Rochester, Minnesota, 55902.

The important thing is to realize that something can be done, and then *do* it.

A Little Love Outside the Bedroom Will Work Wonders in It

1988

In all the years I've been writing columns, I have never written one that deals directly with the subject I'm about to pursue: sex. I grew up in an era when nobody even talked about sex. As young people, we got our amazingly inaccurate sex education from each other. Our pornography was in the National Geographic. The virtue of modesty was so impressed upon me that I dressed in the closet the first twenty years of our marriage. After that it didn't matter.

Kids get more sex education in one episode of a soap opera or one movie than we did in all of our growing up years. Magazines are available everywhere that could be used as gynecological text books.

The kind of ignorance in which some of us were raised was not good. Not at all. But casual sex as an indoor sport can be totally destructive. There has to be a happy medium.

Times are changing, but not because we've suddenly come to our moral senses. According to a recent TV special, a whole generation of young people is being "Scared Sexless" by the fear of AIDES. Sexual relationships, experts say, are again becoming monogamous. Generations of people, who were sufficiently titilated by watching Rhett Butler carry Scarlet O'Hara into a bedroom and *shut the door*, will swear to anyone who'll listen that it's not a bad way to go. But even sex in a monogamous relationship has it's problems.

> *Mrs. Burney: I thought only women had the excuse, "I'm too tired" when their husbands talked about sex. But I am frustrated because my husband, this past year, has been using that excuse over and over . . . . I know he is depressed over the farm situation.*
>
> *So am I. But I feel we should try to maintain our togetherness and that a happy sex life would help. What suggestions do you offer when he says, "I'm too tired". I've even thought of looking elsewhere, but I love the guy and want to help him . . . . I hope it is not necessary to sign my name, as really I'm almost ashamed to write this . . . .*
> *Frustrated Farm Wife.*

Dear Frustrated: Don't be ashamed. This is a problem that is as common as it is understandable. When men feel like failures outside the bedroom, they have problems in it. It's been more true for women, perhaps, that to have successful sex at night they needed to have a loving relationship that starts in the morning. But a man who's depressed and having trouble with his own self-esteem also needs that same kind of all-day loving relationship. He needs to know he's loved for himself, not for his performance in bed.

A lot of us who should know better still confuse the act of sex with love. To the young people I differentiate as follows: "Sexual infatuation is one set of glands calling to another. It is instant desire. Love is friendship that has caught fire. It takes roots and grows—one day at a time."

The best kind of sexual expression, for young or old, is always the result of a warm and loving relationship. But for a relationship to be warm and loving, it does *not* have to culminate with the act of sex. Studies show that it is a myth that happily married couples are always jumping in and out of bed. They are simply happy together whatever they do.

With your understanding and patience your husband will doubtless work out of his depression. Sharing your feelings would be terrific. (We counselors always say that.) But with some men, communication on the sensitive subject of sex only makes matters worse.

Whether the non-cooperative spouse is a man or a woman, the important thing is to ensure them of your love. Do little uplifting things. Hugging with no pressure to *perform* is a terrific upper. Give honest compliments. Change the scenery with a candlelight dinner and romantic attire. Take a tiny trip together. Our marriage has survived six children and forty years because we took off every so often by ourselves and had an overnight in a near by town . . . and communicated. Professional counseling may be necessary for severe depression. But for most couples, a little patience and a lot of love outside the bedroom will work wonders in it.

Non-Eating Child: A Little Hunger Can't Hurt

1988

I was not a perfect mother. This confession will not come as a surprise to any of my six grown children. They've turned out amazingly well (with a few sideroads into not so amazing), but I'm convinced they would have experienced fewer *sideroads* if I'd had more parenting skills.

Because of my frustration with my own lack of knowledge as our kids were growing up, and because of an expressed need in our community, I've gotten myself certified to teach parenting classes. I'm excited by the results my young parents are experiencing, but I'm also learning that using new parenting techniques, and shedding old habits, takes enormous effort. One of the vignettes in the video I use shows a teen age daughter bringing home her report card. Her father ignores the A's and B's and jumps on her for a C saying *"Your mother and I know you can do better."*

Every time I see that video, I cringe. It looks all too familiar. I hear a *guilty as charged* verdict in my own head. Focusing on mistakes is destructive. Concentrating on what a child does right builds confidence. Child expert, Dr. Rudolph Dreikers, says *"A child needs encouragement just as a plant needs water."*

We encourage children by showing confidence in them, and building on their strengths. We especially need to understand the importance of valuing each child for that child's own unique self, not comparing him or her to other children. We need to allow children to work toward becoming independent by trying things and succeeding or failing on their own merits, recognizing that failure is simply a stumbling block you have to **turn** into a stepping stone. But sometimes we over-react with criticism, which devastates, and sometimes we over-protect, which smothers. It is not easy to allow one's children to experience the consequences of their actions.

> *Dear Joan Burney: This may not seem too important to you, but this situation is driving us nuts. We need some advice, so I'm hoping you will take time to answer this. I have a four year old daughter who just won't eat. Our little boy, an 11 month old, eats everything and is so good. But we have to coax and coax our daughter to get her to take a bite. Sometimes we're sitting at the dinner table for over an hour just trying to get her to eat a little bit. She's a really sweet kid, otherwise, but we just don't know how to handle this. Frustrated Father.*

Dear Frustrated Father. Many parents share your frustration. This problem is not unusual. That sweet kid has simply figured out how to get her Mom's and Dad's undivided attention. She may be threatened because she had this perfectly satisfactory family, and this new baby arrived. It's almost as traumatic a situation for a child as it would be for you if your wife said, "I like you so well, I'm adding another husband to our family."

Understanding this helps, and you may want to try two things. The first is to quit fussing about her eating. Dreikers says there is always a misbehaving parent when a child becomes a feeding problem. It's a child's *business* to eat, and when you quit attending to her business, she will eat. Put her food in front of her, and have a pleasant meal ignoring completely whether she chooses to eat or not. When the meal is over, remove the food, without comment. Allow the child to find out what happens when you choose not to eat. You get hungry. Hunger pangs will not kill, they are simply logical consequences of not eating. When the child complains about hunger you say in a very friendly way *I am sorry you are hungry, but supper will be at six, and you will be able to eat then.* At the next meal do the same thing. Be firm and friendly.

This may take awhile, and go against all your *but a child needs to eat* instincts, so try not to panic. Remember her short term discomfort will make for long term peace in the family. Remain firm *AND* friendly. When she is no longer getting attention by not eating, and she realizes hunger is painful, she will eat.

The second thing is to build her feeling of security in her family by spending special time with her and commending her when she is cooperative. Encourage her to talk out her negative feelings and fears. Let her know that you understand. You'll do fine. You've got love on your side.

Understanding That You Don't Understand, and You Don't Have To!

1988

The topic of working together in harmony brought in the following words of wisdom from a reader.

Giving me another opportunity to stress a favorite topic, the fact that people will be different than we prefer them to be. Learning to live comfortably with that relieves of us a lot of stress.

"People need to understand each others personalities. It's easier to work with someone with a personality like your own. But this doesn't always happen. One of our sons is like me, hyper. It's easier to trip our triggers. The other is like my spouse, laid back. We've learned how to work with each other, but it's too bad it's taken so long to learn . . . . The important thing is to see things with a grain of humor. And

*to talk things out. We always have a round table discussion
when decisions needed to be made. There are times when
the men got angry with each other . . . . but there was never
a thought of severing the family ties. They sit down in the
shade on five gallon pails and talk over weighty problems."*

Solid advice. As the reader suggests, an important step in getting along is to accept the fact that each one of us has a different
personality. We process information differently, we react differently
to stress, we laugh at different things, different things make us
happy. Some of us are laid back. Some of us have triggers that are
easily tripped. *Trying to change someone else's personality is an exercise in futility.* We are what we are. Learning to accept a person's
personality, appreciating strengths, understanding weaknesses, is a
great way to co-exist peacefully.

Anyway, wouldn't life be dull if we were all the same?

The variety of personalities in my own family is mind-boggling.
My sister June and I are the best of friends. But we have very different personalities. I tend to rush into things with great and sometimes foolish enthusiasm. She thinks everything through. I process
externally, spewing out words as I'm thinking, changing my mind
with every new bit of information. June processes internally. When
she says something, it's all thought out.

We learned about ourselves when we took the Briggs-Meyer
Personality Inventory along with other members of our church's
Family Ministry team. What an eye-opener! We had twelve people
in our group with twelve different personalities. The two who were
exactly opposite on all points of this inventory were June and me,
sisters, born of the same parents, raised in the same environment.

What it made all of us understand is how important it is to
have every combination of personality in any group. One person's
weakness is another person's strength. Different personalities com-
pliment each other. And one never can predict. People who are
alike don't always get along, and opposite personalities do attract.

Look how many neat people marry messy people, for instance.
The bottom line is people have a right to be different then we prefer
them to be. And there are some people we will never understand.
We just need to accept them as they are, appreciate their unique
qualities, and live as harmoniously as possible. Just understanding
that we won't always understand everybody—we understand them

better than not understanding them at all—we keep trying to. Because we never will.

Do you understand?

The secret of getting along is communication, having a *round table* discussion or sitting down in the shade and talking over *weighty problems.* Or better yet, talking things over before they get weighty. Discussing differences, we work them out. Feelings stuffed inside fester.

Thank you, dear reader, and God Bless.

Eighty-Year-Old Martha Is Lean and Mean

1988

My friend Martha, a sweet little lady pushing eighty, bowled a 202 the other day, and had a three game series of well over 500.

She may look like the rocking chair type, but when bowling she's mean and lean. Martha's fiercely competitive team, some of whom are in their eighties, regularly wipes out my *much younger* team. I confessed to my colleagues that I hoped to bowl as good as Martha when I got to be her age.   They looked at me incredulously and said, "You don't bowl that way now!" Martha and her friends keep enthusiasm in their lives. When they hit 75, they all went to the big city and had their ears pierced.

It's just like Mark Twain says, this business of aging is mind over matter—*if you don't mind, it doesn't matter.* Many otherwise intelligent people start disintegrating when they hit a certain age because of the erroneous assumption they are supposed to. It's nonsense. They start thinking old, acting old, and pretty soon they've got it made, they're old. They sit around contemplating their aches and feeling sorry for themselves, and they practice creaking.

Not the Martha's of this world. They practice bowling. They understand that age just wrinkles your skin, but it's giving up enthusiasm for life that wrinkles your soul, and they have 16 year old souls.

The good news is that we're becoming a nation of Marthas. *Psychology Today* cited studies showing that the elderly person of today is physically active and intellectually stimulated and will be a force to contend with.

Alleluia.

But all of us who are aging (and who isn't?) have to work at it. It's not easy, as the following letter shows.

Dear Joanie: I hope you'll excuse me calling you Joanie. I've read your columns for so long I feel as if we're old friends. My problem is my "old" man. He's not so old, actually, only in his late sixties, but he sure is starting to act that way. He retired a couple of years ago and we thought it would be wonderful. We could do everything together. Problem is doing everything together has been far from wonderful.

He's depressed and under foot all the time. Always "helping." I miss the time I had to myself. I'd miss him terribly if he was gone forever. But if he'd leave for just an hour or two, I wouldn't miss him at all.

Am I being terribly selfish? Signed: Frustrated.

Dear Frustrated: You're being terribly human. Actually, so is he.

Many men are depressed by retirement. For many couples a little togetherness is wonderful, but too much is too much. It doesn't mean you don't love each other. It just means you each need your own space. The few times weather has forced Kip to stay home from cattle sales he has *helped* me. He rearranges my cupboards and my closets and throws important things out. My only salvation is when that road clears he's out of here. Kip's lucky, because like most cattlemen he'll never have to retire. They can keep going to sales until they fall off the seats into the ring and die happily 'mid the pungent smells they love.

It helps to understand what the men who retire and find it *far from wonderful* are going through. We all need to be needed. We need some place to go and/or something to do. The Martha's of this world make their own excitement. They choose activity over depression. They not only go bowling, they golf on the senior's tour, travel in motor homes, taking courses at Elder Hostels, and they are invaluable as volunteers.

So what you might want to do is sit down with your husband and kindly and calmly share your feelings. Tell him you love him, but you don't love what his retirement is doing to him and to you. Talk to him about options. Figure out some things that you know he might like to do, and that you might enjoy doing together. Be sure there are choices so he can feel in charge. My guess is just thinking about alternatives will get the old fire in the furnace glowing again. I'm excited for you because you say in another part of your letter that you are both healthy and *comfortably fixed* so your options are many.

Have fun!

"We're All in This Together" is the Best Way to Confront Problems

1988

On a recent visit to our house, our three-year-old (almost) perfect grandchild, Kate, put on a pair of my high heels and announced that we would play her favorite game. She would be the mother, and I would be the child. This time, however, the game took a new twist. "Child," she said to me, in a serious little voice, "your father is divorced now, so you won't be able to see him hardly at all, but it will be all right because I love you very much."

"What's this about?" I asked her Mom. Turns out several children at Kate's day care center have parents who are divorced, so the teachers talked to all the children about it.

Divorce is a reality for Kate.

I've received a number of letters asking me to write about the best way to deal with children in a family crisis, especially in relation to economic problems. One such letter asked:

"How can we protect our children from the grim reality of what's going on in our life?"

The answer is, you can't. What's more, you shouldn't. In an era in which three-year-olds need to understand about divorce, we have learned that it is better not to attempt to *protect* children from the realities of life.

Children are enormously resilient when they understand

what's going on. In any case, there is really no such thing as pro-
tecting them, because they intuitively know when their family is in a
crisis. The problem is, if you don't give them the facts, they will
make up their own. They may also figure that they are some way to
blame, no matter how ridiculous that might be. When children
don't understand, they are afraid. They often respond in the only
way they know how, by acting out at home or at school. But if they
understand what's going on, children can adjust. There is a wonderful strength for children in the sense of family as a team. Whether
it's a single parent with one child or a two parent family with a
dozen children and a couple of live-in grandparents, *there is great
assurance in the feeling that "we're all in this together".*

Every family has problems. Life is difficult. If kids understand
this, they can become part of your problem solving process. It's
healthy, for instance, for kids to know that parents can disagree,
talk things out, and arrive at a compromise. When they listen to
parents struggle with a problem, go over their options, and arrive at
a solution, they've learned a skill that will last them a lifetime.

One way to involve families in this kind of interaction is by
scheduling a weekly family conference. This can take some doing
but it is well worth the effort. The meeting can be structured, with
rotating chairmen following Roberts Rules, or unstructured. It
really doesn't matter as long as *each and every* member of the family
has an opportunity to share.

It works. Several families who adopted this practice have said
that the attitude of their children changed completely when they
explained their struggle with finances. When they understood the
facts, the kids *wanted* to be part of the solution, not part of the
problem.

When we over-protect children we are saying "we don't think
you can handle this." We undermine their self confidence. When we
show confidence in them by sharing, they have more confidence in
themselves. We all make mistakes. We all have problems, but the
message we give to them is that mistakes are for learning, and
problems are for solving.

I will restate this for emphasis. Children KNOW when there is
a crisis. In times of crisis parents have enough to worry about without attempting to "protect" their children. Share, listen, and share
again. Make it a team effort. Go gang go!!

Grandma's Have To Stand Up for Their Rights!

1989

There was this woman who became a grandmother for the first time. When her darling eldest son asked her if she'd baby sit on a Saturday night so he and his wife could go out and have fun, she said "of course." She loved it. But it got to be a habit. Every Saturday night, without so much as a by your leave, Grand-child arrived, with an endearing grin on his face. The plot thickens. Eldest son had two other children, and eldest daughter came along with two, and now all of them, with endearing grins on their faces, were dumped at Good Old Grandma's *every* Saturday night.

Grandmother loved her grandkids very much, but she began to feel put upon. And that made her feel guilty. So Grandma suppressed her emotions, because she was a *good* mother, and a *very good* Grandma. But on Saturdays Grandma got crabbier and crabbier. Not with the children, or the grandchildren, Heaven knows, but with Grandpa. Grandpa would work outside all day Saturday to avoid Grandma. She was going mean on him. When Grandpa suggested that taking care of the kids might be too much for Grandma, and that he'd like to have a little fun on Saturday night himself, Grandma blew up. What kind of a Grandpa was he?

Until one day Grandma went to a lecture and heard about a Grandma who was being used just like she was. The lecturer said something quite interesting to Grandma. He said Grandma's have a right to their own life, but sometimes they have to insist on it. "Only one person can change this situation," said the learned lecturer, "and that is the Grandma, herself."

With a sudden sense of revelation, Grandma called her son and daughter and said, "I love you very much, and I really love my Grandkids, but starting this Saturday, Grandpa and I are going to start having our own fun." You know, her kids understood. They really did. This story is true, altered to protect the guilt-ridden. I share it in response to a letter which made the following request: *"I would like to hear your views on what is a parent's obligation to grown children—as in money expected, baby sitting, etc., etc."*

My views are simple. Once children are grown, parents no longer have any obligation to provide them with money, or baby sitting services. Our job is to provide children with roots and wings. When they get their wings, their job is to fly, free of our pushing, propping, and meddling. I know this is true, but what I do, sometimes, is something else. My instincts are to be a smother mother.

I have learned, the hard way, that if you constantly fight your kids' battles, they won't learn to fight their own. So we need to say to our kids, "This is a tough situation, but I **know** you can handle it." And they handle it. We cheer them on.

Children learn in the womb how to manipulate parents. It's their job. First they whine, then get mad, then sulk. They know how to poke our buttons. When they get big, the tactics just get more sophisticated. But if these tactics don't work, you know what happens?

They grow up. They may be crabby for awhile. But someday they will thank us. Many years ago a reader sent me a prayer, sent to her, in turn, by her Baptist Godmother. The prayer got her through many tough moments, she said. It has gotten me through a few too.

I will share it one more time.

Father:
I've been crying over my child's "spilt milk", which is useless. His is the milk, and his is the mess—and his is the responsibility to clean it up. My motherly blubbering will only serve to confuse the issue. He is always my son, Lord, but his decisions are no longer my responsibility. It is essential—for his sake—that I let him alone. I believe in him, in his ability to stand alone. Why do I deny that belief? Besides, I have promises of my own to keep, and things to do before I sleep. Watch over my son, Lord. Amen.

Ignoring the Clods of the World

1989

In the early years of our marriage, when I was at home raising six little kids, wiping noses, mopping up cereal, cooking, cleaning, changing diapers, scrubbing floors, washing and ironing clothes, mending, etc., etc., I used to get phone calls from people who wanted me to do something. They would always begin with these words "Since you don't work . . . . ."

So I have a sense of the frustration "J." is feeling:

"How about writing a few words in defense of the home-makers and farmwives who choose to 'stay at home' rather than pursue a career outside the home. There are clods who act as if a person's worthless if she doesn't have an outside job. This is especially true once the family is raised and has left the nest. Thanks!" J.

Dear J. Gladly! It's ironic, isn't it. There was a time when "clods" focused their dispproval on the women who *worked outside* the home. I've been in both spots. Everytime a clod-like person put me down for whichever thing it was I was doing at the time, I would explain and explain, and apologize and apologize.

What nonsense! The important question is not whether we choose to be fulltime homemakers or to work outside of the home. The important thing is why we give a hoot about what "clods" think in the first place.

The toughest lesson we have to learn in this world, man and woman alike, is to approve of ourselves without the need for the approval of others. *Clods are not the final judge of our worth. We are.* Most of us would like to have the approval of others. Life is more comfortable that way. We do not NEED it. We are each unique, one-of-a kind creations. We have an inner sense of what's best for us. When we're true to that, it shouldn't make any differ-ence what anybody else thinks. But, of course, it does. So we have to work at building a sense of self worth which allows us to say to the "clods" of the world: "I'm doing what I'm doing because I *choose* to." Period. End of conversation.

Somewhere along the line we need to stop looking outside of ourselves for approval and start looking inside. Once we do that, *clods* are no longer a problem.

They are still there, but it doesn't make much difference what anyone else thinks when we feel good about ourselves.

Fact is, people feel about us pretty much the way we feel about ourselves. If we accept ourselves, others will accept us too, no mat-ter how peculiar we are. (And sometimes I'm pretty peculiar.) If somebody is intent on putting us down, we can choose to let them bother us, or we can choose to ignore them. Key word here is "choose."

People don't get in our heads unless we allow them in. We have the right, and even the duty, to be the person it is in us to be. What works for one of us won't work for the other. Women can be as fulfilled being homemakers as working outside the home, and as unfulfilled. So can men, as a matter of fact. I know a couple of house husbands who love staying at home. (Clods have a field day with house husbands. The house husbands I know do *not* listen to clods.)

I have friends who work full time outside the home, by choice. I also have friends who work outside of the home because of economic necessity. Many farm women would love to stay at home, but no longer have that choice. Cash flow gets to be a problem. Putting food on the table gives a job great dignity.

I also have friends, young and old, who choose to stay at home. The older ones have grown kids. Some of them worked outside the home at one time, but don't choose to any longer.

No empty nest syndrome, either. They are homemakers, and they love it. That's where they're happiest. I say "so what?"

We are all different. That's the way it's supposed to be.

We have the right to be who we are. It's as simple as that. In fact, we can't be anybody else.

So why try?

I repeat. The only response we need to make to the clods of the world, if we choose to respond at all, is "I'm doing what I'm doing because **I've** chosen to." Period.

THOSE WHO INSPIRE

CHAPTER SEVEN

Chapter Seven

Inspirational People Who Show Us the Way

I want to you to meet some of the people who've inspired and entertained and educated me on my journey through life. Sue Lammers, Kathy Frank, and Father Arkfeld are living legends in their own time. They continue to inspire everyone around them every day of their lives. And although they have departed from this earth, I continue to be inspired by the memory of such marvelous characters as Margaret Agnes, Ferdie Peitz, Francis Anderson and Hugo Wuebben.

They made such an impact on my life, and the lives of so many others, that their stories deserve to be shared with the next generation, and the generation after that. It's been a privilege to know these people, and a joy to write about them.

Unlimited Gefoobiation and 5-Cent Coffee

1973

Francis Anderson and Hugo Wuebben are practicing Unlimited Gefoobiation in Heaven now, but while they were with us on earth Francis' unique humor and Hugo's extraordinary whittling made an unforgettable impression on the people of Pleasant Valley, and on anyone who happened into the Pleasant Valley Store. They live on in the hearts of those people, and by re-telling their story in my book, I'm hoping they'll live on in a few other hearts too.

A stranger could drive right by the Pleasant Valley Store and never notice it. That would be a mistake. For visiting the unassuming, slightly untidy combination country store and gas station is like a visit into yesteryear. All it lacks is the cracker barrel.

Unlimited Gefoobiation is just one of the offerings of Francis
M. Anderson's unique establishment. If you can understand the
following ad, which appeared in the Cedar County News some time
ago, you are probably a prime candidate for *Gefoobiation.*

> *We hope the following past due press release to the
> nation from the P.V. store is self explanatory: Our non-
> cabalistic utilitarian operation is triparte, fiz, petroleum
> products, haberdashery, and purveyors of subsistance
> necessities.*
>
> *We vend most anything from actysalicylic acid to
> zwiebach. Your indulgence is solicitated if we appear mer-
> cenary, ambidextrous, paranoic or schizophrenic. Cus-
> tomer chicancery intrigues us, we abhor valorization, are
> meticulously scrupulous markupwise and condone tran-
> scendentalism. Caveat Emptor titillates us.*
>
> *Headquarters   for   unlimited   extemporaneous
> Gefoobiation is our creed, motto and slogan. Come again.
> francis m. anderson.*

This self-proclaimed headquarters sits in a hollow on the
northeast corner of the junction of Highways 81 and 84. An astute
observer might be intrigued by the outhouse door blowing in the
wind, underneath the Mobil sign which borders the highway. Or
the hangman's noose hanging under the outhouse door. ("Never
can tell when we'll need one of those," says Anderson.)

Beneath the sign there is a grave marked "Sadie Hawkins."
Two of Sadie's boots stick out of that grave, unceremoniously, and a
totem pole stands beside it. The pole was carved by Pleasant Valley's famed whittler, Hugo Wuebben.

The boss himself or his faithful employee of 35 years, Albert
Nelson, wait on the gas customers, and swiftness of service depends
upon whether you are interrupting a chess tournament or a
sheephead game.

Anderson, a crusty 76, almost always displays a poker face.
But the twinking eyes that peer through his glasses like a wise old
owl's give you an indication of the ingenious humor of this man
who sets the tone for the *store.*

He could have been painted by Norman Rockwell, with the bill
of his ever-present work hat sitting cockily at angles with his promi-
nent nose, and, indeed, even looks like Rockwell.

The atmosphere of the store is most apparent at the coffee

hours and at the noon meal. Delicious food at an unbelievably low price is taken for granted. The fun is the conversation. Cheerful insults fly between the cooks and the *regulars*. Everybody in the little room, with its counter and two tables, gets in the act.

Part of the store's popularity as a coffee stop is the fact that he has never raised the price of coffee "and won't as long as I'm owner of this store". It is still five cents.

"If we went to a dime," says Anderson, "we'd sell half as much coffee and not get to see nearly as many people".

So, it's not the profit that counts at Pleasant Valley. It's the people. Since it is a regular coffee stop for many of the area folk, there is a camaraderie that exists that makes a visit there comparable to dropping in on a big, happy family.

An important member of that family is Hugo Weubben, whose *whittlings* dominate the eating area of the store.

Hugo has on display over 300 items, ranging from a chain, intricately carved out of a toothpick, to a full-sized spinning wheel. Overhead hang nearly 100 plaques. They are replicas of state seals, emblems of organizations, many of Hugo's own devising. Such as the official seal of the Pleasant Valley Store.

He has the seal of Nebraska carved from black walnut trees which were planted by former Governor Dwight W. Burney. Governor Burney planted the trees when he was a boy, for his mother. Wuebben presented four gavels made of that same wood, and appropriately inscribed, to Burney's four sons.

Wuebben's latest carvings have included gavels made from each of the 47 different types of wood found in Cedar County. One is a crooked, gnarled, beat-up little gavel, boldly designated *Watergate*.

Hugo has been offered some *fancy prices* for his whittled objects, but he's not interested in selling. "I'd just have to do them over," he says, and he wants to do new things. He is a member of the National Carver's Association, and is proud of the rosary which he has on display in the organization's museum at Colorado Springs.

Typifying the mellow living and the hospitality of the past, the store is open all day, seven days a week. "Wouldn't do it any other way," says Anderson. "Only way to run a country store."

But Anderson's establishment is more than just a country

store. Hugo Wuebben's Pleasant Valley emblem portrays the extra-curricular activities by displaying the card games and the chessmen, the baseball games and the bowling teams, the radio antenna and, of course, Sadie Hawkins' grave.

Sadie was buried, symbolically, to observe the death of Pleasant Valley's *Sadie Hawkins Day*. Anderson started this "day" during the depression, "so folks would have something to do to cheer them up, that didn't cost much." Anderson adds, "It got to be a big thing."

Local people, remembering the crowds at the ballgames, picnics, and dances of bygone Sadie Hawkins Days, call that an understatement. Returning affluence, of a sort, made *Sadie Hawkins Day* unnecessary, so it was abolished in 1951. But the spirit of neighborliness lives on.

The Anderson radio transmitter, for example, monitors school buses and contacts people who have no telephones during emergencies.

The store is divided into two parts. The front area is the dining room which boasts, besides Hugo's whittlings, a *famous person* wall. The Everly Brothers, a dairy princess, radio personalities, and The World-Herald's Tom Allan are among the many names that appear. Former Gov. Norbert Tiemann's name used to be there, but "some Democrat erased it," says Democrat Anderson with unconvincing sadness.

The shoestring that Anderson "started the store on" is displayed on another wall, and a clock that runs backwards, "Sets the tone for the place."

The other section of the ramshackle, brick veneer building contains a surprising variety of dry goods and other items. "If we don't have it, you don't need it," says Anderson.

The ever-present card table is usually occupied by chess or card players, with interested onlookers sitting in the overstuffed sofa against the wall. Famous chess players have come by to play with local experts, and if Anderson is busy, customers wait on themselves, write up their bills and leave the money.

A large blackboard offers words of wisdom to passersby ("If women can drive better than men, why don't they?") and also serves as a bulletin board for the whole community. Funeral services are announced and contributions taken up for memorials when a local man dies.

One reason for the relaxed atmosphere of the store and for its continued popularity is Anderson's philosophy: "Always cooperate with the inevitable". It is because of this philosophy that Anderson feels, at 76, that he should start thinking about selling.

"Business is good and getting better," he says (Especially if he thinks you are a prospective buyer). With the development of the Lewis and Clark Lake area, Devil's Nest and Hideway Acres, Anderson says, "the cash register never stops ringing".

But it is almost impossible to imagine that the man who started *Sadie Hawkins Day* and invented *Unlimited Gefoobiation* could be replaced. As long as Francis Anderson is the proprietor of the Pleasant Valley Store, and Hugo Wuebben is whittlin', the spirit of Sadie Hawkins lives.

Every Town Should Have a Ferdie Peitz

1976

> *Ferdie Peitz was a legend in his own time. Simply an amazing man. He died a prolonged death battling cancer, and lived his final days with dignity and humor, entertaining the Hospice volunteers, and directing them personally in the intricacies of his care.*
>
> *One night when I was on duty I asked Ferdie if he'd like me to pray with him. "If you think you have to," he grumped in his gravely voice. So I attempted spontaneous prayer, something I'm not very good at, holding his hand and looking soulfully heavenward.*
>
> *When I got done I looked at him for approval, if not amazement. He just laid there and grinned. Didn't seem too appropriate to me. Then he said, with a chuckle, "Girlie, you better stick to the Our Father. You don't do that near as well as Kathy Wintz."*

Every town should have a Ferdie Peitz.

There's a story going around Hartington that ends up with Ferdie standing on a balcony beside the Pope in Rome. One fellow says to the other, "I don't know who the tall fellow in the little red cap is, but the other one is Ferdie Peitz."

Well, that might not be true in Rome, but it would be in Northeast Nebraska, because Ferdie Peitz, whether he's handling his beautiful Belgium draft horses or crying a sale in his distinctive gravel voice, is probably the best known and most popular figure in the area.

No wonder, he's got a string of stories and a line of palaver that's hard to resist. Suppose you're a lady a little beyond your prime walking down the street with your husband of many years, and this friendly rotund gentleman with the shiny dome approaches, beams at you and looks dourly at your husband, and said in a sincere voice which originates somewhere in the vicinity of his toes, "What's a good lookin' young gal like you doing with an old codger like that?"

One can't help but beam back and feel like a *good lookin'* young gal—if only for a few minutes.

Ferdie spends a lot of time "just trying to do a little good." Making people feel good is only part of it. If someone is sick, Ferdie is there. If a kid has a problem, Ferdie takes him under his wing. If an old man needs a place to sleep, Ferdie just happens to have an extra bedroom.

Always available for community service, Ferdie has served on the Cedar County Agriculture Society for "too many years to remember," most of those years as its president. He has been the mollifying oil on the troubled water of many a meeting, and gruffly says, "There's good in everybody, just that it takes a little time to find it in some."

Ferdie has the unique quality of being able to accept folks as they are. He says, "there's nothing new under the sun," and believes firmly, "Kids are no better or worse than they used to be."

Consequently, he doesn't judge. He does offer compassion and counsel, and he's there if you need him.

A lot of people say a lot of good things about Ferdie, but not to Ferdie. He won't have it. "A lot of damned foolishness," he'll grumble, "making a fuss over an old man like me!"

In spite of his own appraisal, however, he has received an Ak-Sar-Ben Good Neighbor award, and just recently the Hartington Chamber of Commerce Community Service Award.

He is a lovely man, a real humanitarian, but he claims to have been a holy terror in his youth. He was born in 1905 and his mother died soon thereafter. He went through three families ("I ate too much and cried all the time") until he ended up with the John Stappert family in Bow Valley.

He lived there for seven years until his Dad remarried. When he talks about John Stappert, who was a huge man—300 pounds and over 6 feet—his voice gentles and his eyes soften.

"John was a wonderful man!" Ferdie said, with a deep-throated rumble somewhere between a chuckle and a growl. "It's a wonder they didn't just drown me."

Ferdie had beautiful blond curls as a youngster. The Stapperts dressed him in a fancy little suit and gave him their love. He used to stir up the bees which lived in the "little house behind the house," and when he was about 4 he burned down three of the Stappert barns.

Ferdie ran when the barns caught on fire. "I was dumb," he said, "but I wasn't dumb enough to stick around." John found him, and "You know," Ferdie said, "he didn't mention that fire to me until I was about 35 years old. He was a wonderful man."

Maybe it was the compassion with which he was treated as a youngster which makes Ferdie the type of man he is today. He knows everybody. One suspects he would know everyone even if he were a coal miner, but the fact is Ferdie's access to people has been enormous.

He has operated two dance halls, appeared in numerous parades and programs with his beloved horses, and been an auctioneer since 1932.

Of his auctioneering, Ferdie said, "I've sold an awful lot of junk in my life, and you'd be surprised how much of it turned out to be antiques." Ferdie started auctioneering when an old sales slip showed a hay rake selling for 45 cents and two sows and 10 pigs bringing a total of $24.75.

Since that time he's seen the prices rise and fall many times. He's dealt with all kinds of people. Many a young auctioneer got his start with Ferdie. He watches over their careers and fusses about them.

Gerry Miller, successful Hartington implement dealer, is one of those. Gerry, who keeps up with his auctioneering because, "It's an outlet that keeps me sane," says that Ferdie's been like a father to him, and Ferdie will say, "Gerry's like my own flesh and blood."

Not to each other, of course. They both kid a lot, and when they cry a sale they are more like Mutt and Jeff than father and son, keeping the crowd entertained with a constant barrage of stories.

In his concern for his fellow man, Ferdie is aided and abetted by his wife Em. She was Emelyne Vlasek when she married Ferdie in 1928. Since that time she has become noted for her good cooking, her genius with plants, and—most of all—for putting up with Ferdie.

Ferdie and Em have opened their home to more kids than most people have on their own. They've loved them all, but take special pride in their adopted daughter Jo Anne and their foster son Bill.

Jo Anne's mother was Em's sister. She died when Jo Anne was just a few days old. Ferdie says she's, "the greatest girl there is." Jo Anne married Don Dendinger, and they live in California with their six children.

Foster son Bill lives in Hartington with his wife Jean and their three children. Bill is an insurance agent, who at this moment is following in Ferdie's footsteps organizing a Bicentennial program. "Do the boy good to get his feet wet," Ferdie says in a pleased garumph.

Bill came to the Peitzes when he was 9 years old for "a week or 10 days," and he never left. Bill says it's an unbelievable experience to be raised by a man like that.

"It's hard to express my feelings toward him. He not only treated me like he was my father, he IS my father."

Ferdie got into the dance hall business in 1945 at the behest of some friends.

"They couldn't find anyone to run the Homewood Park dance hall, so I had to do it." He enjoyed that dance hall business, where he came into contact with all kinds of people, including some of the best known big time dance leaders in the country.

"If you're going to have a successful dance hall, you have to hire the best," Ferdie rumbled, and that is what he did.

Such names as Shep Fields, Guy Lombardo, Blue Barron and Woody Herman found their way to the Skylon Ballroom in Hartington, which Ferdie started in 1951 after the Homewood Park ballroom got in the way of a flood.

Ferdie says the big name bands came to this relatively out of the way dance hall because, "Hartingon's a good town. They liked it."

One suspects they also were intrigued with Ferdie, the small town impresario who "liked them all" and treated them "just like other folks."

Ferdie had a favorite, however, Guy Lombardo. "The grandest man there is." Along with all of the others, Guy would sample some of Em's good cooking, and get a tour of Hartington's highlights. He was obviously fond of Ferdie.

"He even invited me to visit him in Staten Island," says Ferdie, and then—with his characteristic low rumble—"But I'd be as much out of place there as I would in a convent!" So, he didn't go.

Ferdie is always either telling stories or making pronouncements. "I tell you one thing," he'll say, "there are two things you should never love, a woman or a horse. They'll both get you into trouble." He loves both. His obvious affection for Em, whom he sometimes calls "Pete," comes out as he fusses and rumbles about her.

And his horses—well, "It's a lot harder to find a good horse than a good woman," he'll say, "and don't forget that." All this with a sideways glance at Em, and a grin.

Over the years he has had dozens of the Belgium draft horses, but now he's down to one team. "It's nothing for these teams to cost four or five thousand dollars," Ferdie said. "Some of them have been known to sell for $25,000."

He has used his teams to pull his various wagons, antique and new, at fairs and parades, and he has used them to farm his land. He has an old fashioned beer wagon, a stage coach, a one horse open sleigh, and many many others.

Seemingly, Ferdie remembers everything. He can tell you a story that happened 60 years ago as if it happened yesterday, and he can tell you what happened yesterday.

"I worked as a boy in Hartington's own brick yards," Ferdie said. "Lot of buildings in this town are made of those bricks," and he watched the cigar manufacturers make cigars, and remembers the excitement when the train would come to town.

Ferdie says he didn't go to school much. "In those days we got off for corn planting, and for corn picking, and we lost out on a lot."

Ferdie, however, didn't miss out on much. A recent trip brought him in contact with an Arab sheik, which must have been a memorable occasion for both. "I always wanted to meet a sheik," Ferdie said, "so when I saw this fellow with the turban, I just went over." They had a good visit, and the sheik expressed a desire to visit Ferdie some day. "Wouldn't be surprised if he did."

"Funny thing about this sheik," Ferdie said. "He could have four wives and all the girl friends he wanted, or five wives and no girl friends at all."

Ferdie has received his various awards sputtering with indignation. "I haven't done anything anybody else hasn't done," he grumbles, "only they've done it better."

Author at 90 "Gives Flowers to the Living"

1978

When I get old, if I have that privilege, I want to be just like Margaret Agnes. What a joy it was to know this lady, and what an example she continues to be to me. She died several years after this story ran, and I considered printing the column about her marvelous funeral full of Irish songs. But I know Margaret wouldn't want us to shed more tears about her death, she'd want us to celebrate her life. So, here's Maggie.

NORFOLK, Neb.—Margaret Donohoe Agnes is 90 years old, she has written her first book, and it's in its third printing.

A remarkable lady of Irish descent, she has a sense of humor and a gift of blarney which have taken her a long way. "And I'm still having a heck of a good time," she said, her Irish eyes alight with amusement.

Margaret has not had an easy life. But "does anybody?" she asks. "You have to let go of the past, you know. Learn to enjoy the present. Everybody's moving too fast. We have to learn to take time for the little things that are so important. We have to give flowers to the living."

Margaret's past accomplishments, however, are impressive. A resident of Norfolk, Nebraska, she's been named "Duchess of Norfolk," had an avenue named after her, and received the state title of "Merit Mother of the Year."

She was also named, "Woman of Achievement," by the Sioux City Journal, in the forties "near as I can remember." She does remember that the Journal had a "big whoop-de-do" and everybody involved had a "whee of a time."

Margaret's book, *Maggie First*, is a warm personal account of a large Irish family growing up in O'Neill, Nebraska, and additional accounts of Duchess Maggie's life. It captures in short, concise paragraphs the indomitable spirit that permeated that era, with a style that harks back to Margaret's teaching days when she used to tell her English students, "keep your incidents small and tell something out of your hearts as well as your minds."

She started writing the incidents down when her daughter suggested it. "My kids don't know anything about the Donohoes or the Irish.

"I couldn't have that!" said Margaret Agnes. The project was started. Being a night person, she wrote from eight p.m. to—sometimes—two a.m. "You know when you get old the past is sometimes clearer than the present." The various events would come back to her "clear as a bell." But "I knew I had to get them down in a hurry or I would lose them, and I didn't pay much attention to English structure."

Events that came to her are described in catchy sub-titles in the book, taking the reader through the humor and pathos of her childhood, through her fifteen years of teaching in O'Neill and Omaha, her beautiful marriage to her "beloved" George Agnes, her years as Norfolk's official hostess mothering over 6,000 newcomers, to her retirement years in the Odd Fellows Manor at Norfolk.

Her marriage to George Agnes brought her a ready-made family of three with "no labor pains." Heart children, she calls them. And eventually, one of their own, "the happiest day of my life."

George Agnes worked with lumber companies. Things weren't easy in the depression. They moved several times, lived a few years in Sioux City, where Margaret's "heart child" Mildred wrote a shopper's column for the Sioux City Journal called "Down the Aisles with Susan." They ended up in Norfolk, where George Agnes, still a relatively young man, died.

Margaret was faced with earning enough money to keep her home and raise her children. She was a teacher, but in those days the school boards did not hire married teachers. So she just "made" her own job. She answered what she thought was a "felt need" and started the Norfolk Courtesy Service, selling herself and what eventually became four services (Newcomers, Bride and Groom, Babyland and Radio) to the businessmen and women of Norfolk.

Always a friendly and outgoing person, Margaret enveloped the newcomers to Norfolk in the warmth of her personality and literally "mothered" 3,500 families in her thirty-one years in business and she said, "I loved every minute of it."

The spunky lady allows herself a moment of melancholia when she described the next crisis in her life. Her home of 30 years was taken over for a school building project. It was a "heart breaking experience," forcing her to part with many of her loved things, such as "the crock my mother kept salt in."

But only a moment. Quickly the grit that characterizes the lady, and the book she wrote, reasserts itself. "I just had to tell myself that part of my life was over and done with. I had to let go of it and learn to live a new life."

So she wrote a book. For years she's been saving $3,000 of George's insurance money for emergencies. "It dawned on me that at my age I couldn't have too many emergencies left."

She decided to spend the money. "First I thought of a trip to Europe, but—you know—when you get to be this age there aren't enough bathrooms along the way for you to take any sizeable trip," she said, with just a hint of wickedness in her eyes. "Then I thought of a fur coat. I have always wanted one." But again, "At this age I don't go out that much in winter. I daren't catch the flu, you know."

So she decided to publish her own book. "I took a chance on it, that's for sure," she admitted. She decided on a paperback as the most reasonable and readable.

Weren't her children pleased? She laughed, "how would you feel if your 89-year-old mother decided to write a book? You'd be wondering just what in thunder she was going to say, wouldn't you?" But her children were supportive.

The book got written, with secretarial assistance from Margaret's beloved friend Marie Huck, one of the newcomers Margaret mothered many years ago.

Margaret thoroughly enjoys the notoriety accompanying being an author. She especially enjoys the mail she gets. "You'd be amazed at the reasons people order my book, and—oh!—I get such wonderful comments after they've read it."

Typically, she's not resting on her laurels, but thinking of "maybe a little fiction, based on some of the episodes in my book."

But whatever happens she is sure she's in the "hands of the Lord." A woman of firm Catholic faith, she puts every incident in her life in the hands of a favorite saint or of the Blessed Mother. For instance, an upcoming autograph session which was worrying her was "in the hands of St. Anthony."

As strong as her faith is her pride in being Irish. She quotes with glee her "sainted" friend, Rev. Bernard Strasser OSB, who said to her, with a German accent, "Margaret, there are two kinds of people. The one's who are Irish and the one's who wish they were."

Father Strasser said about her book, "When I read what you say about 'mama' I cry; and old men shouldn't cry."

Other reviewers said nice things, too, talking about her "beautiful memories," and saying Margaret, "writes warmly and with sensitivity."

But Margaret is a realist. "My book really has limited appeal. After everybody I mentioned in the book buys it, it might not interest others." But the sales are "flying with the geese," and again at the age of 90, her investment in herself paid off. The lady is a lesson to us all.

It's appropriate somehow that her *retirement* years are spent on the fifth floor of the Odd Fellows Manor, in an attractive apartment overlooking the city of Norfolk. "I've been in every one of those homes," she said, gazing out of her picture window with a bemused expression on her face. "I've seen the children grow up and have children of their own."

Then she sits down in her favorite chair, with a shamrock plant by her side, lights up a cigarette ("they fuss at me about my smoking, but the doctor hasn't told me yet it will shorten my life") and talks about getting old. "Some people shouldn't get old. They wouldn't want to. They'd make dreadful, crochety old people."

Her eyes light up and her face belies its 90 years with a saucy grin. She makes what has to be the definitive statement concerning Margaret Agnes Donohoe's life, "But you know, I've loved every minute of it."

In My Head I See

1984

Since I wrote this story, the Franks have moved to Wausa, Nebraska, where they live in a big house "two blocks from church and two blocks from down town."

Kathy was reluctant to leave the farm, but says, "I don't miss the farm like I thought I would. It's great being in town, I'm going on cane travel again and I'm all over town." She still does all her own housework and takes care of her garden. But she doesn't take her talking books out to the garden as she did on the farm, because, "If I'm reading something like the three recent John Jakes novels I just finished, some of those scenes might shock my neighbors." Kathy's active in her Methodist church, and is looking toward finding a job, perhaps in telemarketing, at which I predict, with her upbeat personality, she'd be a whiz.

Twenty years ago, on a sunny day in October that was to change her life forever, Kathy Frank and her husband Fred set out with friends on a pheasant hunting expedition. They headed out to the beautiful country west of Verdigre, Nebraska, the town in which Kathy taught kindergarten and Fred worked as a garage mechanic and a school bus driver. Kathy was twenty years old, and the young Franks had been married two months.

Kathy's not exactly clear as to what happened to this day, and doesn't want to be. But a gun misfired, and the shot raked across her face. Kathy was sitting behind the steering wheel of the car, and she said, "I turned to look at just the wrong time. It was buckshot and it tore the covering on my eyes." It that instant, although she didn't realize it at the time, Kathy lost her eyesight.

Kathy tells this story calmly and with much humor to audiences all over the midwest. A striking brunette with considerable poise, she stands in front of the group of people exuding a sense of joy and appreciation for life which sets them immediately at ease.

"There are two kinds of ways to look at what happened to me," she says, "I choose to be positive. When we're growing up, most kids pray to be something special. This is not exactly what I prayed for, but it's the answer I got. You have to admit," she adds with a wry chuckle, "it makes me special. After all, if I weren't blind, what would I be here talking to you about."

The term members of the audience always use after hearing her is "inspiring." She describes herself as "stubborn". The attribute that shines through always, and that she says probably saved her, is her indomitable sense of humor.

"I've always had that," she said, "and I don't know where I'd be with out it." In fact, under her picture in her Wausa High School Year book these words are inscribed, "She puts all her troubles in the bottom of her heart and sits on the lid and laughs."

After the accident, Kathy was taken to Sacred Heart Hospital in Yankton, South Dakota. "I didn't have any idea how much damage had been done," Kathy said, "I kept thinking when the eyes healed I would see." The realization came to her gradually, and she said, "I was blessed by the positive people around me, Fred, my family, and especially Dr. Tom Willcockson and Sister Irene. They were very encouraging, and insisted I'd be able to go ahead and do things. They made me believe."

That belief has sustained her. "People are always asking me, 'don't you get depressed?' " and I answer, "don't you?"

"Of course there were times when I was really down," she said, "but I'm stubborn, and it's my nature to think positively. When I get depressed I just know I have to work it out, and I do. I have so many things to be thankful for."

It was also a great help, she thinks, that she went straight from three weeks in the Yankton hospital to a training school in Minneapolis for the visually impaired. "I didn't have time to think about it," she said. That is where her positive attitude took over. As she remembers it, "It just evolved."

"Being around other people who were blind helped me," she said. She remembers, laughing about it today, an incident which helped her make the turn. "There was another former teacher at the school who was blind. During one of those first weeks we both somehow got in the middle of the floor of the class area, and neither of us knew where we were, or that the other one was anywhere around. We ran into each other. We said simultaneously, 'I'm lost!' and then we just stood there and laughed."

Fred also went to Minneapolis where he worked at a filling station. They spent four months there, and in that time Kathy learned to use Braille, the system of printing for the blind where characters are raised dots to be read with the fingers. She also learned "orientation and mobility," including cooking techniques and house keeping in an apartment set up for that purpose. She learned how to use a cane, and she said, "I learned how to knit and to sew. I sewed some before the accident."

That deceptively modest statement took on more meaning when she added, "I sewed my wedding dress."

The Franks moved back to the Wausa area where they now live on the farm that was the home of Kathy's parents, Mr. and Mrs. Dalton (Doc) Gillilan. Fred works for RADEC construction of Hartington, and is gone on constructions jobs at times. But Kathy manages "just fine."

She gives a lot of credit to her family and her friends who allowed her to do things herself. They were "wonderful!" she said, "It would have been easy for them to over-protect me, to do things for me, but I was lucky. They understood that I had to learn to be independent. It must have been very hard for them."

Thinking about it all, Kathy shakes her head impatiently, "Of course there are times when it's frustrating. It's a big nuisance to be blind. But I'm not that limited. In my head I see."

For instance, she can visualize the things in her kitchen. A light touch tells her where she is as she moves about pouring coffee, getting cookies out of a cookie jar, and answering the phone. "I can tell some things by the size of their containers," she said, "and some things by their smell. The cans and other things I can't figure out, I have a sighted person help me, and I mark them with a Braille label."

As well organized and oriented as she now is, sometimes she

still goofs, and the results amuse her. "Once I made a pot of coffee for our card club, and I did it in kind of a hurry. It turned out to be hot tang."

Then there was the time when she learned late one morning that she was going to have extra men for the noon dinner, a common occurrence on a farm. "I'm always ready," said Kathy, "so I pulled a casserole and a pie crust out of the freezer, with a package of frozen apples to make the pies with. My Mom came in and said, 'what kind of pie is this anyway?' Turned out it was carrot. The men ate it and didn't complain too much. In fact, we all got a good laugh out of it."

Kathy takes great pleasure in "reading" up to four books a week, especially in the winter. "In a way I'm lucky," she said, "because I can read while I'm doing all my other work." She reads via a record player in the kitchen and a tape recorder in the living room. "The National Library for the Blind supplies me with the records and the tapes."

Her stubbornness flares when she talks about how well she gets along with her other chores. "It may take me a little longer because I'm blind, but not much," she said, "I firmly believe that blind people can do almost anything with a few adaptions."

She willingly assumes the responsibility for many of the chores outside their farm home. "I love to be outside. I have the feel of this place. I can hear the pump jack, so I know where to go to plug it in. I know how to get to the barn and the chicken coop, and when I get there, I know where things are. I feed the ponies, and in the summer I even work in the garden," she said, "I enjoy it. I'd a lot rather be outside than sweeping and dusting furniture." She uses her other senses to the fullest, and says she doesn't think they started out more acute then "normal peoples" but they've "been trained" in the last twenty years.

What Kathy describes as her biggest blessing and challenge has been the raising of son Jeff, now 16 years old. "When Jeff was a baby, I got along very well. Any mother can tell you that after changing diapers a few hundred times you can do it with your eyes closed." When he was a toddler, she said, "I put bells on his shoes so I could keep track of him. Of course, he got so he was smart enough to take his shoes off, but we managed." She kept track of his whereabouts outside by a light harness with a length of rope attached. "You do the best you can." she said, "whatever works."

Jeff being 16 has been a blessing, because one of the things Kathy can't do in spite of her indomitable spirit is drive. "Jeff's very good about driving me places," she says.

In answer to the question "don't you find raising a teenager challenging?" Kathy says, with the look of a lawyer resting her case, "didn't you?" She adds, "Being a teenager is really tough sometimes, and it doesn't make much difference whether you have a mother that's blind. They have to learn to assume the responsibility for their own actions. It's not an easy time."

Kathy does not think of herself as inspirational, or even courageous. She thinks of herself as a survivor. If the story of her survival with blindness can help others, she tells it willingly. She has a gift for it, and admits being a lifelong ham. "I was a cheerleader and in all the plays in high school," she said, "and usually making a spectacle of herself." In recent years, Kathy has had parts in the Wausa Melodramas. "I really enjoyed that," she said, "and give the director credit for patience." She used squares of carpeting and furniture to keep herself oriented, and said "Only once did I miss a door."

Kathy shares her experiences with her audiences, and shows them the Braille books and the equipment she works with. "I can sense the audience's reaction," Kathy said, "and I usually get a pretty good response. At least, I've never had anybody come up and say 'you did a crumby job.' "

Not likely. Audiences know a class act when they see one. Kathy's audiences pay rapt attention to her low key presentation. Her mother, who usually drives her to her various speaking engagements, says Kathy is always nervous about going, but thoroughly enjoys herself after she gets there. In recent years she's leaned to play the guitar, and added a mellow-voiced song or two to her presentations. Her choice of songs are "primarily religious because I do most of my singing in church" but she also admits to liking a little rip-roaring country western music, such as "I'm Going to Hire a Wino."

Kathy's method of survival is epitomized with this quote, "A person does what she can do, as well as she can do it. Being blind doesn't seem to get me out of doing anything. Last summer, I even cleaned the barn. It wasn't too hard. I just kept cleaning until I got down to the cement and then I quit."

Father Rick Is Going Home

1987

The story of Father Rick was written in April of 1987 and printed in the Catholic Digest and the World Herald Magazine of the Midlands. As this book goes to press, in the summer of 1989, Father's cancer has stayed in remission, and, miraculously it seems, he is still actively serving the Archdiocese of Omaha as pastor of St. Micheal's parish in Coleridge. "I wonder why God is allowing me to hang around so long," Father Rick says, "but then I run into some person, or some family, that really needs to hear my message. And I say to myself 'that's why I'm still here.'"

Father Rick Arkfeld stands in front of St. Francis Church in Randolph, Nebraska, with a grin on his face, his eyes sparkling with humor. He spars verbally and cheerfully with a passing young man who is on his hit list of prospective converts, and he asks the photographer, as he stretches himself to his full five foot six inches and strikes a pose, "does this make me look thin?"

There is a serenity and a sense of humor about the 52-year-old priest which is seductive, and belies the fact that he is a dying man. And to witness him in church, pronouncing joyfully to one and all "I am a son of the Father and I am going to the Kingdom, and I'm terribly, terribly excited," makes it impossible to believe that this man of luminous and magnetic faith left the active priesthood in 1974 in an agony of self-doubt. He returned in 1978, after a dramatic spiritual awakening, and since that time he has, like a modern day pied piper with benevolent militance and great good humor, led numerous fallen away Catholics and many converts "home". (With no end in sight.)

Father Rick (as he's known to all) is a guitar-playing priest, who can break your heart with his soulful rendition of Danny Boy. Although there was some doubt he would make it, with the malignant tumor in his lungs gradually snuffing out his life, in March of

1987 Father presided over a glorious celebration of his 25th Jubilee as a priest. The church was filled to the rafters with people who loved him. In May of '87, his doctor's gave him a *good report* suggesting it might be possible that he would "live until Fall." Joyfully, he continued to use his *borrowed* time to agressively pursue people who are hurting and "need my God."

His happiness has not been diminished by the fact that he is dying of cancer, he says, it has been enhanced. He sees his approaching death as an "opportunity" and says, "God's task for me now is to teach people how to die peacefully with acceptance and joy." Father Rick , who had smoked for 29 years, learned of his cancer in February of 1986.

In the Spring of '87, after an operation and treatments, his lung capacity is about one fifth of normal. His breathing capacity is greatly diminished and he has to make adjustments. For instance, Father Rick had for many years been the Omaha Archdiocesan Spiritual Director of Cursillo. As he looked out over his many close friends at an emotion-packed Mass to celebrate his 25th Jubilee, he could foresee a problem. He asked his Cursillo friends if they would forego hugging, not an easy thing for them. He just didn't have the strength for it, but he said with glowing warmth, "I'd be glad to shake your hands." Although he still functions as pastor of Randolph, he sits to say mass. He will continue, he says, "as long as I have the breath to do it."

"When I heard that I had cancer," Father Rick said, "I don't know that I was prepared for it, but I was excited about it. I was excited because it was a new way of teaching and preaching." In a homily to his parishioners after he returned to his parish, Father Rick said, "I asked my people not to pray for a miracle, not to pray that I would be healed. If God wants to heal me, He'll do that, I'll live as long as he wants me to live. I said to them 'I want you to pray that I will give a good example.' "

He told of a young man in his parish by the name of Brian Meyer, who, due to an accident in his senior year, is a quadraplegic. "I got to know him and be with him, and found out that he just totally accepted that he would never walk again . . . . . and he laughs and goes on and plans for what he can do. I told my parishioners if I did anything less than that facing this cancer, I would be ashamed to face Brian Meyer. I really meant that."

In many ways, Father Rick believes he's a lucky man. "What if I'd been run over by a truck, I would never have been able to experience this enormous outpouring of love." To date, Father has received over 3,000 cards and letters, with more coming in every day. "No way can I estimate the good that has been done by my being allowed to have this experience," he said, "I got the warning to get ready, and I have had the wonderful opportunity to teach others how to die gracefully. I really have never cried. I have never been sad. I have never been angry or anxious. Oh, I have cried when I've heard a song or something that moves me, because I think if it can be that beautiful here, what will it be like in heaven. I have cried for the sadness of those who think I'm leaving them, but just to cry for myself . . . . . I haven't done that."

Six weeks after surgery, when the doctor told Father Rick that he had a very agressive cancer in its advanced stages, Father Rick said, "I drove home without any hardship at all. I wasn't bent out of shape. What was hard for me was talking to my brothers and sisters. They cried."

His acceptance and excitement at his approaching death sometimes even puzzles him. "I don't understand exactly why, but I think grace comes when you need it. People that doubt—well, they haven't gotten the grace yet." Father Rick, who likes imagery, explains it this way, "We all plan and look forward to something. Most people are looking through a window called life—looking to building a house, buying a car, having a baby. All these things pertain to life. I'm looking through a different window. I'm looking through a window called death. Cancer is just putting into action the process of getting ready to leave. When I look through the window of death, I realize I'm going to be with my mother and father, St. Teresa, and Mary Magdalene, even Elvis Presley and Judy Garland. Imagine going up to Judy Garland and saying 'will you sing for me.' It's just a different window. It gets almost to the point of 'hurry up.' "

But not really. He says, "I'm having a lot of fun. Nobody has more fun than I do. I would like to be around for forty more years. I've enjoyed every minute of it. I wouldn't stop on purpose. I wouldn't sit down and cry because I'm not dead, but I'm not going to sit down and cry because I am dying either. I firmly believe that God is using me to teach people how to die without being afraid."

Part of his acceptance comes from his belief that he is not leaving anybody because his love will keep him with them in spirit. "They will be without me physically, but I will be totally aware of everything and every one. I think I would be in worse shape if I thought I was leaving, but I have no intention of leaving anybody."

In Christmas letters to his parishioners and friends he told them that he hoped that he could become for them "a symbol and a sign that death, as life itself, is nothing more than a means to become one with God and one with each other forever." He reminded them "to pay a little more attention to the people around you, to their goodness and the gift they are in your life. We get so stretched out about so many things of so little importance that we sometimes fail to see the gift of the present."

People have suggested to him that they think he's suppressing his feeling, or just not facing them. He says that's not true. "I live in a house all by myself, I'm alone a lot, and if I was suppressing it there would be times when it would get the best of me. It just hasn't happened. I have never had a bad dream, been anxious, worried, or fearful—anything. Never. So I do not believe that I am running from it, in any way, shape or form." Father startles everyone when he says, "I really didn't know it would be so much fun to get ready to die." But he means it. It's fun he says, "from a lot of different directions. The correspondence I have received has just been thrilling. People have taken time to write me the darndest things, things that happened 20 years ago."

This man of luminous faith has not always been so. Father was ordained a priest May 26, 1962. In June of 1974, in an agony of conscious, Father put away his Roman collar and quit. "I went away because I had a lot of difficulty being a priest. Everything was hard. Preaching was hard. Dealing with people was hard. Dealing with other priests was just impossible. All of these things were such a handicap that I was getting to be angry, and I know a few angry priests. I didn't want to be one. I wanted time, and I took the time. When I came back, it went from night to day."

For four and a half years, from June of 1974 to November of 1978, Father Rick owned and operated *The Olde Furniture Store* in Fremont, Nebraska. He dealt in unfinished furniture, repaired furniture and stripped and refinished antiques. He kept very busy doing for furniture what he was destined to eventually do for people.

Father remembers with awe the spiritual awakening which led to his return to active priesthood. He lived on a lake near Fremont, where he made great friends of the family next door. Their daughter, a delightful, laughing young girl, was killed in a tragic automobile accident.

These people were family to Father Rick and he was devastated. When they came to him and asked him to say the funeral mass, he could not refuse. He got permission from the Archbishop, and prepared for the Mass. "I wanted to do this," Father Rick said, "but all of a sudden I realized I had to preach. This was the thing I agonized about the most while I served as a priest. I hadn't preached since I left the altar. I found I could not prepare one word. I read the Gospel, which was four lines long, and the 700 people sat down." He remembers saying a few words about the gospel. Then he described what happened. "In my head, I went over and sat down with the other priests, and listened to myself preach a sermon I'd never heard before. I heard concepts and ideas that never occurred to me. It was amazing." People remember the inspiration and comfort that came from that funeral homily in which Father Rick talked about God as a farmer who sometimes sowed seeds which will be harvested early.

Father Rick said his ability to speak those words made him realize what his problem had been. "I finally got the message. I learned that if I got out of the way, the Holy Spirit would take over. I'd love to teach anybody who is ordained to quit worrying about selling themselves, quit pushing themselves. That's what I had been trying to do those first years. We must let the Holy Spirit take over. You'd be just amazed how I don't prepare for homilies. Where it comes from, I don't know. I just get out of the way. After I came back I never wanted to get out of the pulpit again. I just kept talking." The realization that washed over him at that funeral caused him to walk across the threshold of *The Olde Furniture Store* and say to the five men working for him, "This store goes—I'm going home."

One year later, on the 3rd of November 1978, four and a half years after he'd laid down his Roman collar, he put it back on. He was sent to Ewing as pastor. Ewing became home in every sense of the word. Father talks about his experiences with the serenity of a man of deep faith who knows his God's in charge. He leans back in his chair in an office full of recording equipment and pictures and tapes, and says with confidence, "When I got rid of my hang-ups, God could use me. "

God certainly is using Father Rick. His many converts are only part of the story of his ministry. His five and a half years in Ewing were memorable ones and his impact on the Ewing community was substantial. An outgoing, loving man with an impish grin and a wealth of wit, he has especially reached out to hurting people. "I can look in a person's eyes and see a world of hurt. I go right up to them and say 'if you can't talk to me about it, for the love of God, talk to somebody.' " His approach to a prospective convert is friendly but direct.

Whether in a bar or wherever, he simply finds out if a person's not going to church, and he says, "You know, I don't want to tell you you should be a Catholic, but would you do me a favor? Would you give me a chance to tell you what I think about God? At the end, if you still think something different, or you're not interested, we will be friends for life. Maybe you'll like my God." Couples in mixed marriages were special targets in his benevolent quest for converts. "I'd grab a six-pack of Michelob, call ahead and go to their homes. When I walked in, I would invite them to have a beer, and say to the person who was not a Catholic 'why do you sit at home when your wife is going to church? Is there something you don't like?' " One by one, he'd answer their questions. Of the 27 couples in mixed marriages in Ewing, 22 were no longer mixed when Father left.

He chose to move, not because he had to, but because he intuitively sensed, after seven some years, it was time. The Randolph parish became available. "If I had to move—and I knew the time was coming when I would have to—I wanted to go to Randolph."

But the tears that do not come at the thought of his approaching death, do glisten in his eyes when he talks about leaving Ewing. "One of the reasons I know how to die was because I went through the grief of dying when I left Ewing. I drove away from all those people I loved, and I cried." The pain of leaving Ewing will always be a part of him, but Father has built a very special relationship of love with his parishioners at Randolph and they with him.

Because of his precarious health, the people of Randolph planned Father Rick's Jubilee celebration for March 1st of this year, rather than waiting for May when it was originally scheduled. There was doubt that he could make May.

There was a time, before Christmas, when he thought he'd have to give up his parish. The cancer was steadily growing, and his breathing became more labored. "I tried chemo-therapy a couple of times, and decided that was not for me," he said. Then his doctor put him on steroids, and the growth not only stopped, the cancer seemed to regress a little.

So he's kept his parish, and continued to be a living example of dying with grace. His almost exultant approach to dying overwhelms those who love him. Father is the youngest in a close-knit family of nine brothers and sisters, and they have trouble sharing that joy. Father says, "I have **made** them laugh with me. They are getting good at it. When I told my brother the cancer could spread anywhere, even to my brain, he said 'it would die of starvation.' But I know this is not easy for them. My sister Mary says the day after the funeral, the laughing will be over."

One of Father's greatest joys, after coming back to active priesthood, has been the brotherhood of his fellow priests. Father Rick's sermons are intensely personal, filled with stories from his own life, and of those of his parishioners. He told his priest-brothers at a jubilee mass to celebrate his twenty-fifth anniversary, "we are part of the greatest brotherhood among men, the priesthood, ... any one of them will give you his time, his energy, his heart."

He told them that death really brings life, and, he said, "I think that every priest would feel the responsibility to teach the gospel by his personal acceptance in the knowledge of his approaching death. I don't feel unique in anyway to this dedication. But to be given the chance—to be called by God to teach others how to die gracefully—is better than any sermon we'll ever preach, or building we'll ever build. There are so many people who fear death. They need to hear a convincing message, or see hope unveiled before their eyes." He carries the power of conviction about life hereafter in his words.

Father Rick's funeral is planned right down to the minutest detail. He has chosen his casket. His tombstone is already inscribed. He will be buried in the family plot, between his mother and his grandmother at St. Patrick's cemetery in his hometown of Battle Creek.

With his characteristic and sometimes outrageous humor he tells people, "I'm going to be transferred soon to be the chaplain of St. Patrick's cemetery in Battle Creek. It will be underground work." His casket is made of solid oak, and is raw wood. Typical of Father Rick, when the distributor warned that the casket should have some kind of coat put on it because touching it would leave finger marks, he was delighted. Instead of a floral display on his casket he will have a sign that reads "This is unfinished wood. It absorbs fingerprints. Please touch." Father Rick's epitaph will continue to encourage those who love him and who have given his God a chance.

He printed a promise on the back of his tombstone, a promise he's made to people for many years. It reads: "I will be standing on the bank of the river of death, and I'll be watching and waiting to take you home."

Sue Lammers, An Extraordinary, Ordinary Girl

1987

Sue Lammers, a vivacious young woman with a great sense of humor, graduated with honors from Wayne State College on May 9th, 1987.

Then 22 years of age, Sue was like a lot of other young women. She liked to to go to the movies, to dances, listen to loud rock music and do a little partying. She was also doing the things most kids do when they're getting ready to graduate: complaining about tests, working on her resume, going to job interviews, and preparing to say goodbye to her college days.

There was one big difference. Sue is a quadraplegic. But by the time she graduated, this was old news to her. She'd come to grips with her handicap painfully, with determination and humor, bolstered by a deep faith, and the prayers and love of her family.

With a double major in math and computer science, she had prepared herself to go out into the world and earn a living. "I think

I can do the job just as well as anybody else," she said, "But—of course—some people may not hire me because I'm handicapped." But "give me a chance," she said, and "I'll show them!"

Show them she has!

With this kind of grit and determination Sue, the daughter of Donavan and Jeanette Lammers of Hartington, Nebraska, has reached the goals she has set for herself, earning her own living, and buying a van which is specially equipped so that she can drive it herself. She's come a long way from the hot day of July 16, 1980, when the car Sue was riding in with her sister Peg hit a rut, skidded on loose gravel, plunged into a ditch and hit a tree. Sue, going to be a sophomore at Cedar Catholic High School that fall, and her sister were coming home from *walking beans* (pulling the weeds from a soy bean field) at a neighbor's farm. The youngest of a family of two brothers and four sisters, Sue retells the chilling story calmly. After the accident she said "Peg got out, and I saw this arm laying there. After awhile I figured it was mine. I couldn't feel it or anything."

Although she couldn't know it at the time, she'd broken the 5th and 6th vertebre in her spinal column. The road she'd travel from now on would be an arduous one. Damage to her spinal cord did not allow messages from her brain to reach the rest of her body. With no use of her legs and very limited movement of the upper part of her body, Sue has learned to do all her own writing, wearing a specially fitted brace. Another brace allows her to work at computers, at which, according to her teachers and classmates, she is a whiz. Although it takes her only a few minutes to whip her braces on to demonstrate how effective they are, Sue said it took her hours to learn to do it the first time. She persisted, she said, because she had to. "You learn how to do things differently, to use the muscles you have to get things done." To get to her classes, Sue rode in a specially equipped electric wheel chair, which she also uses to get to ball games in the summer, and to church. Her home town of Hartington wasn't an easy place for a person in a wheel chair to get around. "There are very few cut curbs," Sue said, "and old buildings with steps that don't allow a wheel chair access."

But Sue was determined, and painstakingly, Sue learned to be pretty independent. However, just to get up in the morning, comb her hair, put on her clothes and do many things other people take for granted, she requires an assistant. The four years she attended college, her assistant, good friend and fellow student Teresa Mauch, lived in a room adjoining Sue. "It worked out really good," Sue said, "She got me up in the morning and helped me in the cafeteria."

The full impact of what the accident meant to her life dawned on Sue gradually. Which, Sue said, "was a good thing." The pretty young woman was an avid athlete before the accident. She loved track where she "ran the distance, usually a mile or two miles." She liked volleyball, and jogging, and took long walks through the grove of trees on her father's farm. She fed the chickens, helped with the milking, played in a tree house and romped in the snow with her sisters. She and Peg and Teri, the two sisters just older than Sue, were "very close."

They still are. If anything, her accident brought them closer together, Sue said. Her family and her friends have been the main reason she's been able to persevere. "They've always been there for me." Others call Sue's invariable good spirits and sprightly sense of humor inspirational. Sue laughs outright at that. She says "They should talk to my Mom." Her Mother, she says, has had to take the brunt of her frustrations. "She's very patient. She puts up with me. I take a lot out on her because I know she'll always be there." She admits that occasionally she gets down, but she says "I just call one of my sisters, or listen to loud rock music."

The long period of rehabilitation began with a three week stay in the Sacred Heart Hospital, where surgery was performed. Sue then flew to Craig Hospital in Denver, a rehabilitation hospital for patients with spinal cord injury where she stayed for three and a half months. She's had two additional operations since that time, one for bone infection, and one for a cyst on her spinal cord, which she says "is real common for spinal cord patients."

In Craig, Sue had physical, occupational and recreational therapy. She worked in groups and on an individual basis. In the afternoon there would be wheel chair classes where, "You go on endurance runs with your wheel chair. It's rough. There's a lot of work."

They pushed Sue at Craig. But, she said, "It's a real secure place. All the people out there are in the same predicament you are, and you get to know the people. They are really nice. But then you start going on outings and you realize you have to get back into the real world." Was she discouraged? "Well, yes, there would be times. I'd get sick a lot, and every time I'd sit up I'd faint." For one thing, she wasn't used to the altitude. There were times, Sue said, when "it just felt like I'd never feel good again." She adds with a grin. "I got over that too."

Her spirits begin to revive at Craig. "When you're out there, it's a lot easier because there are a lot of people worse than I was. You see these people that have come back and are leading normal lives. You realize it's not going to be that bad."

She emphasizes how important the support of her family and friends was all during this time. "My Mom was always there," she said. "A lot of people came to see me and sent cards." She has a special feeling of gratitude toward Monsignor Cyril Werner, who would not let her give up. Monsignor came out to Denver twice to see Sue during that first long period, and brought along groups of her friends. "He's kind of like a second Dad," Sue said, "he's real easy to talk to."

Coming home was an adjustment. After Thanksgiving in 1980 she came back to school. "The kids had never been around a person in a wheel chair." she said "There was no one around that I could talk to. I was the only one." For reinforcement she kept contact then, and still does, with the good friends at Craig. Sue couldn't write her own lessons yet, and although Cedar put in a wheel chair ramp at the front of the school, classes were scattered out on all three floors of the school. There were a lot of things to contend with. "But everybody helped me a lot." Sue said.

In fact, a small army of her classmates took Sue over, and when it came to stairs, "My girlfriends would just take me up. They got really good at that." By her junior year, with the help of a brace, she was doing all her own writing.

Things started to fall in place. Still, Sue says, it was tough to see her friends running and playing volley ball, but "the hardest was not being able to dance."

Sue loves music, and continues to go to dances, where "a lot of people just visit anyway."

Gary Dunn, Principal of Cedar Catholic, remembers those days. "There was a camarderie among the girls that took care of Sue that was extraordinary. It was good for the whole school," he said. Ironically, according to Sue, her grades got better, "after I quit sports and had more time to study." Another "good thing" about her being in a wheel chair, Sue said, was that whenever the family went shopping, "they could pile their packages on me." When Sue graduated in 1983, she was "really scared" about going to college. She chose Wayne State because of it's proximity to home, and because when she went there on a school visit "the people were so nice."

She said "I started as a math major, and after my first year I decided to go into computer science. I really liked to work with computers, and I thought it would be a good field for me to get a job in." Her college days were a success by anybody's standards. On campus she was in computer club, and the scholastic honorary society, Cardinal Key.

She even became something of an activist working with the handicapped committee of the Newman Club that lobbied for better access to campus buildings, and was instrumental in getting electric doors installed on buildings like the library, which would open by pushing a button.

Her first years were made easier by a fellow guadraplegic, Brent Chase from Allen, Nebraska. "He would let me know which way was easier to get to a building and things like that," she said.

Sue rode back and forth from school in a specially equipped van driven by fellow students from Hartington. That's when she started dreaming about having her own specially equipped van so that she could drive herself. "I tried driving last summer in Denver, and I really loved it," Sue said. But first she had to get that job and earn enough money to buy it.

To that end she sent out resumes, and went through interviews. It took from May to December for Sue to land a job. She didn't ever give up, but she admits now that she got a little worried. "I was afraid I'd forget everything I'd learned," she said.

Metro-Mail of Lincoln, Nebraska, a large company that handles mailings and does telemarketing, hired Sue to do Computer Programming, and she was on her way. "I really do like working there," Sue said, "there are a lot of good people, and many of us are about the same age so we get along really well." Sue lives in her own apartment, with a Chinese couple, Chouquan and Dongxiu as live-in companions. She's waiting for the delivery of her specially equipped van, so she can start getting around on her own. "I'm a little nervous about that," she said, but she's more excited then nervous, because she says, "Once I get a little experience I'll be able to get myself to things. Lincoln is a pretty accessible town for someone in a wheel chair. It should be fun."

Sue hasn't given up hope that she will walk again. Her surgeon in Craig told that because her spinal cord was not cut they may someday find a method to get through the scar tissue.

"He told me that there's all kinds of research being done on injuries like mine, and it's possible that within my lifetime they'll find something that will help."

Sue hopes that her story, a success by any measure, will be encouraging to the many people who have handicaps like hers. "Everybody has problems," she says, "and yours always seem worse. But there is always somebody worse off than you. You've just got to keep working at it, because things always turn around. Things get bad, and sometimes they get worse for awhile, but they always turn around. Eventually. You just have to believe that—*that things get better.* You just have to have faith in God that they will."

"Look after Each Other"

1988

If you compared the people in a community to the pieces of a patchwork quilt, in which every part, no matter how dissimilar in size and shape, contributes to the whole, Gene Kathol would represent the thread that holds that quilt together. He was not the kind of a fellow to be standing at a podium, but the kind who, responding to his father's counsel, *"Take care of each other,"* did just that for his family and his community.

This barrel-chested, robust man of great good humor died in 1988 at the age of 48, personifying the kind of unsung hero who keeps a community running smoothly without making a fuss about garnering honors.

As the manager of Kathol Plumbing and Heating, Gene managed to keep his customers cool in the summer and warm in the winter in spite of the antiquity of their equipment. His customers came first, except when the fire whistle blew, and then—his mother Clara said, "I always knew just what he was doing." As president of the Hartington Volunteer Firemen, he'd be streaking for the fire truck to fight yet another fire.

Almost everyone knew where he was on the opening morning of pheasant season. He and four of his brothers, *the legendary Great White Hunters*, would be sitting in their car drinking coffee and smoking—near the patch Gene had patiently scouted as the best spot for pheasant hunting in the whole country—waiting with what brother Bob described as *anticipatory goose bumps* for the first rays of the sun so they could begin their traditional systematic depletion of the local pheasant population.

As much as he loved hunting, that much he also loved his work. Brother Bob says, "I never could talk him into taking a manager's position and hiring others. Gene said, 'that might be for you, but I like to get out with the people.'" Gene's wife, Jolene concurred. "He hated sitting at the desk," she said, "What he loved was going out on service calls. When he fixed something for someone he'd be thrilled to death when he came back."

But Gene was far more than just a fixer of things, he was also a fixer of people. He didn't talk much about his faith. He lived it. He was always available to patch up the equipment at the church, convent, and rectory. He served as Grand Knight of the Knights of Columbus, and could be found in the middle of any of the *good works* going on. The Saturday before he died, he and Jolene went to confession.

Doris, Gene's sister, said that in his bluff, good-natured way, "He had a special concern about the elderly and the widows. We used to kid him about this. He hovered over them like a mother hen with a bunch of chickens. They are so lost with him gone, we almost feel as if we should be the ones sending sympathy cards to them."

Typical would be an invalid's report of her air conditioning service call the week he died. "Gene said he'd just as well look over everything as long as he was here. Since the water softener was empty he'd just as well put salt in it. Then he sat along side my bed and asked me how I was doing. He said I looked mighty good considering what I had to deal with."

So it's understandable why the question that's been posed to Jolene most often since Gene's untimely death has been: *What are we going to do now?* The day of Gene's funeral when the air conditioning system in the church went on the blink, Monseignor Werner asked that question.

Gene and Jolene would have been married 29 years this month. For twenty of those years they've lived in a house they built almost entirely by themselves, where they raised their five children—Callen, Sheila, Stacy, Chad and Sherri, the youngest, who's still at home. "Gene worked until two and three in the morning on this house," Jolene said, "trying to get things just right. He was very fussy. When you start out really poor, and work so hard for things, you are a little fussy." Jolene just might be a little fussy too, she admits. Gene used to say, "You clean things that are already clean." Perhaps that's why they've always been such a good team.

Gene and Jolene worked together at home, and for the last eight years Jolene managed the office.

She loves it. "Gene insisted I learn a lot of things," Jolene said, "that I thought he'd just as well do. Now, I appreciate that." She also appreciated it in 1981, when Gene fell through a roof he was working on and severly damaged his head and she had to take over.

"Those were rough times. He was a long time getting over that," she said. Brother Danny said Gene's accident brought the family a lot closer together and, "we began to appreciate how precious the family really is." Gene was "our rock," Danny said, "and in a way, since that accident could have killed him or made him an invalid, we should feel fortunate to have had him as long as we did."

Ironically, it was Danny's own battle with a life threatening illness this past fall that brought to Gene a greater realization of the importance of family. He was "so worried about Danny" Jolene said, that he began to have "uncharacteristic" bouts of sentimentality.

For instance, Gene began to brag about his grandkids "even during business conversations," Bob said, and he talked a lot about his family and his wife. "He probably never told Jolene this," Bob said, "but he really was proud of the way she took hold of things. He told me, 'She's tough. You know, I not only love her, I really, really like her.' "

One of Gene's treats for *Lucy*, his pet name for Jolene, was to take her out every Friday night for fish "whether I wanted to go a different night or not," Jolene remembers with a chuckle. "Sometimes we'd be home in bed before ten, but we **always** went out on Friday night. "Gene approached life on a dead run, working just as fast as he could and just as hard as he could," Jolene said. He said exactly what he thought in plain language, and he did what he said he was going to do. He was "the most basically honest person I've ever known," according to Bob. He was not a formal man, which is perhaps what endeared him to so many. The only time he would put on a tie and a suit, according to Jolene, was for a wedding or a funeral, "and that had to be a very close relative."

His brother Bob was *more than just a brother*, the two were best friends. After their father, Leo, died at the age of 56, these oldest sons in the Kathol family, who *fought like hell* as kids, but won soap box derbies together, were in constant communication about the business. Gene, the rugged outdoorsman, worked night and day to keep the then struggling business alive for his family, and most importantly for his mother, with the constant support and advice of Bob, the urbane Omaha Investment Firm executive. It was an uphill effort. With the loyal help of Gene's uncle, Urban Kathol, who'd been in the business with Leo and remained with Gene, the men built the business into the success it is today.

No story of Gene would be complete without more than a passing reference to the adventures of The Great White Hunters. Competitive to the hilt, brothers Gene, Bob, Lee, Danny and Stan have been together for the opening day of hunting for over twenty years. From their point of view, all the times that Gene made his service calls, or installed his furnaces and air-conditioning units, he had a more important mission, *scouting the countryside for pheasants.* So when opening day came, the boys had nailed down some of the best hunting spots in the country, and when no other hunter could get his limit, the Great White Hunters did, or *made a hell of a dent in it.*

They take along one *outsider* and that is undertaker Jim Wintz "for his canny wit, and because he knows everybody in the country and can get us permission to hunt almost anywhere". The brothers look forward to this event all year long.

"Gene might not have said this," Bob said, "but I knew he felt this way. He loved to hunt. All the time we were hunting he had this silly grin on his face". Only Bob didn't say "silly." (That grin is apparent on the picture, which appears in the picture section of this book.) The brothers each had their own dog, Gene's was named Coco, and that turned a hunt into *a real sporting event.*

"On Friday night we'd all gather at the Chief with hunters from all over the country. There would be a certain amount of lying, and we'd put bets on the next day's hunt," Bob said. Danny believes this was Gene's "most precious night of the year", he was so proud of his hunter brothers. Bob said, "It's indescribable, that feeling of excitement when you put your leg over that first fence on opening day, after you've been sitting there in the dark listening to those roosters cackling at you and the dogs whining because they are ready to go. It's hard to describe the power of that feeling."

An important part of the tradition was ending the day at Tooties *trading stories with other hunters* the heighth of *camaraderie* and then, Bob said, "cleaning our pheasants by the lights of the car."

Gene, in his philosophic mood, talked to both Jolene and Bob about retiring at 55. His Dad's death at the age of 56 had been very hard on him, so remembering that, and because of his concern about Danny, he talked about the importance of slowing down, putting it to Bob this way, "We're going to shoot more pheasants this year."

Doris, an officer of the Bank of Hartington, also talked about the "deep talks" they'd had about their lives choices after Danny's illness.

Jolene said she had no warning that Gene was going to die, but in retrospect remembers "he was eating a lot of Tums" and would sometimes seem "awfully short of breath." He worked awfully hard, she said, but whenever she said something about slowing down, he'd say, "I'm the healthiest person around." He always told her, "you don't have to worry anyway if something happens to me, Bob will take care of you."

The autopsy showed that in spite of his bravado, Gene was a heart attack waiting to happen. He had one artery blocked 90 percent and the other 60 percent. Some of those close to him, with whom he'd had "deep talks" think that he might have had a premonition that something was wrong.   A strange thing is that the morning before he died, according to Urbie, Gene whistled everywhere he went. Leo, his dad, whistled all the time, and Bob whistles, but up until the morning he died, Gene had never whistled at all.

Had he chosen to get a check up, surgery might have prolonged his life. He also might have lived longer had he not lived life quite so robustly. But Doris echoes the rest of the family when she says there's no use going over the "what ifs." She says, "We will never know what would have been in store for him if he'd had the surgery, or if he'd had to curtail the way he lived, because Gene wasn't much for curtailing anything."

"He was the kind of a person he was. He lived the way he wanted to live."

As far as Dan's concerned, that's an attitude Gene would have appreciated. He'd like us to remember to "hug each other once in awhile," Dan said, and that, "saying I love you isn't so hard to do. Gene would not want us fretting or stewing over his death. He'd say, 'just keep the family traditions going and I'll be fine' ".

So that's what the Kathols continue to do. On opening day of pheasant season, the Great White Hunters, with Jim Wintz now the designated pheasant-patch-scout, will be again waiting in *goosebump anticipation* for those first rays of sun. Gene would want it that way.

Brother Stan says, "Those first pheasants will always be for Gene."

Index of Selected Columns by Content

Photo by Marianne Beel

No Matter How Dark the Night Gets
The Dawn Will Come

The Dawn WILL Come!

215